occupational hazards

hazards

jonathan segura

SIMON & SCHUSTER PAPERBACKS
New York London Toronto Sydney

Simon & Schuster
1230 Avenue of the Americas
New York, NY 10020

Copyright © 2008 by Jonathan Segura

First Simon & Schuster trade paperback edition July 2008

SIMON & SCHUSTER and colophon are registered
trademarks of Simon & Schuster, Inc.

For information about special discounts for bulk purchases,
please contact Simon & Schuster Special Sales at
1-800-456-6798 or business@simonandschuster.com.

Designed by Kate Susanna Moll

Manufactured in the United States of America

10 9 8 7 6 5 4 3 2 1

Library of Congress Cataloging-in-Publication Data
Segura, Jonathan.
Occupational hazards / Jonathan Segura.
        p.   cm.
1. Journalists—Fiction. 2. Conspiracies—Fiction.
3. Omaha (Neb.)—Fiction. I. Title.

PS3619.E416O33 2008
813'.6—dc22   2008000887

ISBN-13: 978-1-4165-6291-7
ISBN-10:   1-4165-6291-5

for mom and dad

<u>one</u>

Could be I'm still drunk. Or maybe this is the hangover that'll do
me in. Bottom line: shouldn't be speeding to cover a hostage situation. But it's early Monday, deadline's Wednesday and it's been
a slow week, so.

Began this errand at home. Got the car started on the first
try despite the subzero temperature. Headed downtown, flipped
on the scanner and heard the chatter. So it's north I go on 16th
Street, out of our two-skyscraper downtown (the taller of which,
at forty-some-odd stories, was erected a couple years ago) that
hugs the Missouri River and where Union Pacific, ConAgra, Gal-
lup and First National all have their HQs, and into the poor black
neighborhood. Locals call it "North O" because four syllables
are two too many. About 90 percent of the city's black population lives up here, and 100 percent of the unarmed black dudes
cop-shot to death are buried up here, too. Other direction, not
surprisingly called "South O," is where the growing Hispanic
population lives and works in the few remaining meatpack-
ing plants. Used to be the slaughterhouses paid decently. Now
they've got union busters on retainer for the couple times a year

when the immigrants get funny ideas about a living wage. Rest of the city, west of, say, 42nd Street and all the way out to 172nd or however far this burg sprawls, it's reserved for white folks. If you drove out there, you'd notice the curbs aren't crumbling and the streets are wide and lit up reliably and you'd see these tracts of minimansions—miles and miles of the fucking things— and you'd want to know where the money came from and you might wonder, momentarily, if you'd ever end up in that sorta spot and, if so, by choice or misfortune, and, in the end, how in the fuck you'd hack. It's in this town that I've been left to carve out a life.

Anyway, according to the snippets I've caught, some freak-show went on an ill-advised holiday from his antipsychotics and has convinced himself that his 13-year-old daughter is the Antichrist or some fucking thing. Stepping out of the car with the Canon strapped around my neck and my notebook and pen in hand, I find the cops have cordoned off a two-block radius around the action, and all the TV jocks and wire and daily nerds are congregating around Lieutenant Dick Savage, the cop spokes-man. Savage and I don't get along, which is a story for another time. Hang loose at the rear of the posse and listen to the latest: negotiations haven't been successful and the guy's been spotted through the windows of his house alternately shoving a long-barreled pistol down his daughter's throat and rubbing his tem-ples with it. Which is enough for me, really, so I walk down the street past a handful of rotting cracker-box houses and start hop-ping fences and cutting through backyards.

I finagle a decent spot behind a tiny hedgerow across the street from the house. About a half-dozen cruisers are lined up on the street and twice as many cops kneel behind them with their guns drawn. Lift the camera to my eye and use the zoom glass to scope out the action. Kinda worried the photos might turn out blurry—telephoto's maxed out and being held by these shivering mitts.

Someone I can't see because of the glare opens up the dormered window on the second floor of the house and throws something small and black into the street. Can't quite make out what it is. A guy who I assume is the negotiator steps out of an unmarked cruiser, rubs his chin and says a few words to the sergeant next to him, then makes a phone gesture with his hand and shrugs. So negotiations have failed. Lick my lips because they're chapped as hell, and the fuckers must be bleeding, because I taste copper. Suddenly there's a torrent of screaming. I scan the house with the camera and see the front door's open. The girl, still wearing blue plaid pajama bottoms and a Huskers sweatshirt, is thrown out onto the porch. She's screaming and crying. Her face is red and swollen and there's blood dripping from beneath her right eye. Snap a few shots of her as she stands up. Two tripping, running, horror-movie-esque steps toward the street, and— shit—that familiar crack meets the shutter click as a chunky pink mist erupts from her head. Soon as her body falls, the cops open up, the trigger-happy juveniles, and I'm clicking away, the speed winder buzzing, egging me on, till I see a bearded and bloodied face drop just across the threshold of the front door. Black and crimson holes—two in the forehead and one in the cheek. Shoot till the film's expired.

Follow my footprints through the snow back to the media corral, where Lieutenant Dick is talking into a tangled nest of boom mics. His face looks plastic under the sun guns blazing down on him, the prick. I consider stopping for a quick quote, but this will get covered all to hell and back, so I can snake whatever I need from what's going to be printed on it in the morning.

Besides, by the time we hit the street with it on Thursday, it'll be stale. But it's hot—and mine—for the moment.

En route to the office, my cell phone rings. Caller ID shows it's from my apartment, so I don't answer. Check my voice mail after plugging the meter, and Allison's going to be working late, so go ahead and get dinner without her. Can do.

The only way into the office is down a steep flight of fire hazard stairs illuminated by two bare bulbs. At the bottom, I step into a puddle of melted snow deep enough that it splashes my socks. Door's a heavy sumbitch, solid wood with a plate of frosted glass dominating the top half. *Omaha Weekly News-Telegraph* written in Magic Marker.

A dim, miserable place, the office. Used to call it the orifice, but gave that up because it's such a gimme. The walls here started out white, but years of cigarette smoke have turned them yellow in some places and brown in others. There's only one window, and it's a good twelve, thirteen feet up and no bigger than a broadsheet.

Swagger like the cowboy I'm not across the sales area. Our five reps call it the killing floor. A noisy bunch, these guys. Yammering loud and fast and dinging that goddamned sales bell whenever one of them closes a deal. You'd think they were trying to impress someone with the show they put on. Wink.

My home is in the back, next to the pisser and below the sign that reads: *Enchant. Deceive.* Secondhand metal desk and a '70s-era orange IBM Selectric typewriter. Used to have a computer, but I got hooked on the rhythmic clatter one afternoon at a vintage store waiting on an ex to finish perusing the junk.

"Morning, boy." It's Manny, the implausibly titled Chief of News and Marketing. I know, how can a newspaper maintain its integrity with that power structure? Answer is: at least we're not pretending. Manny's called me "boy" as long as I've been working for him. He thinks it's funny, for a middle-aged black guy to call a college-educated, just-past-30 honky his boy. "Tell me you got something on that shooting this morning."

I spin around in the chair and hold up the can of film. Manny's shirt's already halfway untucked from his triple-pleated Dockers and his tie's loosened. Horrible damned tie, too: puppies square-dancing and drinking moonshine from little brown jugs. He can say what he wants about my appearance, I've got two things going for me: my shoes are always polished and my ties, when I wear them, don't fucking suck. "Have it written up by Wednesday." Spin back around to confront the pile of press releases. One on top's from Savage's office, says the police locked up a local Catholic schoolteacher this weekend after a dozen kids accused the guy of paying them each 25 bucks to jerk off and shoot their loads into salt shakers as part of a study he's doing for the university. Attached to the release is an itemized list of everything taken from the guy's apartment after a search: 22 containers of suspected semen, a Jumping Jolly Pussy, Anal-Ease, a Realistic Vibrating Pleasure Face with Sucking Action (Dishwasher Safe), *Cum-Filled Sorority Bitches, Part 7* and a Nikon Coolpix 885 digital camera.

"Got a minute, boy? We need to chat."

I fold up the press release and slide it into my pocket. "Let me get a coffee real quicklike."

"Meet you upstairs," he says while pretending to read whatever it is he's holding. Since we don't have a conference room, whenever something needs to be aired somewhat selectively or covertly, we talk upstairs, which is a euphemism for on the sidewalk.

I don't think I'm in trouble, because I can't remember having fucked up anything recently, so maybe I'm getting a raise. Which would be the first one since I signed on fresh out of school eight years ago.

Coffee shop on the corner gives us coffee because we give them a free ad every week. I take two houses with milk, tip a buck because I'm a nice guy, have a quick *hey-how-are-you* with a guy who calls me Tommy and I'm out the door.

After crossing the street, I set one of the coffees on the sidewalk and kick the window to let Manny know I'm waiting on him. He's grumbling something about heart disease when he gets to the top of the stairs.

"You should cut back on the pork rinds." I give him the coffee from the ground.

"Got a burner?"

I pull out my pack and hand him one, then light us both with my Zippo, that white trash standard-bearer.

"Where you at with the expressway piece?" Manny asks.

Fuck. Caught. A *big deal* public works boondoggle story he threw at me a week or more ago that I've recently deposited in the doomed-to-never-be-finished drawer in my file cabinet. It's got plenty of company in there: an exposé on the broken juvenile justice system, the obligatory gang violence tearjerker, an interesting-as-wet-carpet piece on how the county's funding formula for its elected officials screws over the public defender's office in favor of the county attorney. Name it, I've half-written a story on it. So I throw out one of my standards. "I'm playing phone tag with the engineering firm. Guys are hard as hell to get on the phone, you know." It's not that I'm lazy, but trite, systemic shit fails to start me up.

"Keep on 'em. This one's going to be big."

I nod and shrug simultaneously. It could be a big story, but it won't: nobody reads our fucking newspaper, and I get paid the same whether our circulation is four or 400,000. The fantasy world in which Manny lives, though, is disturbing. Maybe it's easy for him because he hails from the sales world. Ten, fifteen years ago, he sold computer hardware and networking equipment. Made a killing on routers and servers when the whole dot-com thing blew up. The technology boom exploded at about the same time as his old man's heart. And because his pop was a newsman from the old school, Manny thought he'd do the right thing by him and start up a brick-and-mortar business selling tangible information. That he hasn't given up and sold out, you could or couldn't call that admirable, especially now, when small papers are shuttering every day and the big boys are steeped in revenue shortfalls. He still thinks he can make a difference the old-fashioned way. He can change things, create community dialogues, reverse the century-old traditions of racism and hatred and separation and distrust that are Omaha's hallmarks. He's older than me. He's been to more places and seen more and met more people than I have. So why is he the blindly idealistic one? What's he seen that I haven't?

"But," he says, trying to tuck in his shirt while holding his coffee, "I've got an idea for something else that you might actually write. Remember that Park-Leavenworth story you never did anything with?"

It was supposed to be a big goddamned deal. Profiling a once-golden neighborhood that'd fallen to shit and was back on the proverbial upswing. I invested about two weeks into that story and let it die. Back when the neighborhood was at its worst, I lived there, so writing about it shortly after vacating made me feel like an opportunist asshole, rubbing everyone's noses in my steaming pile of movin'-on-upitude. Besides, neighborhood makeovers make for tedious reading. And yes, I'm fully aware the Baltimore *City Paper* won some bigshit alterna-rag award for a similar story. The *News-Telegraph*, however, is not the *City Paper*.

"Think it's time we revived it. Got a peg now with all the apartment renovation going on downtown."

"That's a trend, not a peg."

"What I said, ain't it? You've got that, the new elementary school on 19th and whatever, the prostitution cleanup"—he taps his index finger on his coffee cup with each alleged point—"the new shops and stuff opening up. That's a story."

"Blowjob."

"Not if you do it right."

"Mouth's a mouth, Manny."

No reply.

"Well, shit." I chew on my lip and look over Manny's shoulder. It's what I do when I pretend to be thinking about whatever it is he asked me. The problem here, or at least the main problem, is that Manny's idea, as usual, is nebulous as fuck. It's like trout fishing using a whole leg of lamb as bait; there's so much shit to chew through you'll never get to the hook. "How about," I say, "we narrow the scope a little. You know, laserlike focus."

"Go on."

"Instead of hitting all the bases, why don't we hit one of them. But hit it really fucking hard."

"Developer profiles."

He loses points for not putting that in the form of a question. He loses more points for letting his sales flag fly.

"What's say we do something about that neighborhood watch group that's turning the area into a war zone by way of making it safer for the crackers? Couple guys got arrested little bit ago for beating up a kid. Thought he was a dealer or something. Turned out he was a Mormon doing that thing Mormons do. Daily did a tiny brief on it?"

"That's got nothing to do with redevelopment."

"Thing is—your story's boring. Mine isn't."

"Look," he says, "I know you'd be perfectly happy skulking around crime scenes forever, but I need something on this redevelopment push."

I make a fart noise with my mouth.

"I want you to do this story. I know you don't, but for me, okay?"

This for-the-Gipper shit's always trouble. "Why?"

"Because it's a story is why. When's the last time a neighborhood in this town got gentrified?"

"Never."

"See? Story."

"I don't buy it. What's the deal, seriously?"

"Boy, not everything everyone does has an ulterior motive."

"Not true, my proud brother. Not true."

"Think whatever you want, so long as you write me a fat centerpiece story for next week."

"Gimme two weeks, and you, sir, have a deal." That's generally the amount of time it takes for him to forget the specifics about what he's assigned me. He'll ask about how that one thing I'm writing is doing. And I'll say it's slow but steady; give me another week. And by then, he'll forget about it, and I can go on doing what I do best: writing the seedy shit he wishes I wouldn't.

"I need it next issue. We have a huge hole."

"Yank something from AlterNet."

"AlterNet ain't exactly our friend right now."

Someone neglected to cut a check. Again. We're not really fly-by-night. More navigated-by-the-blind.

"Can't you get Donna to do it? Features, you know, that's what she do."

"This story has Cockburn written all over it."

"Maybe the one I have in mind. The one you want has advertorial written all over it."

"Shit, boy, it's the end of the year. Everything's slowing down. Wouldn't it be nice to do something light? Take a break? Get some extra cash in the door so I can maybe float you a Christmas bonus?"

Okay, so one of the few things I still have that I give a shit about is my integrity. And for all my I'm-so-jaded shit, this still matters: I am what I do. Gimme a scent, let me loose and I'll come back at the end of the day with a story hanging limply from my clenched chompers. Or, rather, there was a time. And I'd be remiss if I didn't say I think I've still got it in me. I'd be further remiss if I didn't say I'd like to find out whence that part of me's hidden itself. Why? Moments like those I witnessed this morning—that spark. It's been faint as of late. I'd communicate this to him, but I'm not one for disquisition. I already have a pretty good idea of what he's up to: he's got an ad package set up with whoever the fuck owns a bunch of real estate around there, and the deal's contingent on him delivering up some slobbery complimentary-with-an-e copy. We've had these debates countless times, but it matters fucking not; he refuses to see that what he's doing is plain fucked. "This why you brought me up here? To give me a bullshit assignment?"

"Didn't want you to throw a fit in the office."

"Maybe if you'd change my diaper more often—"

"Just get this done."

"Big mistake, to count on me."

"You'd like me to think so."

With nothing left to say, we stand and smoke in silence like a pouting baby and his fill-in father.

When Manny's smoke is down to the butt, he grinds it between his thumb and index and middle fingers until the cherry falls to the cement. He takes the butt inside with him when he goes to throw it away. Mine dies beneath my heel on the cement.

I could follow Manny back in but opt instead to check in on the pervo teacher. Since he was picked up this weekend, his bond hearing will be this afternoon. Figure by the time I'm done with that, business should be picking up down on Leavenworth Street enough that I shouldn't have a problem finding a nefarious character or twelve to chat up.

two

Bond hearing was a yawner. Deputies trooped in the guy, prosecutor asked for remand, public defender mumbled her perfunctory request for a low bond, judge refused and then off went pervo-fucko. Full gallery, but nobody got worked up. Couple teary-eyed mother types hugged each other in the rotunda afterward like they'd survived a fucking tragedy. Little gold crucifix necklaces they wore got tangled up during their warm embrace, so when they separated, both chains snapped.

The corner where I am right now, 19th and St. Mary's, is located just outside downtown proper and comprises a tiny chunk of the concentric circle of poverty that surrounds downtown, like the triple ring on a dartboard if the bull's-eye is the First National tower. It's from here on any one of the numerous hilltops that you can look east and watch downtown inch upward while the reconstruction crews work their magic on the riverfront, and you wonder why none of that money finds its way here as you trip over a hole in the sidewalk and land on either a spent needle or an empty pint of Thunderbird. And when you get up and dust yourself off, the filth gets splashed back on you, more than likely in the form of overflow from one of the EPA trucks that's cart-ing off the lead-filled soil that fills the yards of most homes in the eastern third of town. It's also one of those pockmarked pockets you'll find in any city where you can find a fix for whatever you need, so long as quality isn't foremost on your mind.

Had the chance to leave here. Twice. First time was for col-lege. Scholarship at Northwestern. Passed because I'd just been belatedly trusted with the knowledge that Mom was on her way out. Couldn't leave the old man alone after that, either, could I? Knocked off undergrad in just over three years. Graduation presented another natural opportunity to flee. Job offers from Dubuque, Norman and Jefferson City. So, report on the county fair and the greater tricounty knitting club's scarf-and-hat roundup or take a job at this start-up weekly run by some dude sans news background, where I could cover what I wanted in a metropolitan area of just under a half million that cranks out a good forty—fifty murders, couple hundred rapes and another couple hundred arsons annually. (The math on those puts all of these, per capita, comfortably above the national average. Ditto the poverty rate among blacks; last census numbers had us leading Detroit by an impressive margin.) Plus, booze is cheap. Which very nearly fucked me. But, another story for another time.

I wedge the car between a couple snow mounds about a block away from my old apartment complex. The snow on the sidewalks has been packed into a sheet of ice, so I walk on the street as far as 20th and then cut across a vacant lot. Broken glass and rusty metal and construction debris make walking a hazard. The apart-ment buildings around here used to be grand little places. Now they're mostly boarded up and crumbling. Ahh, and here she is, the Baron Square, home sour home. Eighteen months ago, the complex's sixteen buildings were on the verge of falling over. The landlord had been testing the limits of the term *livable* for years before that. I was the last legal tenant, convinced to move after waking up one morning to a rat gnawing on my sock. Rest of the place was flops, shooting galleries, maybe the occasional meth kitchen. Nobody gave anybody any grief. Good people, in a way. Now it's in the final stages of a huge renovation—a first for the city, to give a neighborhood a makeover. There's so much space out here in the heartland that it's cheaper to keep on thrusting westward into virgin land than to rehab something rotten. One of my sources in the Planning Department said this project is sort of the starter pistol for the immediate area's overhaul. The vision, he said, is to transform the place into an arts district, Omaha's Soho, if you will. So before any of these derelict spaces begin to think about transforming into yuppie lofts and martini bars, the cops are going to scrape from the street the hookers and winos and pushers, while at the same time taming the wild bunch that is the neighborhood watch. And if that isn't the seed for a viable, if not mildly entertaining story, then I don't fucking know what.

Near 22nd Street now. A thrift store's the only life on an otherwise dismal street—one of those that gets darker the farther it runs. Traffic on Leavenworth Street here is pretty steady, but there's nobody on foot. I cross, moving south, to check out the action on the backstreets. Doesn't take more than two blocks before I find my quarry leaning on a "No Dumping or Standing" sign. Acid-washed jeans and a purple Vikings parka. Her body's got that used-up hollow look for which, if real estate developers ever found a way to gentrify bodies, this lady'd make a prime candidate. Approaching her, I slip on the ice and nearly eat it.

"Hey." Be cool. Smile in a non-sex-offender way.

"Yeah?"

"What's going on?" I'm such an imbecile.

"You a cop?"

"Even better. I'm a reporter." Tool.

"I got nothing to say."

"Oh, come on, you don't even know what I'm going to ask you."

"Don't care." She loudly smacks her gum and glances over her shoulder down the alley. Nothing back there except a dumpster and a broken tricycle.

"Look, I'm writing a story. Maybe you can help me out." Pull my hands out of my pockets and stick ol' righty forward. "Burn."

She looks at my hand like I'm holding out a fistful of foreskins.

"I'm not a cop," I say. "I swear."

"If you was, you gotsta tell me. Trapment."

"Here." Hand her a business card. This is fucking ludicrous. Giving a hooker my card. I'm sure she's impressed. "I think we can help each other out." Sometimes the I-scratch-you-scratch tack softens up people. Newspapers, see, are a gateway to fame, an institution dedicated to chronicling the feats of the extraordinary people who define our times. But the truth is that very few of us have something worthwhile to contribute. Every last one of us could just as easily blow off our heads tonight and leave nothing behind except a headstone that nobody visits, and the world will keep on turning and burning without so much as a hiccup. That thought—that you've done all you can do, and even *that* wasn't even worth the effort—is paralyzing for more than a few. So the shot-at-glory-before-death I peddle is enough to make some people jump up and dance. The kicker here is I can't stand the thought of possessing anything that even remotely stinks of significance. I'm content with my emotionally, financially, matter-of-factly marginal existence. If I were to suddenly matter . . . Well, I'd rather not.

She reads the card. Then laughs. "Cock-burn?"

Ahem. "Co-burn."

"I never heard of this paper."

"It's a thinking man's paper."

"So what you want?"

Bingo. The kid's still got it.

"Ever had any problems with the neighborhood watch?"

"Why would I?"

"You tell me."

"I ain't gonna play games. You wanna score or what?"

"Not that I don't appreciate the offer, because I do, really, but I have a girl, see—"

"What makes you think I turn tricks?"

"You just asked me—" Shoulda had another coffee this morning, because it occurs to me now that she's trying to sell me— what? Crank? Smack? What's hot this week? Get it together, kid. "My mistake."

Her eyes narrow to slits. "I ain't no hooker."

"You said—"

"I don't care what I said!" She steps toward me and jams her hand into her pocket, where, presumably, she has some sort of weapon. An inexperienced wordman might be scared right now. But, see, I've interviewed all sorts of whackos. When I was just starting out, I went to the house of this guy suspected in a hockey-stick-related murder. Fucker answered the door with a mean-looking something featuring a pistol grip and a banana clip leveled at my chest. Took a little doing, but soon I was sitting in his living room politely declining the tea he offered me. He was later charged, tried and acquitted.

I apologize and turn around. And why the fuck is she so mad, anyway?

"Hey, motherfucker," which sounds like *mo'fugga,* but who am I to correct her, "don't turn away from me!"

I try to make my departure look graceful. Ice and snow and gravel and sand, and these fucking dress shoes provide no traction. Not the sort of situation one would expect to find one's self in after having heard his chosen profession-to-be repeatedly described as *a calling*. I was young then and didn't know that *a calling* meant "shitty work/no money." Instead, I imagined manila envelopes changing gloved hands in parking garages, covert late-night phone calls, rye lunches and gin dinners, shouting into pay-phone handsets *Get me rewrite!*

"Come back here, dickhead!" She chucks a rock at me. It misses.

If I could believe in God (and, at moments, I do so wish I could), I'd pray he make my feet sprightly and my steps nimble and accurate. All it'll take is one patch of ice, then—*bang*—brained by a rock. Not the way I'd planned on going.

She screams behind me, cursing, hoping I die soon. Bottle of soda whizzes past my ear, exploding when it hits the trunk of a rusted Eldorado. Scented purple sugar-water soaks my coat. Traffic's still steady on Leavenworth. A warehouse lines the north side of the street, its crumbling facade taking over half the sidewalk. And to my right are stores that are never open. I fumble down to 20th.

The residential blocks are more of the same. Tiny, dying houses with jerry-rigged porches and blankets and sheets over the windows. Broken-down cars in driveways and on lawns and curbs. Three squatty pit bulls behind a chain-link fence thrust themselves at me, barking and snarling and snapping and pawing. Their faces and throats are covered with healed scars and fresh, bloody gouges. Fighters. Maggie's, a tiny, unlicensed dive bar. An Italian restaurant. Cracked concrete and more snow piles. My breath crystallizes and rises and swirls as I tap a lit cigarette held between my thumb and index finger. Snot trickles out of my frozen nose.

And there she stands: contestant number two. Not entirely ugly, but no prize, either. Her face bears the tracks of the thousands who have marched through her. She's definitely seen better days, but looks like she'd clean up decently enough if a stylist had a week to kill in the name of charity. Take the frizz out of her hair, scrub the hell out of her skin, clip her fingernails and throw on a heavy lacquer of makeup to cover the pockmarks.

She looks me up and down. "Cop," she says, her breath redolent of bleach.

"I hate cops more than you do." I shove my hand into my pocket and pull out a card. "I'm a reporter, working on a story about the neighborhood."

She takes the card and shifts her weight onto her left hip. Leopard-print tights. Military surplus parka with faux-fur-lined hood.

"What's your name?" I ask.

"What's yours?" She hasn't looked at the card. A crooked, toothy smile crawls across her face.

"Cockburn."

"Luka."

I would say that's an unfortunate name, but I don't have much leverage in that department.

"You smell funny. Like candy."

"Cologne."

"So, what," she says, "you wanna talk about you or me or your sick wife or how tough it is working and coming home to a kid with cerebral palsy? You just need to relax, right? Let loose."

"Tempting, but, curious if you know anything about those neighborhood-watch guys cruise around here at night giving people trouble."

Is that disappointment I see in her face, or is she just looking ragged? "That one's going to cost you."

"Sorry. Can't help." Badass, grizzled journalists like myself never have to pay. We're the Canuck Mounties of information.

"Too bad. I got all kinds of stuff to say." She sucks in and bites her lower lip.

"How about you give me a price list." I pull out my notebook and a red pen.

"That doesn't look like a wallet."

I know bullies. You would, too, if you had my name. I keep the notebook and pen out, but don't let the two come together. Call it a compromise. "How much?"

"I'll suck you off for twenty-five, fuck for fifty."

The dogs bark and rattle the fence behind me.

"I don't have that," I say.

"Twenty," she says.

"Look, I don't want to fuck you—"

"Twenty's for head."

"Whatever it's for, I'm not interested." Really? "What I am interested in, however, is your take on these neighborhood-watch dudes."

She puckers up and sucks in some frozen air. My terseness, it seems, amuses her. She looks up and to the left as her fingers tap the musky olive fabric covering her right forearm. "Tell you what—you come back here tomorrow, and if the dickheads haven't offed me before then, we'll talk all you want. But you're buying me lunch."

"What time?"

"I'm always here, Cockburn." She waves my card at me and walks around the corner.

"Co-burn," I shout after her.

<u>three</u>

Give my shoes a quick buff, then mosey on into the living room, where I try to find something to do as an ancillary to the Old Crow. Half an hour till the late news, so the TV's out. Throw on the first Clash record, and, you know, this is one of the few bands that didn't turn into mockeries of themselves after the second record. (Which ain't to say *Sandinista!* didn't suck. It did.) Grab the broom—which does not at all currently substitute for the guitar I wish I had and knew how to play—and sweep up the plaster flakes that've peeled from the ceiling. Flip the record, smoke a couple smokes, eyeball the Journey greatest hits record (if asked, I'll loudly deny owning it) strategically wedged spine-in between *Paganicons* and *Young, Loud and Snotty*, and wonder what I was doing fifteen years ago when I shoulda been learning git-tar. It'd be pathetic to pick it up now, I think, as I stow my not-rockstick in the closet.

Anyway, I head on over to the dark nook by the kitchen where Allison's set up her cute little white cupcake of a computer and clear my inbox of the day's porn spam. Couple lonely, early evening e-carousing sessions a month or so ago when Allison was pissed at me and spent a few nights over at her sister's, and I'm bombarded with ads for penis pumps. She asked me about all the e-mail I'd been getting, so I came clean, and she thought it was funny that I jerked off in the high-back chair. Then she wanted to know what I did with it—the semen—when I ejaculated. (Which are the words she used, *semen* and *ejaculated*.) So I said I shot it into a pair of her underwear and I'd never tell her which ones.

Pour another jolt of the Crow and get situated on the couch with my TV notebook. Part of the job is keeping tabs on the local TV news jokers. Sorta like working day care, if the little mongrels got clothing and cosmetics allowances. Channel 7's new-as-of-last-summer lurid blue and red color scheme (we ran a bit on it, I'm sorry to report) is flashing across the tiny Trinitron when I hear the tumbler tumble, and in Allison walks.

"Hey," she says once the door's shut.

I respond in kind and return my attention to the tube. Flip through the major affiliates (the Fox newscast, which is on an hour earlier and features a newsreader with a harelip, is on par, reportage- and production-quality-wise, with something out of Albania twenty years ago), and Allison throws herself down next to me. Local ABC's leading with the dead girl from this morning. NBC, CBS, ditto. Not a shocker.

"You cover that, too?" Allison asks.

"Sorta," I say.

"What a sicko," she says.

"He's dead now."

There are a couple other stories before a short piece on the Catholic school guy. One clip of the attorney talking outside the courtroom, and, hey, look, there I am on the edge of the frame, taking notes. Allison sees it, too, and nudges my leg with hers.

"You're a star," she says.

"One born every minute, right?"

She mutes the TV when a buyer-beware about a used car dealer out west comes on Channel 3. "What else did you do today?"

"Knock it off." I grab the remote and hit mute again. We have this tacit agreement that I run the TV, if I'm home, at six and ten.

She leaves my notebook and me alone on the couch. Illustrative, this, of how we tolerate each other. Nutshell: don't wanna end up like my folks. You know, together. With child. Maybe in love. Maybe not. Die early. Figure living with Allison is okay, so long as we really don't share anything or care all that much. Nice, though, to have someone to joust with. Easier this way, too, than picking up trampy young thangs at the bar. Which would require a prolonged feigning of interest in someone's life. Here, we both know it's perfunctory bullshit, and, truth be told, there's a small degree of comfort to be found in the idle patter. Told her when I moved that she could set up shop if she wanted, but under no circumstances should she misinterpret that move as me taking even the first awkward baby step toward respectability. *Whatever*, she said.

"You wanna get me another?"

"Not really."

But she does. Barely a finger, so it's like she didn't. "Tease," I say.

Channel 6 is onto sports, so I hit 7 and 3, and they're in equally lame territory. Off goes the TV. On comes the banter.

"Your day was?" I say.

"Busy. Today was order day, so I did that. Toby was there, and he was all cranked out, so he went through and sorted all the misplaced records."

"He's the smelly one, right?"

"No, that's Nick. Toby's the one you keep calling a fag."

"If he wouldn't fuck dudes."

"He has a girlfriend. You've met her." She scratches behind her ear.

"You cut your hair?" The sly dog I am.

"Nope."

"Washed it?"

She draws in a breath and shoots it out of her nose. "What else'd you do today?"

"New assignment." Sip. "Next neighborhood over's got its own paramilitary outfit."

"So?"

"Excellent question. Don't have an answer yet."

She gets this exasperated look but stops short of rolling her eyes. "That job," she says, "is beneath you."

"And you aren't?"

She grabs my glass and sucks down the dregs. Melted ice, mostly. "Not often enough."

So, really, she's not all that bad. "Yeah. Well." I hit the bathroom, where we keep the household pharmaceuticals. Color-coded bottles, so you don't have to think. Black. (Mine.) Red. (Hers.) Orange. (Misc.) Shake out a couple downers—both are blue, but one's a capsule and the other's a weird doughnut shape— before pouring the last of the Crow.

The pitter-patter of dainty feet grows louder. "Think you really need those tonight?"

"Probably."

"Maybe you could try one night without." Allison examines my loot. "Or just one or the other, even."

This, from the girl who got me all fucked on blow—fun as it

wasn't—back when. "Something going on I oughta know about?"

"Do whatever you want," she says. "My guy got arrested, so you might want to conserve."

Like there'd ever be a supply issue. "What's his name? I'll look him up. Maybe write a brief brief." I dump out a third, pop the trio of Burn's little blue helpers and wash 'em down with the last of Burn's little brown helper. Wasn't *necessarily* a fuck you, but it appears, to the professional observer, there's some genuine hurt in her eyes.

"So I guess you're going to bed," she says.

Try to kiss her on the cheek on my way past, but she ain't having it. Not a problem. There's plenty of others out there, because she, apparently, has turned a corner. Found Christ or some bullshit. We're not so entangled that I couldn't effortlessly ditch her. She seems to be ignorant of this fact.

On the nightstand is the copy of *Molloy* I've been trying to read for the past four months. Really, where *to* begin? Get to the part that isn't much different from the other parts when I start to feel the tug. TV chatter from the other room's sounding tinny and faint, so I dog-ear a page I've dog-eared before and hit the light. Fighting with the wadded-up sheets and blankets, saying something about fucking asinine jersey knit shit, when Allison ambushes me.

"Didn't hear you," I somewhat say.

"Because you're shitfaced and yelling at the sheets, perhaps?"

She undresses, and I'm halfway to gone when she lies down and nuzzles up next to me like she hasn't done in about forever. Maybe she, too, senses the doom in the room. The sleep's really pulling on me, but the Emasculator, shockingly, is sniffing around down there, and I'd be an idiot to pass up the opportunity. A little good-bye wrestle, plus it's been a few weeks and looks like it'll be more than a few more. So we're a little out of practice. Clumsy. And I'm fucked up, but she's into it, moaning and biting my ear and neck. Almost wish I'da hesitated or just waited on those pills, because I can't just beg this off and pass out. It's an asshole thing to do, but I put my face in the pillow over her shoulder and go to work. Doesn't take very long till I lose my hard-on. Rolling off her, I know she's saying something, because I can sorta hear her, but fuck if I can tell; I'm wrecked.

four

Ate a greasy breakfast and drank four cups of coffee this morning, but my brain is still wrapped tightly in gauze at about quarter to noon when I step out of the car just south of Leavenworth on 19th Street. I walk around the neighborhood for the duration of a cigarette before spotting Luka near 20th and Howard as she steps out of a rusty truck with Illinois commercial plates. Closing the door, she points east with her right hand, scratches her head with the other, then shrugs. I keep my distance until the truck drives off, spitting out behind it a cloud of sludge and salt and frosted exhaust. Wearing the same clothes she had on yesterday, she steps back onto the sidewalk, crosses her arms and looks around. Acting like she doesn't see me. I wave and yell a monosyllabic greeting that's somewhere between *hi* and *hey*.

She ambles toward me over the icy concrete.

"Time for a break?" I ask.

"Got a little time. The lunch rush is over." She looks down and up the street.

"Where to?"

"You're buying, so you pick."

"Think there's a new place a block or so down. Been there?"

"What do you think?"

"Me either. Shall we, then?"

The restaurant is one of the few new businesses that've opened up around here in at least six years. Tattoo shop around the corner, but it didn't last very long. Indie bookstore-slash-café. Convenience store. Place we're dining is prototypical, I imagine, of what the neighborhood's going to be like in another year or two, so I figure what I'm really doing here is facilitating a changing of the guard. Besides, might be fun to needle the land-grabbers a little.

Place's got a real minimalist vibe, beginning with the name, Bistro 1742, which is derived from the street address, moving on to the décor, which consists of simple two-top wire and glass tables with matching wire chairs and ending with the fact that other than us, it's deserted. We sit at a window table that has a rectangular glass ashtray on it.

"So," she says, her chin propped up on her right fist.

"So I'm working on a story about the neighborhood." That's it, start out nice and vague.

"And?"

"And how you've got the Huns roaming around trying to keep the peace."

An Olive Oyl–looking waif wearing all black steps up to the table. Can't tell if she's bored or pissed. Course, it could be something simple, like she isn't thrilled I brought a prostitute into a reputable place of business.

"You want to hear today's specials?" she asks, begrudgingly.

"Just a menu," Luka says.

"Two," I say.

Ms. Oyl places a sheet of blue-marble paper in front of each of us and then disappears. *Menu Changes Daily,* or so it claims.

Lots of encrusted and infused and drizzled shit to choose from. I settle on the only menu item I can picture based on its description: lamb burger.

"Know what you want?" I ask.

"I think. What's arugula?"

"Prick for 'lettuce.'"

Luka's still looking at her menu, so I seize the opportunity to set out my tape recorder. Sort of a dirty trick, but. Some guys actually connect a wired mic to their sources during interviews so everything's on the level. But the less someone is clued in to the process, I figure, the more natural the conversation's going to be. Or I could be full of shit.

"Okay, I got it," Luka says.

I wave over Olive, who scrawls down our orders on a little notepad. I get the burger and a coffee. Luka orders—and I'm glad I'm taping this, because otherwise nobody'd believe me—the lemon-basil-infused grilled swordfish steak with mango chutney, walnuts and smashed (not mashed, mind you) yams. "And an iced tea," she says. "Lots of ice."

"Didn't have you pegged as the iced tea type," I say when Olive walks off.

"You were saying?"

I chat her up about herself so she gets comfy. She talks about the good spots to cat and, somewhere in there, trots out that tired fucking *ain't selling my body, just selling my time* line. I half expect her to start yakking about the night classes she's taking at Metro and her dream of *earning* that associate's degree in nursing technology so she can do something with her life. Mercifully, she doesn't.

"Yeah, so about this vigilante neighborhood watch that beats up Mormons."

Olive brings the drinks and a small plate of olives, which is just too *too*.

Luka swirls her tea around with the straw, making the ice cubes clink against the glass. She takes a sip and says, "What you wanna know about 'em?"

"For one, you ever had a problem?"

"Nah. I know some people who have, though. One girl, a few of them chased around with baseball bats. Another one, the other day, they drove by and threw fish guts all over."

"They ever do any real damage? You know, something irreversible?"

"Kill anyone, you mean?"

"If I had to, I'd settle for a good wounding."

"If so, they're hiding the bodies real good. Think they're afraid to go whole hog."

I milk the silence for a few seconds to see what else she might spit out.

"It's not like I pay taxes or nothing," she continues, "but a body's a body, even if it is a lowlife's. Tell you, though, word is they're starting to get bold. Giving the street-level guys a hard time."

"How so?"

"Travel in packs with, like, bottles and pipes and knives. They scare off the johns, get free ones. Shaking down the corner guys, but they ain't got the balls to do anything real."

"So it's an annoyance?"

"Yeah," she starts up again, "and it's not like anyone can call the cops, and plus, I guess, there's this new thing going on where they're putting all the names and license plates out on the Internet."

Oh, how I love it when they're articulate and informed. "Of the guys who get picked up for lewd conduct?"

"Yeah."

"How long's this been going on?"

"I don't know. Few months, at least."

"You sure about that? Because I've never heard of it, and I like to think I know what's going on."

"It is. I know."

"You know because how?"

"One of my regulars."

Regulars? Love it. "So a"—pause—"client of yours told you about it? He get written up or get a blackmail letter from the neighborhood watch or something?"

"Nope. He's one of them. The watch group."

"The same one that's trying to run you out?"

"Uh-huh."

Olive fucks up my flow and brings the food before I can ask what the regular's name is.

"Fresh-ground pepper?" Olive brandishes one of those pepper-grinder things that looks like an ornate billy club, and I could be wrong, but it looks like she wants to use it to brain my sporting friend and me.

I decline; Luka doesn't.

"Is there anything else—"

"No," I interrupt. "We're fine, thanks." Again, I wait to continue until Olive extricates herself from my precarious discussion here. "So, this boy of yours; what's his name?"

Luka's got a mouthful of swordfish. She holds up her index finger, chews fourteen times before swallowing and says, "Not telling."

"You can tell me. I'm one of the good guys."

She cuts another chunk of fish, pops it into her mouth and shakes her head. "I've had better," she says. "Swordfish."

"I'm not going to bust him. It's just that I'm going to have to hang out with these yahoos sooner or later, and I kinda like to know ahead of time what I'm going to be up against."

"Forget it."

"Give me something. What's he look like?"

"Tall, white."

"Married?"

"Like all of 'em are."

"Good job?"

"Good enough."

"You said he's a regular, so how regular?"

"Couple times a week."

"And how's he manage to stay off the most wanted list? Rest of the watch in on it, too?"

"Nothing like that. They're too dumb to run a cover-up. He comes to my house, and nobody knows nothing."

"You trust him that much, huh?"

"He wouldn't do anything stupid. He's got a family."

"Point, but regarding the list thing—he told you about it. Why?"

"He tells me everything. Why I never had a problem is I always know where they're going to be. But, I mean, we just laugh about it, really."

"And other than him telling you about it, you've heard nothing of it, right?"

She smears smashed yams on her fish, cuts a chunk, says, "Yeah," and, before she closes her mouth, slides in the food.

"See, thing is, unless your average Joe and Jane know the information is floating around out there, it's useless, get it?"

"But it *is* out there."

Yet another reason I'll never have children. No patience.

"The list, right? The only way it works as a weapon is if there are obvious and direct consequences for anyone unlucky enough to end up on it. And the consequences that come out of something like that are public embarrassment and maybe a ruined marriage. But, again, if nobody knows that this thing is floating around out there, then it might as well not exist, see? I mean, I love this kind of shit, but if I don't know about it, how's some housewife out in west Omaha going to?" That mild buzz in my gut cranks up a dozen notches, because, hey, easiest scoop yet. A shame it's lacking in the significance department.

"I see," she says. "Guess it's better off this way, then. For me."

"Yeah, probably." Time for a quick redirection, get her thinking about something else before she puts it together that I am, in fact, going to fuck her over. "Look," I say, turning off the tape recorder. "I'm pretty hungover. I can barely see straight, and the last thing I wanna do is work."

"So?"

"The food's already here." I gesture at my untouched plate. "So how about we have a nice lunch and chat. Just two people chatting. How about that?"

"It's your nickel."

"Dime."

"Whatever."

"So tell me about how you ended up in this line of work. It's not for the story, so you can tell me the truth." I'm getting antsy now, my feet tapping on the floor. Need to get moving on this. Soon.

"Nothing special. I ran away from home when I was fifteen. I lived in a little town a couple hours from here. Then I got here and I had to work, so I did food jobs and lived in a flophouse for a while. Then I temped and got an apartment. And that was fine for a while, then the agency closed and the new one couldn't get me anything that paid more than six an hour, and I had some other problems, and I lost my apartment, fell into some more problems, and the next thing I know, I have a kitty cat and a new apartment and there's some guy buying me lunch and asking me to tell him my story."

Fucking *kitty cat?*

She pokes the greens on her plate with her fork. "You want some?"

Apparently, my face registers the disgust, because she drops her fork, slouches back in her chair and crosses her arms.

"You think you're special?" she asks.

"Nah, I know how low on the ladder I am." I smile as broadly as my face will allow.

She's still slouched back in her chair, catting for an apology or an offer.

"Smoke?" I ask.

She doesn't say anything, just sticks out her hand.

"Not that easy. You gotta tell me something."

"What?"

"Your name."

"You know it already." She jiggles her outstretched hand.

"Your name is not fucking Luka. Which, might I add, isn't a very sexy moniker. Kinda clunky."

"What is it with you and wanting to know everybody's names?"

"It's not so much that I want to know, it's that I have to. Otherwise, my editor'll kill me." Actually, he wouldn't. It's for me. I like to know things. "See, if I have to prove to him that you or whoever else really exist, I can pull a birth certificate or a rap sheet or whatever."

"So you need me to help you cover your ass."

"Exactly. So?"

"Here's a hint—*Luka* is Hawaiian for?"

I light up and blow smoke her way. "I look cultured?" I pull out another cigarette halfway and set the pack on the table.

"Ruth." She reaches for the pack, but I yank it away.

"You gotta be quick," I say. "Last name is?"

"Give me the smoke."

"Not till you tell me."

"I can just go buy a pack across the street, you know."

"Go ahead."

She pushes back from the table, and the chair makes a horrible scraping noise against the tile floor.

"Sit down. Here." I toss the rest of the pack to her. "Keep 'em."

She smiles. "Thanks," she says, and then, after lighting up, "Robeson."

"Well then, Miss Robeson." I tap my watch. "I hate to eat and run, but." Nothing worse than having to sit still and behave when you want to *do* something.

"You got something better cooking?"

"Don't know if I'd go so far as to say 'better,' but I do have work to do."

"I thought you was working on my story."

How cute, she's taken ownership of my job. "One of many. But, look, we're going to have to chat again a time or two more, because we didn't really get shit done today." This would be the *deceive* half.

"You know where to find me," she says before sauntering toward the door, where she grabs her coat off the tree and walks out. I watch through the windows as she cruises up Leavenworth. Barely out the door before someone pulls over and she hops in.

Nice ride—silver Audi, dark smoked windows. For giggles, I jot down the tag.

I settle the bill with Olive Oyl, and my cell rings as I'm stepping outside. Allison.

"Hey." My voice jumps an octave. First I've spoken to her today, and I sound like a fucking elf. Way to look strong and independent, wanker. "What's going on?"

"Not much. I'm at work, about to go grab some lunch—"

Okay, so first thing I gotta do is get in touch with the neighborhood watch and find out about this john-list thing they've got going. "The gym, huh?" Which means I'm going to have to hang out with them and shit. Sucks, but, can do. And, fuck me, the cops . . . Donna's gotta owe me for something, so I can pass that buck over to her.

"—think we should talk."

Hate it when she pulls that rhetorical shit. "Talk?"

"We talked about it last night, remember?"

"We talked about you thinking we need to talk?" Musta been pretty fucked up. "Did I say anything?"

"Just that we have to talk."

"That it?"

"When are you getting home. Five?"

"Probably. Want anything?"

I hang up before I hear the answer, because I know she's going to say no. Yeah, not only can I finish her sentences, but I don't even have to wait for her to start them.

From the bistro, it's only about seven blocks to the Park-Leavenworth Neighborhood Improvement Association headquarters, its location divined from a quick phone call to the office. A short drive, really, and it gives me just enough time to think that maybe she—Allison—has decided to finally suck it up and find someone respectable so she can pursue that full, satisfied life shtick. She's, what? Couple years younger than me. Probably getting bruised by her maternal pangs. I have, I realize, scant evidence of this. But she's never given me flak about getting fucked up. If anything, she's encouraged it. Call it a working theory: that she wants to *talk* is really her wanting to ditch. Which is fine. Saves me the trouble. One might wonder why. One might also not need to wonder why.

Pulling up out front, I find the address is also that of Hacker Catering, and it throws me a little. These places normally come in one of two flavors: the tiny, dedicated storefront that has maybe a conference room in the back and a donated Tandy or two up front, because access to technology, no matter how dated and faulty it may be, is tantamount to empowerment. The other way they come is what I expected to find here: something offensively low-budget that's based at a folding card table in the corner of someone's dark, musty, unfinished basement. But it appears the fine working folks who live around here have found a happy medium. So good for them.

My entrance to the shop is marked by a thin metallic clang because the bell that hangs over the door is missing its striker. The lobby, or whatever you call the space up front at a catering shop, is furnished with a couple random discarded restaurant tables and mismatched chairs. Few framed pictures of Italy or somewhere else photogenic nailed to the eggshell walls. Other than that, pretty dreary in here with the sallow sunlight filtered through dirty windows. Ashtray on the countertop with a few brown butts in it, so don't mind if I do.

Nobody's around, for all I can tell. No noise from the back room, so I give a cursory "Hello?" Nothing doing. The Cockburn of Last Week would say something like "Well, fuck it, I tried" and walk out at this point. But since there's blood in the water, I figure I can stick it out till I at least finish the cigarette.

Couple-few drags later, there's a thumping, wheezing disturbance way in the back of the place. "Hey," I shout. The thumping stops.

"Someone there?" a longtime smoker asks.

"Nope."

"Good." And the thumping starts again.

"I lied," I shout. Pause till the thumping stops. "Someone's up here."

Couple phlegm-filled hacks and coughs. "Who'sit?"

"Opportunity." Because why give the spiel to someone I can't see?

A guy who doesn't look nearly old enough to be carting around that oxygen tank walks in from the back. Guy's probably not even forty-five. Wearing all white, from his carpenter jeans to his thermal top to his blank, mesh-backed baseball cap. He squints up at me from behind round, rimless glasses and wipes his brow with, of course, a white handkerchief.

"Bernard Cockburn. I'd shake your hand, but the counter here"—I pat the top to demonstrate—"is prohibitively tall."

"Denny Amsterdam," he mumbles more than says.

"I'm with the *News-Telegraph*."

"Yeah?"

"And I'm writing a story about the neighborhood."

"Lots here."

"Yes there is. And this address is listed as the neighborhood association headquarters."

"That it is."

"And I understand the association organizes a night patrol of sorts."

"That we do."

People love to talk about themselves and the insignificant projects and hobbies they adopt to give a tinge of meaning to their otherwise dismal lives. So the fact that this jerkoff's just standing here, blinking and mumbling like a doofus, could mean a couple things. It could mean that he is, in fact, a doofus. But what it probably means is he's in possession of information he knows I want, but he doesn't want to fork it over. So, how to spin it? Give him the reins. "I can come back another time if you're busy."

"Now is fine." He pulls out a brown cigarette and lights up. Takes a couple seconds before the rotten-to-the-point-of-sweet odor hits.

"Cloves, huh?"

"I prefer them to regular tobacco cigarettes."

"That a fact?"

"It is my opinion that clove cigarettes taste superior to to-bacco cigarettes."

Well, now we're making some progress. So long as he keeps the cherry away from that tank he's connected to, this might move along just splendidly. "I'm more of a Camel guy," I say while stabbing out the butt. "Call me old-fashioned, right?"

"Clove cigarettes date back to biblical times."

"You got me there. So, Denny, my man, what I'd like to do is"—get the fuck out of here before I end up hanging from a meat hook in the basement—"hang out a night or two with the patrol. Think you can set me up with that?"

"I would say, yes, that it is possible." He drags on his clove, and his eyes cross as he does so.

"Think you can tell me a little about how it works?"

He tightens his lips, then noisily pops open his mouth. "We rendezvous here Saturday and Sunday nights at ten."

"And then what happens? After *le rendezvous?*"

"That depends on how many of us meet for the rendezvous. We patrol in groups of two to three in automobiles and maintain radio contact." He reaches beneath the counter and retrieves a wooden milk crate full of Toys 'R' Us–grade walkie-talkies. "I stay here to maintain the registry."

Ding! *Registry*. Love it. "Tell me about the registry."

"This"—he grabs an orange imitation-leather-bound ledger book from the counter's bowels—"is the registry."

The back of my neck tingles. "Mind if I have a little look-see?"

He turns it around, and I start flipping through the pages. For as bottom-drawer as the rest of the operation seems, Denny's definitely a detail person. Goes back about ten months, and each page is divided into columns labeled *make, model, license, time, color, locaton* [sic], *name,* and has room for about forty unlucky guys. Flipping through it, no names of note jump out at me, which is a bummer. Something I do notice, however, is the majority of the tags here are from the next county over, where Offutt Air Force Base is, which makes sense, because the airmen gotta have something to do with their money. Nothing new there.

"You started keeping the registry when you started doing the patrol thing?"

"That is true, yes."

"So, this information in here, what do you do with it?"

Denny's arm falls to his side, and the burning tip of his cigarette swings dangerously close to the hose. "Every Monday morning I make a photocopy of the newest entries and hand-deliver it to our police department contact."

Bet that guy loves his job. "I hear this info also finds its way out onto the Internet."

"I would not know too much about that. That is Bill's project."

Okay, it's starting to get weird how this guy never uses contractions. "Bill?"

"Dunkel."

"You know how I can get ahold of him?"

"If you want to come back here Saturday night." Denny wrinkles up his nose like he's going to snort. But he doesn't. "He will be here then."

"You don't happen to know the website where Bill puts this stuff out, do you?"

Denny bends down so far he disappears. When he resurfaces, he hands me a letter-sized sheet of hot-pink paper. Printed on it in that cheesy faded-brushstroke font is a URL so long the paper had to be set to landscape. One of those http://members.aol.com/something/somethingelse.html sites nobody'd ever find even if they knew precisely what they were looking for.

"Why the flyer?"

"We planned on posting them throughout the city."

"But?"

"Bill said we have to obtain handbill permits before we can do that."

"That's a blue law. Nobody's gonna care if you put these up." Am I scooping myself? Nope. "But you wouldn't want to listen to my legal advice."

"We want to be completely in adherence to the law in our operation."

"That's very noble." I fold up the flyer and slide it into my pocket. "The dough to run this operation, where's it come from?"

He clears his throat. "Grant."

"Grant who?"

"City grant."

Duh. "I hear a couple of your guys got arrested a week or two ago."

"That was unfortunate."

"Unfortunate the kid they beat up wasn't a pusher."

Denny doesn't respond to my feeble attempt at camaraderie.

"You know the fellas who got picked up?"

"They are no longer part of our organization."

Political, this guy. "Denny, it's been great. See you Saturday night, then?"

He doesn't say anything, just turns around and wheels his little oxygen tank behind him into the darkened back room.

five

Back in the office, I poke at the Selectric's keys for a few seconds before feeding it one of last week's press releases from the cops. *Fuckity fuckity fuck fuck fuck.* I stare at the line of type until the words decay into letters and the letters into lines and loops and the lines and loops into blurry smudges. There's something about the office, especially now. No matter how tweaked I might be for something, walking down those steps feels like diving into a pool of syrupy malaise.

"Get with it, jackass." Donna flicks a paper clip at me, and it bounces off my glasses.

"Watch it, goddammit. You're gonna scratch 'em."

She repeats what I just said in a whiny voice, and ends the line, after a brief pause, with "Pussy."

I lean back in my chair and steal a glance at what she's editing the hell out of. Paper looks like a crime scene. "Whatcha working on?"

"If I was some hippie who got paid to write the horoscope? Know what I'd do? I'd turn it in on time and write it in English. What's 'mesmerizing seclusion' mean?"

"You quit again, didn't you?"

"Or how about—I don't know—let's change 'from beneath the scrabbly underbrush, the dark other side of you emerges' to 'your dark side comes out,' or, maybe, 'takes over.' What, did he write this, plug it into some online French D&D translator and then retranslate it back?"

"Smoke?"

"No, I quit again."

So, I light up. She'd do the same to me, bless her heart. As the only two reporters on staff, we lean on each other pretty frequently. She normally covers the lighter stuff, though there's a tiny gray area where our worlds overlap, so it isn't that uncommon for one of us to try to pass the buck. Divorced, with a daughter, she's been with the paper for a couple years, and I've come to like her and trust her judgment-slash-discretion, so, naturally, I do whatever I can to make her time in the office something like an ice pick wedged beneath her thumbnail. Otherwise, I don't suppose she'd know I think she's pretty okay.

While ashing on the pile of fresh-today press releases, I notice the one on top. It's from the mayor's office and was sent at 7:46 A.M. yesterday morning. *MEDIA EVENT: The Mayor will address recently released crime statistics at a 9:00 A.M. press conference TODAY in the Mayor's Press Room. Chief O'Grady will also be available for comments.*

No way out of writing this one. Crime numbers definitely fall within my jurisdiction. I call Seth, the mayor's spokesman. He says he'll fax over the mayor's prepared comments.

"What'd the chief have to say?" I ask.

"Uhh, wait one," he says. I hear him shuffling through the papers on his desk, the inept sixty-grand-a-year prick. Or maybe I'm just jealous. "The Omaha Police Department is aware of the trend and is addressing the issue."

I could call up the cop public-information office, but they don't really trust me, little mishap a couple-few years ago. I'll attribute the quote to Seth. Six minutes to beat out a ten-inch story on the crime stats (violent crime is up, property crime is down) and slide the copy into my outbox. Call my guy at the DMV and give him the Audi tag from earlier. Says it's registered to a security company. Babylon.

"Wasn't that a Meat Loaf song?" I ask him. "By the dashboard light?"

He hangs up on me.

"Donna," I say.

She grunts.

"What's say you pay me back for that favor you owe me."

"I don't owe you anything."

"Sure you do." No, she doesn't. "Think real hard."

"I don't have time. What do you want?"

"Need you to call up the Southeast Precinct and talk to who-ever does the community liaison thing there about how his Park-Leavenworth children are running amok. And get a copy of their weed-and-seed grant paperwork."

"Your story. Why should I help you?"

"I'll copyedit the hippie for a month."

There's a prolonged silence. Then a paper airplane sails over the file cabinet that separates our desks. It's the horoscope.

"Love you long time," I say. And, no, we never have. She's not my type: meaner than me, taller than me, has a kid, uses the word *eclectic* in her stories too often. But I dig the cut of her jib. "I need"—I clear my throat—"another favor."

"Fuck off, already."

"Can't you go home or something? I gotta use your computer."

"Use Manny's."

"It's broken." Not really, but the last time I used it, I sorta poked around and found a grip of barely legal-slash-fatty porn. Some things, about some people, are better left unknown. And if I hop on his machine again, I'll end up snooping some more. It's a sickness.

She says "Retard" as she puts on her coat. Sashays out the door without a look back. If she had a younger sister, perhaps.

Finding those jokers who got arrested isn't that big a deal. Run a Nexis search for *omaha mormon arrested assault*, and—bang— you've got Creighton Korbes and James Wozniak.

Couple hits on Korbes. Old story is he ran a smashingly un- successful campaign for the District 3 City Council seat five years ago. Rounded up enough signatures to get him on the primary ballot, but only got 4 percent of the vote. New story is some guy named Leon Calhoun was fucked out of his mind on embalming- fluid-soaked weed (illy, the kids call it) and ran a red going near eighty, T-boning Korbes's car. Five in the morning about two minutes away from Korbes's house. Calhoun died, Korbes nearly did. This was barely a week ago. Calhoun nets a couple pings. Misdemeanor police blotter stuff. Drugs. Soliciting. Concealed weapon. These dingers go back a few years, so how fortuitous for the cleanup crew that one of the chronically unwanted erased himself.

Only hit on Wozniak is from a quote the daily ran back when the Asarco plant was getting shut down. Lead smelting plant on the riverfront, the management of which never felt it necessary to secure a clean air permit. And why should they? Took the EPA thirty years to come knocking. It was a big stink then. Big now, too, 'cause the EPA never left. Eighty years of unchecked smelting, smokestacks pumping out millions of tons of lead and arsenic. Take that and throw in the goons from the now-defunct Brill battery plant who got busted dumping slag all over the north side, and there's your explanation for why sunny River City is the largest Superfund cleanup site in the nation and why the next generation of natives are going to be chud-babies. This worried Wozniak enough that he waited in line at an early '90s public hearing to say his piece. Could be the reporter was taken by Wozniak's delightfully clichéd commentary. Only reason I can come up with why he'd get a direct quote about the "slippery slope these straw-man corporations are pushing us down, and it bottoms out in Pandora's Box." Okay, so he's been a loon for a while.

Look up the duo in the directory, and here's Korbes on Marcy Street off 31st and Wozniak, J-hopefully-as-in-James, one block up. Not a bad way to blow an afternoon.

A brief driving tour reveals an array of small houses. Not shitty ones. Staunchly lower middle class, but only after a couple generations of busting your balls and resenting the frat-boy fuck-heads who rent out the house next door on daddy's dime and keep the recycling bin perpetually filled with crushed Milwaukee's Best cans.

Jam the car into park in front of a pinkish stucco number with a "For Sale" sign out front. Little basket crammed full of flyers hanging from the signpost. Smidge over seventy grand and you, too, can have two beds, a bath and a half, an unfinished basement, a carport and a galley kitchen with new linoleum. *Great starter home*, it says.

Plan is to hit Korbes first, then hoof it over to Wozniak's abode. Alpha order, because there's always a system. Address I have written down is a tiny blue ranch. Privacy fence lines the backyard. What appears to be a recently constructed wheelchair ramp leads up the front steps to the door. Hit the buzzer and wait, but there's nothing doing. Quiet inside and the lights are off. Try the buzzer again, but the result's the same. Mail slot in the front door, so I kneel and peek in. Can't really discern one thing from another. Shadows and furniture. Looks like maybe a giant buck head mounted at the end of the hall. I'm about to give it up when I hear a cough from inside. Sure, I *could* have imagined that, but it's immediately followed by a groaning floorboard.

"Hello?" I venture. "Looking for Mr. Korbes." Pronounce it *Korbs*, because the accented *e*—we don't do that out here. "Just wanna chat a second." So, should I keep looking through the mail slot as I talk? Or would that make my voice too muffled? Put my mouth level with it, maybe? Other option is neither. Guy doesn't wanna chat right now. Get back to him after talking to his former comrades. Fish out a card and slide it into the slot. As I withdraw my paw, I hear a grunt, and then something hard and heavy crashes down on my fingers. I recoil, and it feels like my hand's being torched. Kick the door, shout something about cocksucker-motherfucker. Give my hand a few shakes before examining it. Fingers still work on command, so nothing's broken. Hurts like hell, though. "Fuck, man," I say to the closed door, "just wanted to talk." Stand on the porch a couple seconds to see if he wants to kiss and make up. "Another time, then. Call me."

I half consider skipping Wozniak's place, seeing as how, you know, I'm not in any mood to get entirely chewed up today, but how much fun wouldn't that be?

Place I'm after turns out to be a faded yellow number, bungalow-style and probably mail-ordered from the Sears catalog. Only house on the block with an iron gate and matching grates over the windows—second floor, even. What sticks, though, is the flagpole sprouting from the doorframe. Nothing hanging— just a lanyard blowing in the breeze, banging against the hollow pole. That sound's always bugged me; like it's the last thing a guy would hear before a much louder crack.

I'm walking up the walk when an old couple dressed in black step onto the porch. Guy's wearing a bowler, she a huge-brimmed, veiled thing. Gentleman he is, he hands her a cigarette from his crushed soft pack and lights her before taking care of himself. So I join them.

"Greetings," I say.

"Hello there," says Bowler.

"Chilly, no?" Weather talk. The oldies love it.

"It's what happens in December," says the wife. "Has for years."

A shrewd one, she. "That a fact?"

"Were you a friend of James?" she asks.

"Something happen?"

"Oh dear," says the guy. He drops his cigarette, barely smoked, and steps on it. "James, he passed."

"Passed?" coughs the lady, her voice heavy with indignation or cancer or both, "He's dead. Shot full of holes, and, really, it's for the best." She draws on her smoke. "You live under a rock?"

"Only during high season. You wanna fill me in?"

"Boy'd been rotten for as long as I knew him, which was his whole life. Poor Janice in there, run ragged for forty-four years trying to keep herself together and keep him in line. Should've given up years ago, but she wouldn't."

Ah, Wozniak, J-as-in-Janice. "So James, then, got himself shot?"

"By the police."

Not that I don't believe her, but I don't. That, I'd know about. "In town?"

"Read today's paper. It's all there." Are those ice cubes she's spewing?

"Sorta embarrassing," I say, digging for a card and my notebook, "but I'm with the *News-Telegraph*."

"Vulture," she spits. "Get the hell away from here. Janice's suffered enough."

"But," I say.

"Woman loses her only son and granddaughter the same day. What if it was your mother? Would you want some cheaply dressed schmuck harassing her? Would you?" She drops her cigarette and tugs on Bowler's sleeve. "Henry. Inside."

Those little hairs on the back of my neck, they're standing right the fuck up. James Wozniak, it appears, is my freako from yesterday. So why's he live way the fuck up north and play down here? Plenty of trouble up there. Maybe he loves his mama. Whatever it is, these sad jokers are going to move some papers.

What bugs, though, is I shoulda made this connection yesterday. Weekly deadlines mean the death of hustle.

Hop in the car and lead-foot it back to the office. Not like the information's going to disappear, but why the fuck not? After five, so the place is barren. Run my children through whatever databases I can hook up to: fed court, county register of deeds and assessor. Nothing fed—no shocker there. County land records show Korbes owns his place, but nothing for the Woz. So the guy rented. Like me, so it's less a judgment than an observation.

Weird that yesterday's fireworks didn't turn up on Nexis earlier. I hit it again, just to double-check, and, nope. Run a vaguer search and a story pops up. Reporter didn't drop Woz's name. Looks like I'm not the only one doing less than he should.

Plug Wozniak's address into the assessor's database, and, here we go: WJC Investments, LLC, owns 3497 Redick. WJC goes into the search field, and it's listed as owner of seven other buildings, all bought in the past few months, and all, save Woz's joint, are within a block of one another. WJC's up on its taxes. Have to check with the secretary of state tomorrow to get the scoop on who's holding what in the LLC. WJC—someone's initials. Always is. Whoever it is might have some Wozniak dirt. (W-as-in-Wozniak, J-as-in-James, C-as-in-corporation, coalition, club, cooperative, commission?) Landlords, they know things.

Okay, so what's the story here, kid? Got the city bankrolling a group of miscreants who've seen too many Westerns and bad cop movies. They've gone rogue, but not rogue enough that they don't care about keeping up appearances, hence the ejection of the two guys who got busted for beating up that Mormon kid. And at least one of those two is now dead. The other, well, he's freaked out about someone or something.

All this goes into a half page of typo-filled notes (writing things down—it never hurts), and as I grind out a cigarette on the floor, I notice it's near six, which is as full a day as I've had in months, and I'm not done yet. Still gotta run across town to the color lab, because the Walgreens down the street won't touch my film anymore. Complaints from the kid who runs the photo area that it's too gruesome. Meanwhile, I've seen the greasy prick cruising around the Old Market with the other Goth kids wearing a Cannibal Corpse shirt and eyeliner. Anyway, it's not a bad deal, because the new place delivers the negatives.

Stop around the corner at Leroy the Shine's shop. Across the street from the main library branch, he's the only storefront in an otherwise derelict building. Windows upstairs broken or boarded, Leroy's place isn't much better. Steel-grated, grit-covered window so filthy you can't read the *Shine Shop* lettering. Noxious inside.

Polish, leather, sweat, stale chew spit. Leroy's turned away from the door, ripping the sole off a cowboy boot. Back of his white shirt's a collage of black and brown smudges.

"My man," he says, tugging violently, "you missed the boat on that annexation story last week. Reason the city of Omaha wants that land is because it's owned by a black family. Once the city gets the land, them dirt farmers gotta start paying city taxes, which they cain't. Friend of my cousin's daughter's how I know."

"Probably," I say. Leroy here, he loves a good conspiracy. Or a bad one. Anything to chat about. In this case, he's wrong. Omaha wants to swallow a town out west, but the border between the two has to be contiguous before it can annex. Which isn't very exciting, I know. "Need some black polish."

One final tug and he rips free the sole. Drops it in the garbage and walks over. Plug in his mouth. Radio station giveaway T-shirt. (*Z98—The home of alternative rock!*) Deep-set eyes behind a pair of military-issue glasses. "Them shoes you wearing is brown." Grabs a paper cup from his workbench and spits into it.

"It's for another pair."

"Give it to you for free if you talk to my cousin's daughter's friend about getting the shaft."

"Bigger fish at the moment. Two-fifty, right?" Counting change.

"How about this—you write about how I'm getting run out of my shop after twenty-seven-and-a-third years in this spot."

"Who's running you out?"

"Don't know. Some crackers been through the building taking pictures."

"You ask your landlord about it?"

"Landlord, shit. Motherfucker lives in Oklahoma City."

"Phones work down there, too."

"Do me a solid here, man."

"And find out about the picture-taking crackers?"

"Right."

"The ones you think are running you out?"

"You think I'm batty, but Leroy ain't stupid. Any time white folks go poking around some dump is because they trying to score dope and pussy or they wanna tear it down and put in a McDonald's. And they ain't no pussy or dope upstairs, less you can get high and wet on pigeon shit."

So Leroy's got a point. "I'll put in a phone call or two."

I pocket the polish and step outside thinking I shoulda just given him the cash.

<u>six</u>

"Hey," Allison says. She's sitting at the dinner table, leafing through a magazine. Her hair today is orange. Yesterday it wasn't. So she feels it, too, because cosmetic alterations are what she does when she doesn't want to be thinking about that which she oughta be thinking. "Long day, huh?"

I sit on the couch and kick off my shoes. "Happens."

"You don't look so hot. Feeling okay?" She walks up behind me and rubs my shoulders.

This brashly kind move of hers surprises me. "Like a champ. So, what's up, Tiger Lily?"

"Hold on a sec." She walks into the kitchen and cracks an ice tray. Throws a couple cubes into a glass, it sounds like. I start to feel deflated, like I'm up on the gallows looking down at a cheering mob. Not feeling like the executioner I oughta right now.

Allison sits next to me and hands me a rocks glass filled to the brim with the brown stuff. Twice as much as I'd normally pour, but a gift horse's mouth, right? Draw in a sip and set the glass on top of one of her magazines. "Thanks," I say. "Let's begin, shall we?"

"I'm pregnant."

"No you're not."

She smiles like she just gave me a present she's not sure I'll like. "I took a test."

"If this is a joke, it stopped being funny before it started."

She marches to the bathroom, and when she comes back, she tosses the test box at me. "Satisfied?"

"A mere prop."

She takes another trip to the bathroom, this time brandishing the test wand thing upon her exit. And, sure enough, there's a little blue plus sign in the window. I suddenly feel ill.

"But you're on the pill," I inform the plus sign.

There's a short silence, during which I remember Allison had to pee on this thing. So I set it on the coffee table. "So, what the fuck?" I say.

"What the fuck, what?"

"You haven't made arrangements, then?" Check that. "Yet?"

"No, I haven't. And I don't plan on it, so neither should you."

"Nothing to it. Just like getting an ingrown toenail yanked."

"That's really fucked up, Burn. Psycho fucked up."

What can you say to that? So I nod thoughtfully.

"Anyway, it's early on, so we've got plenty of time to figure things out."

"You-and-I, we?"

"Right, what we're going to do."

"Care to elaborate?"

"One, you'll need to find a job that pays what you're worth."

Dig how she spun it so the move would be for my betterment. "Ahh, no."

"I'm just being realistic, Burn."

"But you don't even like me."

"You're right. I—"

"Don't even."

"What do you want me to say?"

Silent for a bit, and I'm thinking that some things might be unintentional—spilling a drink, slipping on the ice and cracking open your head—but procreation, that's always intentional. At least halfway. "This." I wave at her gravid midsection. "This was planned."

She levels some serious hate eyes at me. "How can you even think that? Accidents happen."

I begin to formulate a retort—it involves a variation on the theme of "my ass"—but my faculties are momentarily lost to a hot swirl of frustration, resentment, anger, desperation and shame. Light a cigarette and drag on it so hard, nicotine syrup might ooze out the filter. Got this consuming, gnashing pain setting up shop. I know it well. It's specific to life-altering moments and carries some ugly associations: Mom, blue-white in a hospital bed. Dad, chewed all to hell. Couple girls I sorta knew back when, in pieces. And now, add this to the stock footage: Allison looking at me like I just pissed on the surprise dinner she spent all day cooking.

It's down the gullet with the remainder of the whiskey. Feel the burn, Burn. Be the burn. "You're getting that thing sucked out, or you can fuck off."

Here, she slaps me. A mean, print-leaving smack that knocks my glasses to the floor and stings like a motherfucker. "Asshole," she spits.

"That's the best you've got, sugar"—grab the specs—"it's best not brought."

"Get the fuck away from me."

I stand and look around at all the shit here that isn't mine and that I never wanted. All the furniture, the rugs, the bullshit faux art hanging on the walls—all hers. Threw out my shit when she moved in. *Cheap,* she said. *Tacky,* she said. *Whatever,* I said. She took a steak knife and slammed it down into my coffee table. Twisted the blade and peeled back the top. *See? Veneer.* Pissed me off and turned me on at the same time, her budding bourgeois tendencies tempered by the violence with which she displayed them. Still, shoulda known.

Grab the coat and hit the bricks for the short haul to the Stuck Pig. Just across the street, really. (And I'd be full of shit if I said the bar's proximity to the apartment wasn't the main reason I acquiesced to moving there.) Group of about fifteen, twenty guys standing around out front, smoking. Weird, because unless the Unicameral rammed through some instant smoking ban in the last four hours, there's no reason these dipshits should be outside puffing butts. At least, not when it's five degrees and the sidewalk's treacherous with scabby junkie fucks from the Warwick Arms next door. Bulletproofed lobby. Stink of cat piss wafts out onto the sidewalk.

As I get closer, I start to make out a few faces . . . guys with whom I have nodding, grunting, at-the-bar-only acquaintances. Couldn't tell you their names, but I know what they drink. I tap the shoulder of the fat guy who wears chef's pants and drinks Michelob Ultra. He turns, nods and grunts at me.

"You guys are outside because a what?" I ask.

"Music tonight, man. That whiny acoustic twat. Doing a surprise show. Surprised?"

"But why are you outside?"

"He and two hundred of his closest friends are setting up in there. Hitting the Niner, man, you should go, too."

"Think I'll rough it." One of my finer qualities, see, is loyalty. Deal it out in small, deserving doses.

As always, my glasses fog up before the door swings closed. Bar's pretty packed. Hunched-over backs as far as the 20-50 eye can see. I perch myself on the last open stool, which is at the end of the bar (next to the package coolers, which might come in handy later) and set my short stack of bills on the mahogany next to my glasses. They're slowly returning to the point of usability. My neighbor looks like he's pushing eighty, which means he's probably forty. He's got a yellow mutt leashed up around the legs of his stool, and the thing's staring up at me like it knows I've been a bad boy. Meanwhile, the old guy's got a copy of the *News-Telegraph* open in front of him. The bar, see, it's one of our distribution points. Cover this week is the 8,273rd feature we've run on that director who films all his movies here. Or, rather, filmed. He's moved on to greener.

"Anything good in there?" I ask him.

He looks at me and I see he's missing the lower half of his left ear. "Read all this crap in the real paper last week."

I yank over the paper, turn to page eight and jam down my finger on the Stuck Pig ad. Gimmick here is the bar runs an ad that features a rock-and-roll trivia question. Answer it correctly, get a free shot. And guess who comes up with the questions. "Tell Mick the answer is Mink DeVille and go fuck yourself." You know how it's okay to torment your younger brother, but when the neighbor kid calls him a pussy, you get pissed, because that's *your* brother? Right.

The old guy dismissively throws up his hand and returns his attention to the exit sign across the room that glows like a beacon in the fog or an exit sign in the thick smoke of a dingy bar.

"Scoop," Mick shouts above the din, "what's happening?"

"I'm fucking parched. Gimme-gimme a Miller Lite."

"Miller Lite? That's total dyke beer. Stock up on it when

the Indigo Girls play town. The lesbians, man, they love it." He reaches down into the cooler and fetches my dyke beer.

"Being a dyke, it ain't so bad, you know," I say after swallowing a mouthful. The mutt's sniffing at my jeans. I spit a small stream of beer onto its back, the cocksucker.

Mick's going through my cash when he asks, "Where's your girlie?"

"Fucking off, last I checked."

"Left you a think-of-me, I see." Rubbing his cheek, he walks off. I put on my glasses and scan the room for friendly faces, but there aren't any. It appears, however, that the bar has been taken over by a gaggle of retards. Not retards like you'd normally hear someone say "retard" out here—which is another way of calling something gay. Actual, no-insult-intended-to-retarded-people retards. Must be the in look among the young indie-rock set. Steak-knife haircuts and ill-fitting thrift-store clothes and greasy hair and pale skin and thick glasses. And still they manage to have hot girlfriends. Guess it's something else I'll never understand. Which is fine, because the kid with the guitar strums a chord and clears his throat. Can't see him from where I'm sitting, but I don't need to.

"If you want to," his amplified, effeminate voice informs the crowd, "you can sit down."

It's like a bad reenactment of kindergarten as the whole mess of them pull up squares of the filthiest floor in town. Once they're all cozy, he starts playing. Some sad, minor-key, two-chord dirge about how much he drinks. The dog howls and I wish music were dangerous again. Anyway, I sip my way through his song, wait for the applause to die, then I loudly tell him he sucks. Disregarding my commentary, he starts on the second song and isn't through the first verse when it sounds like he starts to cry as he sings. Same guy, mind you, that's been nailing that model who was on the cover of *Maxim* last month and who just bought a four-bedroom in Country Club. Breaking my fucking heart, this guy. Or, could be I'm envious.

The irony is not lost on me that I came here to get shitty and internally piss and moan, only to find this cunt, who makes a gajillion dollars moping while strumming his acoustic, doing very nearly the same thing, except he's going to get laid later. This miserable fuckdrip and his fucking wish-I-were-Dylan tunes. I imagine it's the kind of stuff Allison likes. Which doesn't matter. What matters, maybe, is this: I am fucked. And my plan (though I'd consider it a duty, all things considered) to go through this world sans offspring got all but shot to shit thanks to the classic fault of the womb: when it's occupied, it prevents its host from making sound judgments. Or am I being a reactionary shit?

I've got my reasons. Namely, I thought I'd already escaped the doomed life my parents chose. Married and with child by the time they were 21. My dad, a college-educated numbers guy, joined the navy for the steady check and spent the rest of his days calculating risk and acceptable loss. *If x planes fly at y altitude and drop z ordnance at q time, what are the chances of success? How many planes can we expect to lose in a worst-case scenario? How many enemy casualties can we realistically anticipate?* Not that he was philosophical about it, because he wasn't; he was matter-of-fact about how he snapped to it one day that the equations he scribbled down actually, factually meant he was an accessory to sending an acceptable number of men to their precalculated deaths. I've wondered, a time or two, whether maybe, when he was losing it, he ever sat down with a calculator and a pencil and figured up the value of his own life. If he had, it must have totaled out to near zero.

I asked him, once, what he would've done if he didn't have the bad luck to start a family so young. *CPA or forensic accountant or something,* he said, like he coulda been a contenda. Slow the fuck down, crazy man, I told him. *Bernard,* he said, *I ever tell you you were an accident?*

Mom, she was a little different. Dropped out of college before she got her BFA in photography so she could have her precious baby boy. The Canon I use, it belonged to her. Mr. Nostalgia, me. After she forcefully ejected me into the waiting arms of a (more than likely) poorly qualified physician at some military hospital or another, she continued to dabble in pictures for a while, using a young and willing Bernard Alvin Cockburn in her shots as a tiny, angry (and, in retrospect, too obvious) metaphor for everything wrong with her world. That was me, age four, in my underwear, standing on my bed and holding a nightmarish Tiki mask over my face; squatted down in front of a bush wearing an infantry helmet and holding a wilted sunflower; playing dead in the kitchen table's shadow. That whole enterprise was shelved when we were transferred from Seattle to Florida when I was, I don't know, six. Used to think it was my fault, that I ruined it all for her, because after we switched coasts, I headed off to full days of school, leaving her without a model. She went to work as a secretary, which she kept doing after the old man's final orders came through—the ones with Offutt AFB typed on them. She got a gig with a defense contractor and typed reports and filed files and answered phones till her ovaries became fatally corrupted. I gloss this latter development because it happened quickly and I resent how it went down. Seven months, the first four of which they kept me in the dark. Then they were sorry about that and she, his only friend, went and died. He enjoyed a diminishing quality of life for a good seven–eight years, and then there was an incident for which I am blameless. This is all true, though conjecture can hit harder and certainly play dirtier than fact. (*Fact,* that nerdy stepbrother of truth.)

To wit: it's my fault that they lost out on whatever they coulda, shoulda, woulda done. Take the little shitheel out of the picture, and? I'll never know. Just like I'll never know if where I'm at is a plateau or a summit. Ditch? Doesn't matter, because it's downhill from here.

Haven't thought about any of this in a while. But, in light of recent events, fuck it. It's the easiest thing to cop to. The other shit, I'd rather not.

By the time the teary-voiced cockscrubber's done with his set, I've had four or seven beers and a couple shots. The shots were on the house because Mick's a nice guy and takes care of me— I more than cover the tab he runs up at the paper for his ad. So I'm grabbing my leftover couple bucks and the old guy next to me drops his head on the bar. I think for a second that maybe he died, because I'm just in that sorta mood, but his lips are moving, and he slurs out something indecipherable.

Little loose on the walk home, and by the time I reach the bedroom, which does not contain, as I'd assumed it would, a sleeping Allison, it hits me that the apartment has this weird pall over it, like something ugly's gone down here. Or maybe I'm projecting. Planted on the couch, I flip from CNN to MSNBC to Fox News, but they're all doing the same stories—car bomb in Israel, earthquake in Turkey, workplace shooting in Michigan. It's a troubling sort of comfort this nasty shit gives me. So long as people can read and there's fucked-up shit happening, there's a place for me in this world.

Thirsty for distraction, I grab an Old Style, fetch from my coat pocket the flyer I picked up earlier today from the catering shop and fire up the computer. Waiting for the thing to boot, I inspect the pink sheet of paper. It has two blocks of text on it: the 36-point website banner, and then a smallish manifesto printed in

your standard fixed-width font that gives it an underground revo-
lutionary feel. Of course, then you read it:

> We, the Park-Leavenworth Neighborhood Improvement
> Association, have had enough of the illegal and unmoral
> activities that have scourged are neighborhood for too
> long. To combat this cancer that is eating the soul of
> our homes, we, with the suport and co-operation of the
> Omaha Police Department launched this website in the
> hopes that knowlege is power. We know who you are,
> and now the world does to!!

Which is just too easy, so I'm not even going to start. My
foot's tap-tap-tapping away at the floor, and I'm about ready to
gnaw on the chair's legs by the time I punch in the URL, and
what comes up is an online family photo album of "Our Trip to
the Smokeys!!!" Bunch of blurry, compositionally flawed photos depicting a young family, presumably the Dunkels: skinny,
pale white guy, an ogre with a bad perm for a wife and toddler
daughter who's too young to yet comprehend how shitty her
life's going to be. They're at some tourist campsite. What takes
the website to the next level is the photo captions. "Sheila's so
afraid of bears!" reads the one that accompanies a photo of the
wife drinking a soda next to a fire pit. I don't get it, either.

So it's over to Switchboard, where I plug in this Dunkel guy's
name and, zing-zing, here's his phone number and address, which
I write down on the back of his flyer. Not quite eleven, so I punch
the number into my cell and, naturally, get his voice mail. Picks
up after the first ring, so they must have the phone off the hook.

"Hi, you've reached the Dunkels. Bill"—voice switches to
who I assume is his wife—"Sheila and"—hold up the kid—"Julie."

Back to Bill. "We can't get to phone right now, so leave a message at the beep"—Julie again—"and we'll call you right—"

I hang up because anyone sad enough to have that message and that website has got to either routinely beat the piss out of his wife or have some other socially unacceptable habit. Call it a hunch, but it's pretty obvious the guy has nothing even approaching a satisfying day-in-day-out, so his little dalliances on the side are probably what keep him going, which means I should at least try to talk to the guy. Maybe we can compare notes. But why fuck with his wife and kid? Course, at the same time, Bill's little sexual-ethical conundrum would make for some nice texture in the story, so I hit redial and leave a message that Bill should call me. Might as well get the goods, regardless of whether I ultimately choose to write him in. Besides, is keeping his atomic unit happy and healthy my job? I don't think so, either. And I'd be remiss if I didn't acknowledge that fucking with someone makes me feel at least a little better.

Google a few variations of *omaha john list* and *park-leavenworth neighborhood improvement association* but come up empty. Makes me think it hasn't launched yet. So why have a zillion pretty pink flyers printed? Which is a question I can ask this Bill schlub when I see him.

That done, I throw on NOMEANSNO's *Wrong*, crank up the fucker and get out the mop and broom. Couple bourbons later, I've swept, dusted, mopped and otherwise spic-and-spanned the place to a hearty luster. Bored and barely midnight and I'm not far gone enough to think that going out to drink again is a viable entertainment option, so I'll content myself with getting fucked here on Tuinal-bourbon cocktails. Which is fine, just fine.

seven

"Donna, what the fuck is that?"

We're standing by the office entrance at quarter to ten. I just walked in and waved her over after seeing some zit-faced kid sitting at my desk looking dumbly at the Selectric and holding a manila envelope.

"Intern. From the University of No Opportunity. Manny didn't say anything to you about it?"

Ah, the University of Nebraska at Omaha, which, back when I thought I had printer's ink for blood, bestowed upon me my BS in journalism. No shortage of humor potential there. "No. He told you?"

"Day or two ago, yeah."

I eye the underaged interloper and turn back to Donna. "So, what, I gotta show this kid the ropes?"

"Looks that way, doesn't it?"

Am I being paranoid? Is it wrong for me to see this as a threat? To what end, I couldn't tell you, but since when are news and marketing directors prisoners of logic? "Discreetly call my cell in four minutes, would you?"

"Pussy. I'll do it, then."

"Forget it. I got it."

The kid and I shake hands. He's got a strong grip. Good sign, I imagine. He's probably five-six or so, short curly black hair and a constellation of zits on his forehead and cheeks. Clean-shaven, which is a plus, because facial hair is pompous.

"Pete Sanchez," he says. Sanchez . . . Good for the diversity thing. "Pleasure to meet you."

"Likewise, I'm sure. Here." I wheel over Manny's seat. "Sit."

The kid looks at it a second as if he's unsure if it's okay to sit in the imitation-leather manager's chair.

"Go ahead," I say. "Won't shock you. Promise."

He lets out a nervous laugh and sits. Ironed his khakis. Good. Green and taupe golf shirt. Bad.

I say, "You realize we can't pay you."

"That's what Mr. Hertz said."

Mr. Hertz. How adorable. Haven't heard anyone mention Manny's last name in so long I forgot he had one.

"So, Pete, talk to me about why you want to intern here."

"I'm a fan of the paper; I pick it up every week. I like the way you guys do news—straightforward but with a little bit of zip." He stops talking, nods his head, leans forward.

"And you're a freshman? Sophomore?"

"Junior."

"I can save you a year and a half and a few grand right now. Sell you my degree and a bottle of Wite-Out for fifty bucks."

Kid titters. "No, thank you."

"Your loss. Smoke?"

"No, sir."

"Call me Cockburn."

"Okay, Cockburn."

"Gonna offend you if I do?" And I do before he can answer, then continue, "And you don't want to intern at the daily?"

"Are you kidding?"

"Should I be?"

"No. I mean, I guess not. I don't think I'd get a fair shake there. I'd be a gopher or something."

"You might find gophering preferable to how we do things here. I'll be honest, Pete, it's a clusterfuck. Especially on deadline day, which, coincidentally or not, today is."

"I thrive on pressure and do my best work in stressful situations."

That last bit loses him a little more credibility. "How old are you? Twenty? Twenty-one?"

"Twenty."

"And you want to spend the rest of your life working as a newsman?" *Newsman.* I am such a dork.

"Yes."

"Why?"

"I want to help people understand their world and the events that shape it. I want to give a voice to the downtrodden and expose corruption. I want to do something worthwhile, and this is it for me."

Jesus. Is this the best Manny could come up with? I oughta quit and stick him with junior here, see how long it takes him to come begging. "So Staskiewicz is still teaching out there."

Pete nods.

"And you had him for News Writing and Reporting."

Pete nods again.

"What do you think of him?"

"He's passionate. And he remembers you; said I should come out here to get some experience."

"I see he's still big on that pursuit of the Truth-with-a-capital-T garbage. He ever explain what he meant by *truth*?"

Pete sits back in his chair, looks to the left. "Uhh, no?"

"You do realize, Pete, that that's because it's horseshit?"

"I think he's a little idealistic about it. But the idea, I think, is still a valid one."

"Well, we'll see what we can do about shattering that. So, how about you stick around for the day, see if you like it, and if you do, you're welcome to come back tomorrow. If not, no harm done and best of luck to you."

He swallows. "Uhh, okay?"

"What's in the envelope, by the way?"

"My clips and résumé."

"Put that on Manny's desk there." Weaselprick. "Your first assignment is to gopher me a coffee from the place on the corner. Tell them you're with us and it's free. Get one for yourself, too."

He stands up, looks around, and after a moment of what I imagine is an internal debate over what the fuck he's gotten himself into, he extends his hand for a seal-the-deal shake. "You won't be disappointed."

"Never am. Now, milk no sugar."

Waiting for Pete to return with my coffee, I yank a dozen or so press releases from the pile for him to write up. Stuff from the cops, the mayor's office and one from the Republican on the City Council who's leading the charge to abolish the city's living wage ordinance. Mixed in is an envelope from Harrison Color Lab. I take it into the bathroom with me and flip through the test prints. The lightbulb here is a bright white, and it's the closest thing we have to a lightboard. A good half of the frames are motion blurred, but there're a few usable ones, technically speaking.

Every last one of the thirty-six frames is filled with something ugly. Frame twenty-eight is particularly memorable. Wozniak is falling forward, but his head's jolted backward and there's a thick spray jettisoning from the back of his head. I slide the negatives back into the envelope and head back to the word corral.

"Dingus." Donna hands me a few sheets of paper. "Just came over the fax."

It's the Park-Leavenworth Neighborhood Improvement Association weed-and-seed proposal. I take it to my desk and mark it up. Says here they applied a year and a half ago and some guy named *illegible* Chumley signed off on it this spring. And what were they supposed to spend it on? A state-of-the-art mobile communication system, web design and hosting, a laptop and a few random office things. Which makes me wonder what they really spent the near eight grand on. Not huge money, but on felony turf nevertheless. And guess whose signature is at the bottom. My main man Bill's. Follow the money, Cockburn—it's 101 shit.

Dial the number Bill put on the grant app and a receptionist at Curtis Fixtures answers the phone. I tell her I'm looking for Mr. Dunkel, and she tells me to hold. A Muzak version of "Rock the Casbah" plays a few bars before I'm patched through.

"Sales, this is Bill."

"Bill, hey, it's Bernard Cockburn from the *News-Telegraph*. How are you?"

There's a slight pause, barely enough to notice. Maybe he's swallowing a mouthful of spit or coffee. "Doing good. I was going to call you tonight. I've been really busy."

He's got a great phone voice. Deep, confident. "Happens to the best of us. You have any free time coming up? Maybe twenty, thirty minutes?"

"Yeah, hold on a sec, could you?" The line goes mute for a

good fifteen seconds before he comes back. "I'm booked for the rest of the day."

"Won't take long. Grab a coffee after work or something."

He rapidly clicks his tongue a few times. "You know Trudy's? It's on——"

"Yep."

"Right. Will that work? Say five-thirty?"

"On it."

Kid brings me my coffee and I give him the releases. "Make these not suck. Briefly. Then find me whatever you can over at City Hall about the Baron Square project. Memos of understanding—mayor's office, third floor; they got a sweetheart tax deal, so check with the finance department—fifth floor; whatever planning has—eleventh floor."

Then the ringing begins. The phone. Not my ears. Seth calling back. *No, the mayor does not feel this is a good ordinance; it will cost the taxpayers way more than it is worth. No, no, the city law department has not addressed the grievance yet. All right. Call me if you need anything.* Write 'em up. Short, sweet, punchy. Make a call for Leroy, whatever. Learn: part of the downtown historic district, so no Mickey D's. Owner's up on his taxes. Hit something like paydirt with my planning guy—NüCorp's in preliminary talks to renovate it. Planning dept. loves NüCorp. Everyone loves NüCorp. Take the old, make it new. Higher valuations, more yuppie pads, more jobs. Fuck them. *Hi, Bernard, what's your e-mail? For the mug shot. Okay, okay . . . dot-com, got it.* Coffee. *Boy, rewrite that crime stats piece, it's too sassy.* Sassy. Fuck you, sassy. Cigarette. Donna's still trying to quit. *Bernard, press conference today at three. Yeah, the union's going to respond to the mayor's veto of the staffing ordinance. Great, we'll see you then?* Paragraphs, bang clatter bang and my fingers are sore as hell. Run to the deli to grab a sandwich and a bowl of soup. Burns the hell outta my mouth. *City charter says the mayor has the authority to handle staffing matters, not the council. What it means is they overstepped their bounds.* Oh really? *No, the mayor fucked up this time. He fucked up bad. We've got to get him back in line cause the guy's going fucking ape-shit. He thinks he's the king of Omaha.* Yeah, okay. Clean it up and use it. Nah, fuck it, here, let me give you a new one, ready? Pete, here, type these into the computer there, I gotta run. Blinding god-damned television lights and bulging camera equipment. Cables snake all over the place and I damn near knock over the whole lot of them trying to get to a chair. Scribble notes, turn the page, scribble again. Turn the unintelligible scrawls into quotes later. Back downtown. Grab a coffee. New junkie sparring for change on the corner. *Got a quarter?* Funny, I was about to ask you the same question. Note from Donna on my keyboard: *Shitass, call city atty.* You don't say? How many other ordinances have your depart-ment deemed contrary to the charter? No, just this year. Great, thanks for your time. Paragraphs. Seth again. *No, he is not a con-temporary Nero. Who's saying these things?* Me, but he doesn't need to know that. Coffee. Pete, I'm going to call you Nemo from now on. What've you got, Nemo? Red ink. Slash and burn. Here, make these corrections and then transfer the rest of my hard copy to Word. Oh, Nemo, cardinal rule of journalism: source said. Always source said. Never stated, got it? Then you can go home. *Boy, need the news laid out.* Fucking Quark hates me. I hate it more. Text box, picture box, get text, get picture, shazam. Five. Half an hour to go. Go home, Nemo. Yeah, tomorrow at eleven is fabulous. Manny, gotta add Nemo to the mast. Fuck, I don't know . . . check his résumé. In your box. Yeah, Sanchez. Why am I chewing on this cigarette butt? Shoe box of fresh photocopies from City Hall under my arm and out into the cold.

eight

Trudy's is the kind of place you'd expect it to be. Greasy. The waitresses are all overweight with feathered hair and have those change dispenser things on their belts. Slashed vinyl booths jammed up against wobbly tables with decades' worth of abbreviated romances carved into them. The coffee's high octane and there isn't a nonsmoking section. Hanging up front, waiting for my man, and I'm a bit amped from all the caffeine, which means I'm grinding my teeth and tapping my foot. Couple dirty shitheels playing Ms. Pac-Man over in the corner, calling each other dildos and buttwipes. Hey, look, that could be my wasted life. Mommy rounds them up and stops as she hustles past me.

"Got a problem?" she asks.

"Pardon?"

"I asked if you got—"

"Heard you. Nope."

"Stop looking like that at my kids, then, or else I'll give you a problem."

One of her kids, the one whose neck is gripped in her right hand, makes a masturbatory gesture, and it's, perhaps, directed at me.

"Yes, ma'am."

She looks at me a brief moment, maybe daring me to do something. "Let's go," she says, and they do.

There's a light tap on my shoulder. "Mr. Cockburn?"

I turn to look at my guy. Short. Five-seven, max. Brown hair with a freakishly wide part on the right. Flaky scalp shining through. Eyebrows that just won't quit. Pretty nondescript otherwise. Face looks like it was made with tapioca. Round. Soft. This is a guy who'd sell you a used car, and it wouldn't be a lemon. It'd limp and wheeze for years, but it wouldn't just fucking die already so you could in good conscience junk it and buy a new one.

"Grab a table?" I say.

He checks his watch. Digital, plastic strap. "Sure." He holds up two fingers, and off we go to the middle of one of the dining rooms. Small table and a couple chairs, but it's not like we're breaking bread here, so. Order a couple cupsajoe and ready the notebook.

"Whew," he says. "What a day. *What* a day."

"Work. It's a bitch, am I right?"

He grins like he's trying not to cringe at the dirty word he just heard. "I'm a little surprised, to be honest, that the paper's taking an interest in us. It's not very interesting, what we do."

Total dumbfuck move, dipshit. *No, officer, there's nothing wrong here. And there certainly isn't a naked woman gagged and bound in my trunk and I'm not sitting on a hatchet or anything, heading out into the woods where no one can hear her scream.* "So, you're what? President? Of the association?"

"We don't have offices. At least not officially. I guess I'm the get-things-done person."

"Get what things done?"

"I wrote up the funding paperwork for the city, for one. The night patrol was my idea. And I'm working on a couple other, uh, projects."

"Such as?"

"Starting a new graffiti abatement drive. Weekend beautification when it warms up. Trying to make the neighborhood more green. I've been talking to the police about having the abandoned cars towed. Little things, mostly. But they add up."

"To?"

"The sort of place where you'd want to raise a family."

"Family like your friend Wozniak's?" Zing, motherfucker.

His face, it just sinks. "He was a very troubled man, and he was only a member for a very brief period of time. We had to"—he searches for a word—"deactivate him and another one. They had the wrong idea. You don't think—"

"Not at all. But I'm curious—what sort of wrong ideas?"

"Violent ones. End justifies the means."

"And you disagree?"

"You saw what happened to James."

I did. More than he knows. "And Korbes, too. Strange coincidence, think?"

He cuts this crooked, dopey smile. "It's a strange world we live in."

I sit mute, because I can.

"That accident Creighton was in, talk about a freak accident, huh?" he says.

"Was it? I'm not too familiar."

"Picture this—a local drug dealer? He's stoned and driving recklessly. This is not very long after Creighton and the watch parted ways. Anyway, Creighton? He works in a bakery? His shift starts at three or four in the morning? He's driving to work and—

blammo—this drug dealer guy crashes into him. The dealer dies from massive internal bleeding. Creighton's in a wheelchair now, but he's alive. He's a good guy, Creighton, basically."

"Basically how?"

"He is. Not basically. Totally. A good one. Just gets riled up sometimes."

"And the rest?"

"The rest?"

"Of the watch? All good guys?"

"Sure. If you want, I can arrange for you to meet some of the other guys. You'll see. We're pretty normal."

"A little ahead of you there."

"Oh. I hadn't heard."

Bit of a control freak, are we? "What I'd like to do right now is talk to you about this website you're putting together."

"You've done your homework." He picks at a hangnail on his left index finger. "I saw a thing on TV where an association, in Florida I think it was, did a similar thing."

"But yours isn't operational."

"No. No it's not. My wife, she—well, we, actually. We had some concerns about the legality of it."

"But you saw a thing on TV."

"Yes. Yes we did. That was in a different state, though."

"It's a federal matter, Bill. Nebraska's covered by the same laws Florida is."

"I wouldn't know—I'm a salesman, right? That's why we're going to talk to a lawyer. We just want—" The waitress sets his white mug in front of him. "Thanks," he says to her. "We just want to make completely sure." He takes a tentative sip of his coffee, swirls it around in his mouth, and then takes a mighty gulp of the black stuff. "Good stuff," he says, his eyebrows raised in such a way as to make me think that it might not be his beverage he's talking about.

"How you going to pay for that? A lawyer? Pricey, and I saw your grant app—so I know you don't have any cash left if you bought all that gear."

"We have a little."

"Haven't spent it?"

"We spent most of it."

"On?"

"The stuff in the application."

"Remind me. Been a few days and I've seen so much stuff since then that I'm a little fuzzy."

"Two-way radios. Computer equipment."

"Okay, right. Hosting, web design?"

"Right. That's expensive."

"You've got an operational site?"

"Not really advertised." He takes a drink. "But pretty much, yeah. It's a work in progress."

"When do you think you'll have it up and running?"

"I'm not sure."

"Week? Two? A month? A year?"

"I couldn't say, to be honest. I wouldn't want to mislead you."

"Think you're the first. What about privacy issues? Don't you think you'd be, morally, in the wrong for publicly convicting these guys before the courts do?"

"That's a good point. But you've got to consider what this activity does to—"

"What if, say, you ended up on it?"

"If *I* did?"

"Yeah, how'd you feel? A little resentful at least, I'd think."

"I would not, because I'd never—"

"Humor me. If your wife found out? No more trips to the Smokies."

"The Smokies?"

"Took a sneak peek. You've got some vacation pictures up there now."

"I told her not to do that. My wife likes to do that stuff for her family. So they can see what we've been up to."

"God bless the Internet, huh? So, I'm curious. You had a jillion flyers printed up with the web address on it—your own hard-to-find personal site—and you've paid some guy to design it, so where is it?"

"Out there. Somewhere." He checks his watch and opens his mouth to say something about having to leave, so I cut him off.

"But you've reserved the domain, right? What is it?"

"I'd have to talk to the computer guy."

"Aren't you the computer guy?"

"I hired someone."

"He freelance? Work with a firm?"

"Forgot his name. Have his card somewhere."

"But it was your idea to run off the flyers with the wrong info."

He pops his thumb knuckles. "Doing a test run, is all."

"If you got audited next week, you'd be in some shit, Bill."

"Look, I don't know how this stuff works, okay? I wrote a check, the guy said he's working on it, and I trust him."

Spewing seventh-grade subterfuge now. "So, what do you think? It'd fairly screw you over to end up with your name in e-print like that."

"But it wouldn't happen."

"We're talking hypothetically."

"I guess that, yeah, it would be a bad thing."

"So why do you want to do this to some fellas you've never met?"

"Look, off the record? I don't want to hurt anyone. It's my wife, she had the idea."

I probably should tell Billy here that off the record doesn't exist, but I want him to give himself enough rope. "Sounds like she's the one I should be talking to."

"She wouldn't want to get involved."

"But she already is, Bill."

"What kind of story is this you're writing?"

"Not sure yet. Seeing what sticks."

Bill clears his throat. "Well, I have to be going. It's been nice to speak with you, and I hope your story goes well."

"Can't I talk you into staying just another couple minutes?"

He runs his hand down his part, scratching it lightly. "Unfortunately, not tonight. Maybe another time." He pulls a dollar from his wallet, but I wave him off.

"I'll expense it."

He smiles and nods and walks briskly out, his hands jammed in his coat pockets. Toss a few bucks on the table and follow him. I'm parked on the curb, so I watch from the driver's seat as he crosses the street to the parking lot and gets into a late-model white Nissan sedan. Got my motor running and I decide to follow him, either to fuck with him or because I don't want to go home.

A short drive later, he pulls into a garage that's detached from a story-and-a-half, probably two-bedroom house. One of many on the block. Unlike the others, his place is well kept, and it's almost cute with the pink trim around the windows. Wait for him to scurry inside. Humming about how the simple man pays for the bills, the thrills, the pills that kill as I rifle through the mail nobody bothered to collect today. Couple bills—OPPD and Qwest—and a postcard from Fort Lauderdale from cousin Alex saying he wishes they were there and don't they, too?

Stealthily swing open the chain link and walk around back to inspect the yard. Tarp-covered grill and a rusty swing set. The garage has a few windows, so I peek in and find nothing strange, no S&M sets, no extra bed with handcuffs affixed to the posts. Just evidence of an oil leak he should have looked at.

Take a gander in a few ground-level windows. Living room is vacant. No books or bookshelves. Coffee table with three re-motes and a stack of magazines on it. Today's daily on the couch and the walls dotted with family photos. Wedding photo near the hall. By the stairs, Sears value portrait of the trio. Too small to make out the faces from here, but I can feel the awkward forced happiness of the image. Or do I only want to?

One day, I might have to start answering these questions.

Through the slush around to the other side and it's hard to see in, because the window's steamed up. Makes sense: warm inside; frigid, damp and desolate out here. Window in the op-posite corner affords a view if I hop up on the AC unit, which I do. Can't hang out too long or someone might call in a prowler. Dinner's on the table (meat loaf, mashed potatoes, green beans), but nobody's present.

Next room over is full of bright primary-colored plastic toys . . . blocks, what looks like a toy lawn mower, some dolls and a dollhouse. Up on the wall, I can't tell for sure, but it looks like a framed college diploma. Below it is an executive mahogany desk, and it's buried beneath three piles of folded laundry and an assortment of smallish toys.

A light upstairs kicks on. Hop down and skulk in the garage's shadow where the viewing's better. There's my man, pacing and

talking rather urgently into a cordless. He's pointing and gesticulating, then he stops, mid-sweeping-gesture. With his arm
straight out, he just stands there with the phone held to his ear,
staring at the floor. He nods, clicks off the phone and rubs his
eyes. What is he thinking about? Looks like he's talking to himself. Couple exchanges, then he scratches the back of his head,
and off he goes. He reappears downstairs in the kitchen-slash-
dining, and as he surveys the meal, he looks almost despondent.
For a moment. Then the wife walks in, blue flowered muumuu
and all, carrying the kid, and he perks right up. Poor bastard,
he's onstage, only nobody besides him is supposed to know.

Wife (What's her name? Sharon? Sheila. That's it.) puts the
kid in a booster seat. Grown-ups take the spots opposite each
other, throw out a prayer and dig into the chow. Unappetizing as
it may be, the sight gets to me: I'm terminally hungry. But not
for that. Not at all.

nine

Dunkel's house is so close to my apartment that if I hadn't stopped by the liquor store, the car wouldn't have warmed up enough for the heater to start working. There's a part of me—could be big, could be small—that wants to see Allison's car here, too. But it isn't.

There is, however, a note taped to the cabinet where I keep the booze glasses.

B—I'll come by late. A

Deep-six the note, pop the Crow's top and pour a nice tall one over ice. Most of it I drink sitting at the dinner table, running my fingers over the gouges and scratches. There's a lot of them. Can't remember where or when I bought this thing. Donna's given me a few hand-me-down pieces, so maybe this is one. And why the fuck do I care?

Anyway, Allison'll be by later. Probably pick up some of her shit and haul it over to her sister's place or wherever. Wonder how fucked I am if she really is going through with this kid thing.

And she *so* is. Got nothing else solid or permanent in her life, mired in the black, tarry depths of the clock's tick-tocking baby-making years, so why not? Other than the thousands of reasons to the contrary, none of which, I assume, matter to her. Really, I suppose, they shouldn't. Only one should: that life does not a happy Cockburn make. What would? I wish, sometimes, that I had an answer.

I wonder: Did she dump me? Or was it mutual? I mean, she hit me, so I can spin it that way if I catch any shit. Domestic abuse, though, it's not necessarily a get-out-of-jail-free card. Shoulda shot some swollen mugs when I had the chance. Her folks, though. They'll be happy. Open their wallets, as per usual. They'll take care of her. Buy baby junk. Stroller, crib, maternity clothes, bigger bras.

Pour another. Sip. Tell myself this was not part of the plan. Never fucking ever. I've done enough damage. Swallow the rest and wait for the big, smooth nothing.

Not that I need to, but I'm thinking about hitting the shower. Sometimes makes me feel better. The symbolic value of it and all.

There's a pair of red-orange smeared latex gloves crumpled next to a Clairol box in the bathroom trash can, and the bathtub is spattered with droplets of orange hair dye. I fuck with the knobs till I get something satisfactorily tepid. Trying to think, other than the other night, about when the last time was we had sex. Few weeks ago and definitely highlight-reel material. She'd drunk too much wine and I hadn't sucked down enough bourbon to neutralize my end of the equation. After a curried lamb dinner that gave me wretched gas, we tumbled and fumbled into the sack and I kept getting soft, and when I finally came, I fucking farted. Tried to blame it on her, but she wouldn't buy it. So there's that.

Fucking dye's even on the soap. Tiny fetus-shaped blobs. I rub the bar until the orange dots wash off. Why am I getting so worked up? She knows how much I don't earn, and she knows I don't get benefits, and she's not in any better a situation, so getting saddled with a kid shouldn't be even a remotely pleasant idea. Or maybe this whole kid thing is another whim of hers that'll blow over. Soon. She was, after all, in art school when I met her. And what a fucked-up period that was. I'd recently buried the old man, so all I had was my buddy Cliff, which is nothing, really. But he made sure I was continually fucked up, which is something, I guess. And I did the same for him, as his little sister had also recently bitten it. (A painful thing for the both of us for vastly different reasons, which is neither here nor there.) One spring night, he hauled me out to a party some of his friends were throwing at a shitty rented house they shared. So we boozed it up for a while on generic gin and Colt 45, and I was pretty backward by about four when he grabbed my arm and tore me away from the weird urn thing I'd just pissed in because I couldn't find the bathroom.

"Fuck-o," he shouted in my ear above the Dexy's Midnight Runners some asshole was playing, "this is Allison. Be careful around her; she's deadly with a blowtorch." Then he abandoned me with her. Short, pale, little bit chunky (it works for her), and what I'd soon find out were well-represented A cups.

I sidled up next to her and said into her ear, "Blowtorch?"

"I work with iron."

"Must be hard."

"It's metal, so yeah."

"Drink?"

"Vodka gimlet."

I put my arm around her waist and led us away from the urn

and to the bar that'd been set up in the living room. I picked through the bottles, but they were all empty.

"You wanna get out of here?" I said. "They're outta booze and it stinks like piss, anyway."

She lit a cigarette and fingered the bulbous silver locket hanging around her neck like she was trying to tell me something.

"So?" I said.

She grabbed my arm and led me outside. She was saying something, but I couldn't hear what, with the music and the wind and everyone else shouting in everyone else's ears. Thought I heard her say something about *blow*, which was either more shop talk or the not-subtle hint I wanted to hear. When we got to my car, she took off the locket and opened it up.

"You got a light in here?" she asked.

I turned on the dome light and looked over. She was dipping a doll-sized coke spoon into the tiny reservoir of powder held in the locket, so, being the square I was, I turned off the light.

"Here." She held up the spoon to my nose, and not wanting to be a puss, I snorted. My eyes watered and she laughed because I must have looked like the cherry I was.

"Good stuff," I said, even though the only thing that happened was my tongue and the roof of my mouth numbed out. "Been a while."

"Yeah." She snorted, dipped the spoon again and snorted up the other nostril.

Then it zapped me, and something dangerously frenetic kicked in. I mean, obviously: I was tweaking. Unfamiliar turf for a downer guy. Whatever. I drove us to my place and we weren't five steps into the apartment before we were naked and pawing at each other on the floor. I was just about to stick it in when she said, "Better not. Mouse in the house."

"Hardwood floor," I said, knocking for luck. "Easy to clean."

She smiled something crooked before going to the bathroom. Must've been the coke that I sorta started refueling on, but I couldn't get off, so we just went at it till she said she was getting sore. I rolled off her and she hit the head again, leaving me next to a thin, bloody smear, naked and wondering why shit happens to me.

When she came out, she sat on the floor, hugged her knees to her chest and asked for a cigarette. After I handed it to her, she ripped off the filter and I lit us both.

"You're dating what's-her-face, right? Sue?" Allison asked.

"I'm not sure."

"She's really not your type."

"I know."

"Where's she at, anyway?"

"We haven't really talked in a few weeks. I've got some shit going on." Embarrassed by my postcoital blabbering, I looked down and caught sight of the mess on the floor, which reminded me of precisely what I'd been trying to forget. "So how do you know Cliff?"

"That's pretty fucked up, what happened with your dad."

"You always this much a pain in the ass? Or am I just lucky?"

"Know what you need to do? Take me out for drinks sometime soon. Ashtray?"

I handed it to her. "How about tonight?" My knees cracked as I stood. From the kitchenette I fetched a bottle of Old Grand-Dad and two rocks glasses, and we drank and smoked till after I called in sick to work. I knew I'd end up phoning her the next day when we were lying there and our faces were about six inches apart, and she was going on and on about art school, and her breath reeked something like a decomposing corpse in a sulfur mine, but I didn't care.

Those were some good times. I sorta maybe started doing too much coke and hit the Tuinals hard (balance, as always, is key) for a little while as she rode out the last ripples of the wave of her rebellion, having already surfed through all the phases frustrated girls go through on the long path to womanhood: cigarettes and lipstick, rock and roll, hard drugs, backpacking in Europe. No matter what she did, her folks (both of whom, by the way, are tenured professors—she in history, he in chemistry—at my alma mater, and they drive to work together every day in their Volvo, for fuck's sake) never failed to give her their support—financially and otherwise. The apple that is Allison fell pretty far from the tree, but started to roll back toward it not too long after I put away the mop and the bottle of Old Grand-Dad. She dropped art and picked up business school. Did that for a semester, then she switched over to some social science or another, which is where she is now. And she'd be set to graduate in the spring if she hadn't taken off this semester. (Just needed a break from it, she said.) Course, last time she took time off, she switched majors, so she's probably been reconsidering what she wants and how she wants to get it. Now, though, I've inadvertently implanted a desire and given her a direction and a shove.

So this zygote I unintentionally had a hand in creating, it's not unreasonable to think it, too, shall pass. Then we can get back to where we were or weren't. Not that we had anything really special, because we didn't, and either of us coulda had whatever it wasn't with someone else, but I sorta dig what a noncommittal fuckup she is. Was. Rudderless and doesn't (didn't) give me shit. I do my thing. She does hers. Split the rent. Screw every now and again.

Hot water's petering out, so I kill the stream and towel off. Throw on whatever's on top of the clothes pile and hit the computer. Smoke a cigarette staring at the blinking cursor. Light another, pour a second tall one, thumb-drum a surf beat on the desk. What do I have?

- two former cleanup guys all fucked up. One dead, the other nearly. Coincidence? Possibly.
- Bill's hiding something. What's he worried about? That I'll write how he's fucking Luka? Small fries, my man. Small fries. Gotta be something uglier. Fulcrum point right now. All paperwork points to. What did he spend that weed-and-seed money on, anyway? Sure as shit not what he's claiming.
- Figure out who runs that WJC outfit. Maybe nothing. Maybe not nothing. Get Nemo to do that. Kid needs to get used to dealing with bureaucracy.
- If the watch group is as creepy as Luka says, need to hang out. See if they can go big.

If I were the speculating type, I'd think that Mr. Dunkel's bitten off more than he can chew with his crew. Was fine when nobody paid attention. Now, though, the dogs are riled up and could turn on him. That's one option. And one is enough for tonight.

Eye my kicks. They're all scuffed up from my covert op over at Bill's place, so it's shine time.

Grab the brown-bristled toothbrush and dip the tip into the jar of Meltonian No. 78. A regular pair of dress shoes doesn't require that much polish; maybe a little more than the amount of toothpaste it takes to brush your teeth. Some guys apply it in streaks. I'm more of a circular motion kinda guy. Tiny circles all the way around. The tongue, too. Can't forget the tongue. After the polish is applied to both shoes, it's time to brush it off. I've got two brushes, one for my black shoes, one for the brown. The key to brushing off the leftover polish is to make sure all the strokes go in the same direction——none of that careless, all-over-the-place shit unless you want your shoes to come out looking like a blind epileptic took care of them. I like to start out with short strokes, do a once-over, and then finish off with some long, sturdy ones. Last step is the buff. Not that any step is more important than any other, but this is the last one, and it's where the shine comes in, so you don't want to fuck it up. A trick my old man taught me is to use an inside-out sock instead of a buff cloth. Works as well, and you've always got an extra somewhere. So I'm sitting on the edge of the bed, and my right foot's in the right-footed shoe, and I'm giving my shoes a medium-pressure fast buff when the landline rings. Allison, I'm sure. I momentarily toy with not picking up, but decide that's an asshole thing to do.

"Hey," I say.

Pause, and I hear some chatter in the background. Out to dinner and missing me, maybe. "Good evening. Is Mr. Cockburn available?"

"It's Co-burn." Feeling this feeling I've heard described as sinking. "Nope. Message?"

"We'll call back. Is there a good time to reach him?"

"Negatory." I click off the phone. Telemarketers. Probably got my name from the dick-pump people. Peddling Spanish fly or cock rings.

Feeling antsy, so I call up Cliff and tell him I'm coming over.

"You remember where I live?" he asks.

So it's been a while. "Pretty much," I say.

ten

Cliff's smoking and drinking a beer on his front porch with Eddie Fontaine, his nutjob landlord, when I pull into the driveway. The old guy's cracked up, shell-shocked, and rents Cliff the main level and basement of the house for something just shy of two hundred bucks. The low rent allows Cliff to work part-time at a private home for retarded kids and still have plenty of time and dough left over. What's he do with it? Fucks off, entirely. He sorta went downhill after his kid sister ate it big and ugly in a car accident. Technically, it wasn't an accident. Technically, it was a one-car. Technically, she was drunk. Technically, I may have scored the booze for her. Technically, I oughta be in prison right now. Cliff doesn't know the extent of my involvement. Far as he knows, his sister got wasted—which was not an unheard-of circumstance—and took my car out for a joyride. Which is what nearly everyone familiar with the case thinks, if they in fact think about it. I assume they don't, because it's been a number of years now, and the specifics are locked up in sealed records. The very few familiar with the facts, I've got enough scalding dirt on them that all's been quiet on that front for years now.

"Eddie," I say. He's got a huge boil on his cheek. Thing's the size of a walnut.

"Hey."

"Your face is about to explode."

"Fuck you." He gathers up his bottle of Cisco and pack of Merits and walks inside.

"Thanks," Cliff says. "He's been bugging me all day about shoveling the walk. Says his condition won't permit him to do it this winter."

"That thing on his face?"

"Nah, his scrambled head. What a snow shovel and napalm have in common is beyond me. Sit." He motions to Eddie's recently vacated chair. "Tell Uncle Cliff why you look like such a pile of shit."

"I'm gonna be a daddy."

He chokes on the beer, spits, wipes his mouth and says, "No shit?"

"Not even a little."

He hands me a beer from the stash by his feet. "That's awesome."

"How is that awesome?"

"Because I said so." He rubs together his hands. "Know what we need to do? Celebrate. Finish that beer and I'm taking you out."

I do, even though I don't want to go out and get sideways, but even more I don't want to sit around and wallow in my turgid puddle of self-pity, because that's exactly what I'd fucking do if I were alone tonight. "Where to?"

He unnecessarily gives his chin a few strokes and says, "Ruby Tuesday's. I know you're going to say 'Fuck that shit,' so don't even bother. I'm driving, and then we're going to order a friggin' onion and drink Mudslides and you're going to get shitfaced. Finish that beer."

On the drive out, I give Cliff the quick rundown on what happened, and he laughs and punctuates my story every now and again with lines like "That's classic" and "Dude." He actually looks ecstatic when I tell him how Allison smacked me. "Badass," he says. As he navigates us toward a spot in the strip-mall parking lot, a desperate feeling that I want to go home swells within. But he's on a mission, and there's no way to talk him down once he's started.

Stepping out of his truck, I notice it's a T.G.I. Friday's we're at. So I point this out.

"Tuesday. Friday. Whenever. Let's go."

We sit at the bar, and when the bartender, a guy with some seriously gelled hair, a goatee and a name tag that reads *Dirk* comes over, Cliff says, "We want your biggest, greasiest, batter-dipped, deep-fried onion, two shots of your shittiest whiskey and two Mudslides."

"One Mudslide," I say. "I want something fruity, Dirk."

"An Ultimate Piña Colada?"

"Mmm, not a fan of coconut."

"How about an Ultimate Hawaiian Volcano?"

"Sounds like an eruption of fun," I say, quoting the description on the big menu posted behind him.

The shots arrive quickly, and Cliff and I pick them up simultaneously.

"Stella," he stage shouts, for whatever reason. I clink his shot with mine, and then we put them down.

"That *was* shitty," I say.

"So," he says. "What's the plan?"

"Don't have one."

"And you haven't seen her since?"

"Nope. Supposed to maybe tonight."

"And you'll say what?"

"The fuck you think I'll say?"

"You're not fooling anyone with that tough-guy act."

Prick.

"The way I see it," he says, "is you can do one of two things—own up and be a big man. That's one. Two has a lot of variations, but all involve you making yourself scarce. Maybe move. But they'll find you."

"So?"

"So figure it out yourself. Your problem."

"True, but as a trusted associate, you're supposed to proffer sound advice."

He motions with his head to four women wearing business casual and sipping daiquiris. Three of 'em aren't bad, considering, and the fourth is the token chub, which makes the other three even better-looking. "The one with black hair keeps looking over at us."

When this happens, as it does to each of us the few times we hang out, I ignore him. Like I'm doing now.

"See?" He gently pushes my shoulder in an effort to make me confront this woman over the smell of grease and alcohol. And he's right.

Dirk says, "One Mudslide and one Ultimate Hawaiian Volcano. Your onion'll be out in a few minutes."

I turn to see a tall damned cocktail glass filled up with this yellow-orange mixture, replete with a fucking umbrella and a chunk of pineapple. Cliff stops sucking on his straw to say, "Yow."

Not sure how I'm supposed to drink this thing, so I size up the mess, pluck the garnish and take a dainty sip. It's so sweet my stomach churns and knots up after I swallow. "Jesus," I say. "Heinous."

"Tell you what, I'll take one for the team and charm the cockblocker, and you can have your pick."

I light up to kill the citrus taste in my mouth, and as I'm tapping off the first bit of ashes onto the chunk of pineapple, Cliff nudges me. "Whaddya think? Easy out. Just go home reeking of another woman, and, bang, you're free. Works every time."

"Kinda sick of my pecker right now."

"This is golden, man. Come on. For me."

After swallowing another mouthful of painfully tangy booze-lite drink, I say, "Can't we go to a regular bar?" It's shit like this that makes me remember that I really don't even like him much anymore. It's either that he's devolving, or I'm evolving at a rate much faster than he is. But an only friend is an only friend, no matter how much he disgusts you and no matter how much shitty guilt you carry around. "I need some advice here."

Cliff appears to be thinking. Dirk arrives with the grub and I order a beer and battle down a couple handfuls of deep-fried something before Cliff's ready with a response.

"I don't know," he finally says. He rips off a chunk of onion, dips it in the dip, eats it and then licks the grease off his fingers. "Never been lucky enough to knock up someone who has morals. What's that like?"

I'm starting to think this whole exercise is a waste of my semi-precious time. My stomach hurts from this garbage I'm eating and drinking, and the only thing I've accomplished is nothing.

"Maybe it's not what you should do," Cliff says, "but what you want to do. You know that much, right?"

"What I want doesn't matter."

"The fuck? Should be the only thing that does." In goes another chunk of onion.

Thing is, I have what I want. And Allison wants to take it away from me. *It* being this pale imitation of the life I wish I could have. I wanna keep living the ruse—getting fucked up and talking shit and pretending not to care about anything. And, no, I'm not going to come clean about it. Keeping shit to yourself is the only way to keep it.

"Eh," I say.

"Well, sailor, I think you're screwed. Might as well have as much fun as you can now, because your life officially has an expiration date on it. But, you know, if you disappeared, I'd be neither surprised nor unsympathetic."

As the onion cools off, it looks more and more unappetizing, if that's possible. I'm reaching for another handful when someone taps my shoulder.

"What are you doing here?" Donna asks.

"Trying to fucking hide from you." I swivel on my stool, and see she's got her kid with her, which explains the dour look. Probably not a good thing to drop the f-bomb around a seven-year-old. "You know Cliff, right?"

After they exchange pleasantries, I ask her what brings her to this fine establishment.

"I promised Cindy dinner if she aced her spelling test."

The kid's got blond hair that's starting to turn brown, blue plastic-framed glasses that probably don't earn her any friends and a missing incisor. She's already learned that hanging out with her mom isn't very cool, because she's standing off to the side and behind Donna. Actually, Cindy looks a lot like Donna, minus the weight of age and plus the glasses. "I'll buy you a drink if you can spell *pariah*."

The kid looks at her mom like she's silently asking permission to speak to the creepy man. Donna's shooting me a crusty glare as Cindy, in a tough voice that makes me think she'll be just fine, correctly spells it out.

"Close," I say. "There's no *h* at the end."

"Yes there is," Cindy demands.

"Nuh-uh."

"Uh-huh."

"You're sure?"

"Totally."

I shout to Dirk, and when he ambles over and asks what'll it be, I tell him it'll be a Shirley Temple and our bill.

"You gotta be careful," I tell Cindy. "It's pretty strong, so drink it slow. And if anyone asks, I didn't order it for you, okay?"

"There's alcohol in it?"

"Tons."

"Alcohol kills brain cells. Brain cells don't grow back."

"Which is why you should enjoy it in moderation. Ask your mom. She'll tell you."

Donna looks down at Cindy. "You don't want to end up like *him,* do you?"

Dirk delivers the goods. As I hand Cindy the mocktail, I say with a sly-dog wink that may or may not be appropriate, "Remember, I didn't give this to you."

Cindy holds the glass with both hands and gives it a couple sniffs. Could be wrong, but it looks like she's blushing.

"What do you say?" Donna prods.

"Thanks?"

"Go eat."

Donna flicks my ear when they walk away. Cliff, picking through his wallet, says to the accumulated bills and paper scraps, "Look at you, mister natural with the kids."

"Ready?"

When we get back to Cliff's place, I step out of the truck and head to my car.

"We're just getting started," he says.

"Not me," I say. "Shit to do."

"Well," he says, stepping toward me, "if I never see you again, it's been fun." He envelops me in a hug, patting my shoulder a couple times. "All right," he says after he's done mauling me. "See you around or I won't."

I say, "Got anything fun you can part with?"

"Goofballs. Couple hits of acid. Little coke. Some cactus extract I haven't tried yet supposed to fuck you up crazy for like ten minutes and then let you down gently. You getting back into the fun stuff?"

"Mulling my options." I consider the blow. Then I think about how lame it'd be to tweak by myself in my apartment.

"You want a recommend, I suggest the cactus."

"Any straight uppers?"

"Coke."

"Pass."

"Whatever, whenever." Dismissive enough for me.

Hop into the car. Takes a couple tries before the engine turns over, but it gets me home okay. And what should I find in my parking lot? Yep. Allison's Honda.

Walk in, and the place smells like cigarettes. Not the usual residual smoke funk, but freshly smoked. Good sign, right? Pregnant women don't go around smoking much these days. Nor do they drink red wine, which is what Allison's doing in the bedroom. Lying on the bed. Wasted. With blue-black hair. Wearing a lacy black bra and matching underwear. One leg on top of the covers. Her face all fucked up and red from crying or huffing gas.

Excepting the one unfortunate circumstance, I really want to fuck her. Really.

"Darling." Pleasant a start as any. "Looking good."

She flips me the bird. Nice. Nonviolent.

"What are we thinking today?" Soon as it slips out, I realize the faux pas I've made, using *we* instead of *you*. Trying to be charming and colloquial.

"We're thinking," she says, possibly referring to her and that zygote of hers, "you owe me an apology."

"I'm sorry you hit me in the face."

"I'm not." In goes a big gulp.

"I'm sorry you feel that way." Excuse myself to prepare a drink. Salivating as I pour, which ignites a small spark of dependence-flavored worry. One that's quickly extinguished by the 80-proof.

Perch myself at the door and she's fumbling around, trying to light her cigarette and not spill her wine. Chivalrous type I am, I snap open the Zippo and ignite her burner.

"Thanks," she says.

"How much've you had to drink, anyway?"

She looks to the floor, where there's a half-empty bottle. "Bottle. About."

"How long I gotta stand here till you tell me what the fuck?"

"I'm moving out. Found a new place today. I want you to move, too. You don't have to think about anything. Everything's been taken care of. Movers. Deposit. Lease. Everything. You'll just leave here one morning and never come back."

I find myself at a loss for words, which is a strange, unfamiliar place. Just thinking: *What. The. Fuck. Be. A. Man. Kid.* But trying to verbalize this eloquence, it ain't happening.

"So?" she says.

"I'm trying to gauge how offended I am right now."

"I'm being for real."

"You're off your fucking nut."

She gestures at me with the hand that's holding the glass, and no small amount of it sloshes out onto the sheets.

"Nice," I say.

"Little stain going to bug you? Isn't this what you want? Come over here and I'll give you a blowjob, too. Or are you afraid?"

"You really wanna do this?"

"I'll be any way I have to."

I can't imagine things happen this way for everyone. Some, apparently, want the package and, therefore, bypass this or any similar nonsense. So color me lucky.

"How far along are you, anyway?"

"Probably a couple months."

"And you're drunk?"

"Very."

"You intended this, didn't you?"

She drags a sloppy drag. "All the same in the end, innit?"

Truer words, right? Never been more entertaining. "Sum fucking zero." It's down the hatch with the remainder of my drink. "Don't you have somewhere else you can go?"

She rolls over. Pulls the covers over her head.

Hurt my hand hitting the light. Consider the black bottle but pocket the red instead. Snatch Nemo's photocopies from the car and hoof it across the street. Warwick Arms rents by the week. One-seventy up front, cash only. Lobby ATM charges a two-dollar fee, but it spits out the bills. Sign in under Johnny Appleseed. Har fucking har.

eleven

Room's on the third floor with a view of my apartment building and the low, pregnant gray clouds hanging above. Stinks, of
course. Fetid mix of anything and everything sour and rotten. Bed
in the corner's a thin mattress on plywood. Hot plate with black
slop melted and crusted on all sides. Bugs aren't a problem as long
as the lights are on. And they will be.

Sift through what Nemo collected. Not a bad haul. Couple
hundred pages of black-and-white bore-the-fuck-out-of-you agree-
ments, zoning ordinances, MOU's, planning board meeting tran-
scripts and the like. Separate them by departmental source,
dry-swallow a small white pill with either a plus sign or an *X*
etched into it and start reading.

Tossing pages, scribbling notes. Burn through the rest of my
pack. Run to the convenience store for beer and smokes. Allison's pills, though tiny, pack quite a punch. Grinding my teeth,
rifling through paper, circling dollar figures. Picture of the development starts developing. Pull out some bullshit extraneous
legal jibber jabber and scribble notes on the blank backs. Flick
away a couple brazen roaches. *Water bugs,* I've heard 'em called.

Hand flying across the pages. Wonder if this'll be legible or logical tomorrow. Fuck tomorrow. Fuck today, really. I'd fuck yesterday but it's dead and gone. Oh, I so don't wanna be a daddy. Better: I shouldn't. I gave up that right a long time ago. Fuck, man. How was I supposed to know? Few bucks and a favor. Fair enough. I never had a problem handling my booze. Fucking idiot kids. Woulda got it somewhere else, anyway. That's a possibility. Didn't happen that way, but it's possible. It's also possible I could pluck one of these cockroaches from the bed and eat it, too. Spiny-legged monsters. Two inches long and this deep crimson. Swig of beer. Regain focus.

Looking like this: NüCorp's a corp incorporated in Delaware. (As is the *News-Telegraph*, truth be told.) Articles are on file there, and Delaware's secretary of state's office is notoriously shitty to deal with. Thusly, I decide the articles aren't worth a read. Never anything good in 'em, anyway. Continuing: city condemned the Baron Square lot 17 months ago—several weeks after it had begun negotiations with NüCorp about a possible fixer-upper deal. Previous owner is infirm and lives in Turkey. Didn't put up a fight when the city eminent-domained it. Sold it to NüCorp for a buck with the understanding that the Delaware corporation couldn't sell the land for 20 years, and within 24 months of the transaction, would rehab the property and convert it into apartments. Throw in a kowtow to the state and fed HUD by reserving a quarter for low- to medium-income families. Finance pieces together a 15-year tax increment finance package that saves NüCorp roughly a gajillion dollars. In exchange, NüCorp agrees to throw a shit-ton of business to locally owned minority contractors. Planning rubber stamps the plan, City Council green-lights with no discussion on the matter and, bang, overnight, demolition begins.

All very efficient. Nobody tries to muck up the works. Can't get a street paved without someone raising hell about how it degrades the quality of life or endangers the natural habitat of the lesser yellow-breasted tit owl—but this package, it sails right through. Maybe that's how business is done: quietly, quickly, graciously. Hard to believe, but it explains why it's been in the works for well over a year and I haven't written a word about it. Course, if someone had got himself killed onsite . . . Maybe a roofer falls. Resident junkie doesn't wanna go and things turn ugly when the demolition crew shows up. Oh, to dream.

Fist clenched, seeing double. Take a gulp of warm beer. Radiator pipe hissing and spitting. Narrow the eyes and stare across the street. Ugly brown brick building. Three stories. Five apartments. I'm ground floor. Lower third of the exterior covered in dead ivy. Two lights burning at—check the Timex—twenty after three. Feels like sandpaper scratching at the backs of my eyes. Work, boy. Work.

What else I got? Nothing of substance. Not here, at least. Nothing across the street, either. Wonder for a second if this is how things are going to be. Not here. Too expensive. Find a studio somewhere closer to work for a couple hundred a month. Fire up a burner, ash in an empty. Snowflakes falling now. Big, wet ones. All this mess, it'll be covered in the morning.

I leave on the lights and fall onto the mattress. Sheets smell like dish soap. All herky-jerky, I sit up and check the apartment every few minutes, each time expecting the lights to be off. Full-on twitches now. Chewing on my cheek, squeezing my thumbs. Thinking: who's pulling Bill's strings? Guy's a guy who needs a boss. Whoever boss is, asking questions has 'em spooked. Gotta get to Korbes. He'll talk. Eventually. Why's a hooker playing nice with me? Why's Manny got me doing this dumb fucking story in the first place? Why'd Allison have to go and get herself knocked up? Doesn't she know that's how lives get ruined? Even marginal ones. Which covers about all of us.

Fuck this. It's up and out. Slip across the street and hop in my car. Bald tires, fishtailing down Harney. Black sky, gray buildings, white flakes. Jam the car into park across the street from Bill's house. Whole street is asleep. Tippity-tap-tapping the steering wheel. Fidget with the heat knobs. Wonder if Bill can feel the hate eyes I'm shooting at his bedroom window. Asleep in there. Warm, soft wife next to him. Kid down the hall. Hooker slobber dried on his dick. Hope he gets the clap or some shit. Herpes.

Fucktart, what are you doing, stewing? Uppers. Get me wired and irritable. What's the fun there? Is that the goal? Fun? Scratch my scalp. Flake-shouldered, blurry-eyed, ashing out the window thinking this is It.

twelve

Snap awake to a banging noise. Disoriented. Scared. My original position, waiting for the hammer to fall.

In the car. Darkish. Windshield covered in snow. Heavy wet clumps fall from the window where a gloved fist pounds. Roll it down and a sheet of the white stuff falls into my lap.

"Yeah?" Trying not to look too fucked up. Patrol cop. Peering around for probable cause, the cocksucker.

"Can I ask what you're doing here, sir?"

"Sitting."

"You've been here all night."

Not sure if that's a question. I say, "Eh."

"You're going to have to move your car, sir. You're blocking a hydrant."

"Got it." I point forward. The direction in which I'll travel.

"Are you okay?"

"Little tired, is all."

"Have you been drinking?"

"Negatory. Gotta get going. Thanks for not writing me a ticket." It occurs to me, after I turn the key in the ignition and hear this wretched grinding noise, that the car's running. "Long night." Slide her into drive and away I go. Obey all applicable traffic laws, of course, because the cop follows me downtown. Wave to him as I drop a quarter in the meter.

Snow's mostly melted from the salted sidewalks and streets. Pretty meek showing on Mother Nature's part. Slosh through the puddle at the bottom of the steps. Fucking sales bell dings soon as I step inside. One sales dupe high-fives the guy sitting next to him. Wish they'd just fucking make out already.

Nemo's sitting at my desk. Wearing a gray fedora and suspenders. Walk up behind him and knock the hat off his head. It falls onto the Selectric. "Nice hat." Queer.

"It's my dad's," he says.

I want to punch him. Hard. In his mouth. Haven't hit anyone since third grade. "Walk with me, Nemo."

"I don't get it," he says as I open the coffee shop's door. "What's with 'Nemo'?"

"Figure it out. What do you want?" I jerk my thumb toward the barista. Not sure why coffee slingers get special titles, but I play along.

"Latte with a double shot of espresso," he says as if the double shot is a sign of his toughness.

"A *latte*? The fuck is wrong with you?"

"I like lattes."

Caffeinated beverages in hand, we sit at a window table in the smoking section. I offer him a cigarette, thinking he'll wave it off. He doesn't. So I light us both.

"Your dad smoke, too?"

"Not really. Pipe."

"You have other bad habits? Drink?"

"Sometimes."

"And when you drink, you drink . . . ?"

"Just whatever's around."

"Come on, everyone's got a drink."

He has to think about this. Yet another sign he can't be trusted. "Rum and coke, I guess."

Fucking Malibu'd be my guess. "We'll work on it. So, what'd you think yesterday?"

"Is it always like that?"

"Only Wednesdays. Rest of the week is pretty tame."

"That's good. I guess."

"Yes, that's very good. Look, Nemo, here's the deal—I've gotta have ready pretty soon here a big nasty story—"

"I know."

"How do you know?"

"Mr. Hertz said something about it."

"Mr. Hertz said what about it?"

"That you're working a project."

"And?"

"That's it."

"Are you lying to me?"

"What? No. Why would I do that?"

"You tell me."

"I'm not."

"Let's keep it that way. Bottom line, kid, is I'm going to be pretty busy. So you're going to pick up my slack. Starters—call up the secretary of state down in Lincoln, find out whatever you can on WJC Investments. Background is it's some bullshit LLC, so they'll have at least some paperwork on file."

"Okay?"

"Stop being so timid. You'll get eaten alive out there. Lawyers, politicians, your competition, cops—especially the cops—they can smell fear. And when they get a noseful, watch out. They'll knock you down and eat your still-beating heart." I know: *but this is Omaha.* Ever been here? Didn't think so.

He blows on his steaming latte and draws in a noisy sip.

"So, in addition to working the phone with the state guys, today you're going to learn all about the county and district courts. Lucky for you, I can teach you everything you need to know in an hour. Back when the paper started, I had to figure out all this shit by myself." Okay, enough with the crusty old man bit, shithead. "Anyway, after that I've gotta go dick around with some neighborhood-watch dingbats, so you'll be on your own." I snub out my cigarette. "Ask the guy behind the counter for a to-go cup. Time is money, right?"

"Would be if you were paying me."

So this kid's got some potential. Minimal, but.

"Can I ask you something?" he asks.

"Hit me."

"Are you okay?"

I could just hurt him. I just could. "You should, as a rule, ask as few questions as possible. You'll find you'll get better answers if you rephrase questions as imperatives. Try again."

"You look like shit."

"That's a statement. If I were you, I'd have gone with 'Tell me what's going on.' See? Vague. I'd have to guess what you're talking about. And then, based on what I say, you'd know where I was coming from."

His fedora slung low, he says, "Tell me what's going on."

"Nothing. After you." I gesture to the door and follow him.

Before the door shuts behind us, Nemo yells something about

"Oh shit!" I turn around, and he's pointing down 16th Street, where two cops have a knife-wielding guy at gunpoint. My dander would be up if this were going anywhere. But it's not.

"What?" I ask.

"Are you seeing this?"

"If you're talking about the black dude that's about to get wasted, then, yes, I am."

"Shouldn't we do something?"

"Like?"

"Get the story?"

"For fuck's sake, Nemo." Too late. Little guy's already dashed halfway there. Got his hand on his hat so it doesn't fly off. I have to follow him so he doesn't get himself shot.

Two cops with freshly trimmed buzz cuts yell at Knifey to get down on his face. I maneuver around to the street side of the cruiser so I can see the action. Motherfucker's wearing bright pink tights and a platinum wig and is slashing at the air in front of him with a rusty machete.

Stupid kid's creeping up behind the cops now. "Nemo, god-dammit, get the fuck back here. I'm not washing your fucking blood off the fucking sidewalk."

Kid's scribbling in his notebook like he's been touched by the Spirit. I grab him by his coat collar and drag him back a few yards.

"You want to report on this"—I shove him—"do it from across the street, goddammit." He stumbles back over the curb, then runs a few paces. He's probably creaming his little pink sa-teen panties. I lean on a wall and watch the shit unfold like the impartial observer of action that I am. Jerk's waving the knife around, stabbing and jabbing at nothing specific. My jaw clenches and I hear a succinct hissing noise as one of the cops shoots a jet of pepper spray into the nut's face. The guy doesn't scream, but he drops the knife, and falling to his neon-spandex-covered knees, he cups his face with his hands. It's all over now. The cops tackle, cuff and throw him into the cruiser.

Nemo's still writing when I cross the street and walk up behind him. Kid's bubbling over with that variety of ebullient enthusiasm found only in zealots, converts and adolescents.

"You get all that?" I ask.

"Oh man, oh man, oh man."

"Let me know when you're done." I sip my coffee till it's just about gone, stopping when Nemo turns around and gives me a thumbs-up.

"You realize," I say, "all that was for nothing."

"What? That was great!"

"Whatever it was, it wasn't news. If the cops had shot him, yeah, that's news. But pepper-spraying some deranged jag-off who won't drop a knife, that's boring. Let's go."

The next forty-five minutes is a crash course in navigating the court databases and who does what and where their offices are located. Nemo writes furiously in his notebook. (On the cover of which, by the way, he's written his name, *Omaha Weekly News-Telegraph* and the office phone and fax numbers.) Sitting on my favorite bench across the hall from the protection order office, I give him his first real assignment.

"Write down this name: Jason Downs. He's the sick-fuck teacher that's been all over TV for diddling his students. Talk to his attorney, find his parents, find his ex-girlfriends and ex-boyfriends, his ex-pets, find some parents of the kids he fucked with. I've got some notes somewhere on my desk you can look over if you want."

Nemo copies down my instructions word for word. "Got it."

His pen stops moving a good fifteen seconds after I stop talking.

"Couple tricks Staskiewicz didn't teach you: one, no ballpoint pens. Too slow. Go back to the office and grab a roller ball or felt tip. Two, ignore the lines on your notebook paper. Slows you down. Three, you only need to get three or four of every ten words in a quote right. Four, your would-be profession isn't long for this world, so start learning HTML."

I lead us downstairs and show Nemo how to work the computer by running Dunkel through the county court database. Nothing except a speeding ticket, 42 in a 25. Amsterdam's clean, too. Wozniak and Korbes, one each—misdemeanor assault. Luka's a blank. Curious. Very.

"Okay, you try," I tell him.

He sidles up to the machine and types in *cockburn,ber* before I can smack his hand away from the keyboard. "We don't have to time to play. Run that fucko I gave you."

"I was just kidding."

"Ha." Shitbird. "You're going to do that as soon as I leave, aren't you?"

"Probably," he says.

"Go ahead, then."

Apprehensive, he, with me watching. He eyes the keyboard, the terminal, the bulletproof glass divider between us and the clerk. I type it in for him. Up comes the hit: misdemeanor narcotics possession. Reckless endangerment. Show him how to run a query on it.

"See? Here? Where it says NC? Know what that means?"

"No contest."

"Nolo contendere," Run a new query and scroll down a couple screens. "Here's the disposition. Thirty days suspended, one year probation. Got it?"

"Not bad," he says.

Obviously, he's never been on probation. *Très* degrading. "Never hurts to have photos of powerful people doing bad things. Judge Marfisi? Now retired? Everyone knew he was a boozer. Scored some footage from a guy who works security at the casinos. Had him masturbating by the craps table. Security shoves him out just before he pukes. Pisses himself, passes out in the lobby with his thumb in his mouth and his Johnson hanging out. And that sloppy motherfucker was going to send *me* to jail? Cause I had a little junk in my pocket? Your justice system at work, kid."

"What's this? Procuring alcohol for a minor?" Taps the screen like I don't know what the fuck he's talking about.

"Nothing. Some kids got wasted, stole my car and fucked themselves up. Bad. Big fucking mess. Anyway, it was dropped." Legally, true. Might've walked on it, but it still follows me. When I let it. "Anyway, Manny knows about this, so don't go thinking you've got something on me." Which is somewhat true. Manny doesn't know *all* about it. Nobody does. Except me. "Those records are sealed, by the by, so don't bother."

He adjusts his hat. I introduce him to the nice bureaucratic functionary whose little empire consists entirely of records distribution, and leave the two of them to play written-request-and-fetch.

So it's back to home base, where I corner Donna.

"Yeah, what?" she says, turning away from her computer. "Jesus, did you sleep in those clothes?"

Yes. "No. Who's that cop you talked to? The liaison guy?"

"Have it written down somewhere. Chumley, I think. Why?"

"Can you call him again? Have a question I need you to ask him."

"And that is?"

"Ask him what he does with the photocopies that Denny Amsterdam gives him every week. He'll know what you're talking about. And then ask if they've ever done an audit of what the organization's done with the grant money."

"Can it wait?"

"Would I be asking you if it weren't an emergency?" I mosey on over to my desk so she can make the call in what little privacy the office allows, and while I'm waiting on her, I call Allison's cell. Goes straight to voice mail, which means her phone, which is never off, is off. Leave her a "Seeing if you're dead; call if you're not" message. Can't tell if she was trying to be, how might one say, *cool*? last night. Comely, perhaps. Though, if she had just shut up, things very well may have ended differently.

I lean back in my chair and peer around the file cabinet that separates Donna's and my desks, and she's saying "Great, thanks, bye."

"What you have for me?"

"No audits. Too buried in real police work to follow up on that."

"Cops work on an honor system? That's a first."

"Well, this isn't—says he doesn't do anything with the photocopies."

I scribble this down in my notebook. "Whyzat?"

"The cops can't use unsubstantiated information collected by—and this is my word, not his—rogues."

"What's his word?"

"He said 'citizens.'"

"Thanks. Owe you."

"But wait," she says, "there's more. I pushed him a little, because it doesn't make sense that they'd just file the"—she pauses

to let me know she's about to say something ironic—"*information*
if they aren't going to use it."

"So?"

"So I asked him what he does with it, physically. Does he file
it, enter it into a computer, whatever. And he said he throws it
away. Doesn't even look at it."

"Why the fuck he tell *you* that?"

"Because I'm just a little girl," she says in a naughty sex-kitten
voice, "who needs you to help me out a teensy tiny bit."

"Love it. That it?"

"Yeah, and I'm leaving. Kid's sick at school. Probably hungover." She grabs her purse and coat and starts to head out, but I
tell her to wait a second and wave her over to my desk.

"Let me ask you something. Your kid, you like her okay,
right?"

"Don't tell me you got Allison pregnant."

"I didn't say that."

"You did, didn't you?"

"Remind me again why I like you."

"If I had to do it over again? Probably wouldn't. I won't make
you puke with that 'I love her more than I ever thought I could
love anything' bullshit, but it's true. And I hate kids."

"You and what's-his-face, you guys plan her?"

"Total accident. I wanted to abort, but he wouldn't let me.
And then the asshole left us both. Such is life, right, fuckhead?"

"Maybe yours," I say. Grab a directory and find Leroy's number.

"Shine shop," he says. "Leroy speaking."

"No shit, Leroy speaking. You got anyone else working there?"

"Who the fuck?"

"Chill out, it's Cockburn. Got some bad news about the
crackers with the cameras."

"You gonna tell me it's some German company gonna turn this place into condos, ain't you?"

"German?"

"I had visitors yesterday. Some Kraut-sounding name with the dots over the *u*."

"Take 'em months before they can even think about doing anything. Paperwork, negotiating with the city."

"Yeah, maybe. Bottom line is I'm gonna have to move my ass. You owe me two-fifty for that polish." Hangs up.

Flip through the directory, get the NüCorp number. Probably wouldn't be the worst thing to have a look-see at these apartments about which I'm allegedly writing. Couple transfers later, I get a she-flack who says she'll meet me at the onsite office in half an hour. On the case, these people.

Throw on my coat and head out, whistling a tune that started out as "Kick Out the Jams," but by the time I'm on my way out to Omaha's soon-to-be-Soho, it's devolved into something entirely tuneless. I ditch the car across the street from Maggie's, which looks like it's open for business. Walking the few blocks will do me some good. Fresh air. Exercise.

Neighborhood's a fucking mess. Temperature's in the high thirties, so the snow that fell last night is melting and mixing with the sand and gravel. Makes one hell of a sloppy muck for the fast-food wrappers and used rubbers to float around in.

Walking north on 22nd, I pass a beat-up single-story house with a screened-in porch. Three fat, unwashed kids plaster their scummy faces against the mesh and watch me until their mom yells at them, saying the little shits need to be doing their goddamned chores and not lollygagging around. Halfway to Leavenworth, I hear a cracking noise beneath my shoe. I look down at a crushed syringe.

It's getting near the official opening date, so there are a few trucks parked around the Baron Square. Folks moving in. Big *Welcome* banner across the gates now.

Aesthetically, the place hasn't changed all that much since I moved out. Same sixteen buildings with the same dark brick exteriors surrounding the same trees planted around the same concrete fountain in the same courtyard. At first glance, the only things missing are the broken bottles, discarded needles and maybe a bum or two passed out on the stone steps. Doubtless NüCorp has a team of underpaid Mexicans scouring the grounds every morning. At least till all the apartments are leased.

One familiar building has yellow and pink balloons affixed to the door, so I can only assume that's the office. It's the one I used to live in, of course, another demonstration of how perfectly cynically cyclical the world is.

Force of habit, I hold my breath while walking in to fend off the dank, musty stench that used to greet me. Like moldly blankets soaking in stagnant pond water. But once inside, I'm greeted by that new-carpet smell that almost stings your nose. Not sure which I find preferable.

"Cookies?" a chirpy female voice asks.

"With the *News-Telegraph*," I say.

"We chatted on the phone, then. Hi." She's positively beaming. If I owned sunglasses, I'd put 'em on. "I'm Charlene."

"Cockburn," I say. That bitter funk I'm smelling, I can only assume is me. The office here, it's sparkling.

"You want a tour?" She's young, mid-twenties, and attractive with her businesswoman calves wrapped in dark nylons. Maybe this is the type I should go for. Driven. Probably self-sufficient. Course, she probably hates smokers and only drinks vodka cut with juice.

"Lead the way."

Charlene starts in on her spiel about saving one of Omaha's great historic landmarks from the wrecking ball, how NüCorp spent well over eight million dollars renovating all the buildings and how the city planning department is hopeful the immediate area will blossom into a hip little arts district.

"Yeah, so I'm curious about that," I say, playing the ignoramus. "An arts district?"

"That's right. The Leavenworth and Saint Mary's corridors are ideal for little cafés and bistros and independently owned retail shops. And believe you me, the nightlife around here is going to be drastically different by this time next year." She gives me a knowing wink, because we're all fucking in this together, right? "And the Omaha Public Schools has just committed to building an elementary school adjacent to Baron Square."

"You going to import some bohemians, too?"

Charlene grins at me, the heathen irritant. "We're thinking they'll be banging down the doors to get in." She keeps up the patter about completely gutting every building and creating larger, sunnier, happier apartments than the originals.

"Shouldn't have been too hard," I say. "I lived here up till it was condemned. Wasn't very big or bright."

"You did? Which building?"

"Oddly enough," I say, as if there's such a beast as a coincidence, "this one, on the third floor. Had a studio that overlooked the courtyard."

"You just aren't going to believe what we've done with the place."

I follow her up the stairs, and I note the presence of as-yet-uncompleted construction. Unfinished walls. Paper taped to the floor. Random metal and wood scraps next to toolboxes. "You'll be finished when?"

"Officially? Three weeks. That's, as we say, when the last nail gets driven. Most of the buildings have been completed. You probably noticed the movers on your way in?"

I grunt in agreement. These stairs are nothing like they used to be. Don't feel like I'm about to fall through them.

Charlene slides a key into a gray steel door. Used to be my shitty particleboard door. "We call this floor plan the Burroughs."

"As in William S.?" I ask.

"I think so." She pushes open the door. Goddamn right, sunny. With nothing over the windows, it's like walking into a spotlight, what with the white walls and white Berber carpet and pale gray accents. The place is larger than I imagined. Not as big as what I have now, but definitely nicer, and I bet both the hot and cold water faucets work like they're supposed to.

"Two bedrooms, one bathroom, eat-in kitchen with a break-fast nook, cable-ready and wired for high-speed Internet," Char-lene says without taking a breath.

"And, what, a quarter of these are low-income, right?" Not that I'm interested. I'm not.

"The agreement we have with the city and state is for twenty-five percent, but NüCorp, being dedicated to—"

"A third, then?"

"Thirty-three percent."

"How goes that? The income-restricted leasing?"

"Rapidly approaching our goal."

She stands near the door, perky as ever, with a clipboard or something in her hands.

"So, no wait list?" Again, I give a shit not.

"Not at the moment."

"Why not farm out the management?"

"NüCorp wants to guarantee a quality living experience for its tenants. The best way to do that is to see to the management ourselves."

"You mind if I poke around a little bit solo?"

"I'd rather you didn't. Insurance purposes."

"I'm not going to steal anything. And I won't sue if I fall out the window, okay?"

That smile is just etched on that pretty, perky face of hers. "I'd really rather not."

"Can you just stand right there, then, and not say anything or move at all or make any noise whatsoever?"

She mimes a zipping of her lips and the throwing away of an invisible key. I grin my thanks and start poking around.

Near as I can tell, the master bedroom here occupies the bulk of what was my apartment. The glaring exception, other than everything being absolutely and irreversibly changed, is the Jolly Roger I had hung over the window is gone. I was one of the last ones to leave before the city condemned the place, and in my boozy, cokey, Tuinal daze, I fancied myself quite the land pirate. Whatever the fuck *that* was.

So here I am. I should probably feel a pang of sepia-toned nostalgia, but as my shoes sink into the freshly laid carpet, I get antsy and irritated, because more than a couple of my ghosts haunt the shit out of this place. For starters, I got to know Allison right where I'm standing. And two feet to my left, where the kitchenette used to be, that's where I spent many early mornings heaving. Yeah, lot of dark times in here. Don't think I ever turned on the overhead light.

Jesus, the fuckers even took out the radiators. In the bathroom, the faucet isn't dripping and the toilet isn't running. When I flip on the switch, the fluorescent light comes right on instead of flickering on and off and hissing and crackling like in the good ol' days. And the bathtub, well, that's something else entirely. It used to be a tub with claws and a yellowed rubber hose connected to the spigot. Now it's a shower stall with, get this, two fucking showerheads. The floor where I spent so many nights and mornings and afternoons prone, pressing as much of my flesh as I could against the forgiving chill of the hexagonal ceramic tile, has been ripped up and replaced with light gray linoleum.

I suddenly feel like I should be manly—kick the tires, light the fires, that sorta shit. So I open the cabinet beneath the sink and examine the pipes. No surprises here. They look like pipes. I flush the toilet, then fuck with the hot and cold knobs in the shower. The water shoots out of the heads with something just short of gusto, its temperature shockingly responsive to my fiddling.

"How's everything look in there?" Charlene calls from wherever she is.

I put my hands behind my back like I've been caught with one of them where it oughtn't be. "Peachy."

Back in the bedroom, I look out the window, which is, again, different. Replacing the warped glass that used to let in a godawful draft is a two-ply Plexi storm window, probably with a perversely high R-value. It's also the same, in a way. It's in the same spot, and I have the same view. Didn't appreciate it back then, either, but I can see how some could get off on the clear view of downtown's two skyscrapers and a cozy neighborhood bar not a block and a half away. Been there more than a few times. Not a bad place, if I recall correctly. The jukebox could use some work, but they do have a nice patio done up like the deck of a ship. A pirate ship, maybe even.

And, fuck me, either I'm losing my shit or that's Allison in the courtyard talking to some slick suit-wearing monkeyfuck. Asshole has a fucking *mustache*. Looks like he goes to the *gym*. Probably has *abs* and his income puts him above the *poverty line*. Trite thing, to judge yourself by your replacement, but standing up here, my mug nearly pressed against the storm window, I'm feeling like a douche-by-proxy: failed at the life he didn't want, but lacking the balls to admit it's just fucking fine to want something else. Same impulse that has me lingering around crime scenes howls at me to troop it across the courtyard. About-face and thank Charlene for the tour. "Lovely place, really," I say, on my way out the door.

"My pleasure. I have some literature down in the office."

"Not looking to rent." I'm rounding the first turn on the staircase. I hear her hurried footsteps above and behind me, like maybe she's one of the Four Horsemen. Pestilence, I'd wager.

"Background material," she says. "For your story? Are you okay?"

"Late for a chat with the mayor." Granted, guy's a drunk and is probably sleeping one off right now. She doesn't have to know that.

I'm reaching for the front door when she hits me with a "Hey?" So innocent, her tone. It startles me. Teeth gnashing, I stop.

"Here you go." She hands me a manila folder with my name written on it in big dumb cursive.

"Thanks," I say, and possibly mean it. "Question—which of the buildings are move-in ready?"

I get the skinny: nine as of today, five more as of Monday,

the remainder next week. I do a fruity little Cub Scout salute and prowl through three buildings, finding nothing. Fourth one, I hear a muffled voice. No mistaking it. Third floor and directly across the courtyard from my old place. Work a little Liddy action and silently push open the door and there she is, gnawing on her thumbnail, cell phone pressed to her ear.

"Call you back." She drops the phone into her purse. "What are you doing here?"

"Working, actually." I hold up the evidentiary folder.

"The world isn't that small."

"Mine, apparently, is. Where's the guy with the dick smaller than mine?"

"The what? You're sweating."

"The guy you're with? Raoul or whatever the fuck his name is."

"Jesus, Burn. You're spying on me?"

"Answer the question."

"What? You going to hit him?"

This, I hadn't considered. Figured I'd nail him with some verbal rat-a-tat-tat that'd leave him smarting. Because that'd show him what a man I am. "Slap, maybe."

"You are such a little boy. He's with the apartment people."

"Thought you found a place."

"I did. Just taking another look." Got her arms crossed low, so it's not exactly a defensive posture. Pleading, in a way. "Where were you last night?"

"This is the apartment you rented?"

"Has an ice maker."

"An ice maker?"

"Appliance. It goes in the freezer and makes—"

"I know what it fucking does."

"And there's a liquor store—"

"Half a block away."

"Close to work."

"The job that's beneath me?"

"Rent's cheaper than what we're paying now."

Look at her: trying to take care of me. Look at me: not entirely hating her for it. Part of me wants to kiss her and hold her and not let go. Really. Other part wants to torch the building and piss on the ashes. Habit. I deal out a couple smokes. Also habit. She demurs.

"The lease doesn't kick in, you know, officially, until Monday," Allison says. "And the guy's supposed to be back in a couple minutes."

"Fuck him."

"Okay," she says. "Last night?"

"Had some work to do."

"You haven't showered today."

Turn up my palms. *You got me.*

"You slept in the office?"

"I was out and about." Give her my back and have a look-see at this den of torpor and iniquity. Looks just like the other apartment. And, I assume, every other newly rehabbed unit. Shame is it's nicer than where I live now.

"Doing?"

"Work shit. Whatever." Across the way, my old building. Third window from the right, top floor. "I puked out that window over there once." This remembrance of vomitus past strikes me as mildly amusing. Hence the shit-eater I'm wearing. "Sorta hazy. Think I'd just wrapped some story or another. Cliff was there. Called me king shit of fuck mountain. Anyway, it was funny." Move to the kitchen so I can ash in the sink. "I never used my stove here. Not once."

"So," she says.

"So," I say, "what."

She takes the half step over to me and hits me with a deep, wet kiss while she undoes my belt.

"The guy?"

"Shh." She unbuttons my pants. "Go with it."

Toss my smoldering butt into the sink and, for whatever reason, we're both shaking (okay, really, I'm shaking because I'm feeling loopy and tired and thinking: don't-do-this-this-is-a-powerful-mistake. She's probably just nervously excited) when I yank down her jeans.

"Not all the way," she says.

I've got her jeans bunched around her knees. She lies back on the floor and I release the Emasculator, who's showing no small degree of interest in these goings-on. Lifts her legs, her toes pointing at the ceiling so her body makes an L. Got it at the gates when the door opens.

"Woah," he says. "You can't be doing that."

I hurriedly and awkwardly stuff myself back into my pants. "You." I point—with my finger—so we're not confused about who's being addressed. "Fuck the fuck off."

Apparently, my barely concealed boner and I spook the guy, because, without further ado, he fucks the fuck off, abs and mustache and all.

Allison's back in order and I can't tell if she's pissed or embarrassed or thinking this is funny. "Guy's a slimeball," she says.

Give her the pervy leer. What is this? Supplication?

"I don't think so," she says. "Probably just screwed ourselves out of this place."

The feeling I have is one of a bayonet plunging into my stomach and being violently raked. See if I can't fool myself into thinking this isn't the most damaging idea to which I've ever agreed. Course, I did check into a grimy motel room last night. So consider this option B. Pushing myself deep into suspension-of-disbelief territory now, but it's possible signing up wouldn't be exactly like dying. And it wouldn't mean I'd, say, fall off the riding mower I had no real reason to buy because the backyard wasn't all that big. And I wouldn't necessarily then get run over by the thing while my only son watched it chew me to bits. But, certainly, the last thing my kid'd see of me wouldn't be this tired look on my face like *oh, well, what the fuck, anyway*.

But, I do wonder: What is it people *do* with kids? The mechanics of it. You've gotta be around. Watch them. Feed them. What? Go to the park? PTA meetings? Fucking school plays? Hoard pictures? There's gotta be a bigger draw that I'm not seeing. Can't imagine Allison here has a handle on it. It's just *what's done*.

"Lame, anyway. Has carpet."

She walks over to the window and leans against it so she's backlit. When I retell this story, I'll say a crow flew down and perched on a skeletal branch of a tree in the courtyard behind Allison and it looked like it was sitting on her shoulder, because that's where this is headed. Right?

So I pull up a square of Berber. "Something like this goes for how much?"

"Four and a quarter."

"Utilities?"

"Heat and hot water."

"You do realize that everyone else who lives in this place is going to suck."

"Don't care."

"Just got a tour of another apartment in another building, and it's boxy and lame just like this one."

Nothing.

"There's still hookers and junkies all over the place."

More of the same.

"And the other renters, they'll probably have like weird complex-wide barbecues and shit in the summer."

Deep breath says she's running out of patience.

"You'll have to give me head every day. And swallow, too."

"What's it going to be, Burn?"

"Fuck it."

I'm not going to say her face lights up or whatever, but she does look pretty fucking happy. I'd like to think some of her elation's rubbing off on me, but.

"Tonight," she says, "I'll make dinner."

"Tonight," I say, "I'll eat dinner."

thirteen

After leaving Allison, I hoof it back toward my car. The wind's barreling up St. Mary's and Howard, almost so I'd expect to get bruised. Smoke a cigarette and kick around some garbage. Some guy asks me for a quarter, and I give him one, benevolent push-over sop I am. My first thought is that I've really fucked myself now. Second thought is I gotta stop thinking. Call the office. Nemo picks up.

"Gimme-gimme good news, kid?"

"What do you want first? The molester guy or the secretary of state stuff?"

"You already got an answer from the state?"

"Sure."

I ready the notebook. "Hit me."

"WJC is an LLC with three shareholders." Wanker stops talking.

"Haven't heard the good stuff yet."

"Creighton Korbes, James Wozniak and William Dunkel."

If I were at a party, the record would screech to a halt right here. "Repeat those."

He does, and they haven't changed. Simpletons. I write down

Dunkel and *Wozniak* and *Korbes*, again, and underline them five times. You know, because this is important and otherwise I'd forget. "Good thing you're not here, else I'd cram my tongue down your throat."

"Uhh, okay?"

"You know anything about these guys?"

"Nope."

"Did you look?"

"Should I?"

"They're mine."

"You want the lowdown on the molester guy?"

"Write it up. We'll chat tomorrow."

"Manny says he wants to talk to you, too. Important."

"He around?"

"Nope."

"Must not be that important, then, eh?" Pocket the phone. I'm taking what might well be meaningful strides up the hill toward my car. Leavenworth's at the top, and a pair of sporting women are smoking and chatting on the opposite corner.

"Hey," I say from a few paces away. "Looking for Luka."

The one closest to me, a black woman featuring platinum hair with roots that make her look like a negative image of a skunk wearing a purple feather boa over a peacoat, says, "Never heard of her. That her name, for real?"

"Far as I know."

"*Luka?* The fuck kinda dumb hooker name is that? Maybe something like Silk or Candy or Desire or some shit, but, *Luka?*"

Those, I don't tell her, are stripper names. "You know everybody?"

"Better'n you. Shit, if you want your dick sucked, all you gotta do is ask."

"I'm a reporter; working with her on a story about the neigh-borhood cleanup."

Her eyes go big, then start rolling. "Those fuckin' assholes. Did a drive-by last week and sprayed me with bleach."

"You ever see them attack anyone? Shoot someone?"

"I seen 'em with guns. Never seen 'em use 'em."

"That a recent phenomenon—the guns?"

"Old news. Shakin' down the corner boys, bullshit like that. Nothing new. Motherfuckers just get off on feeling like they strong."

"You've seen them, though, driving around armed?"

"All the motherfuckin' time."

This bodes well. "Anything else strange going on?"

"Other than you here talking to me?"

"Right."

"Construction over there." Jerks her thumb at the Baron Square. "Dump trucks all over the place. Guys in white space suits scooping up dirt."

EPA in action. "What about over on, like, Pacific around Twenty-eighth?"

"No traffic there. Couldn't tell you."

"And you don't know a hooker named Luka? Ruth, maybe?"

"Nuh-uh. Maybe you show me a picture I'd recognize her."

"Don't have one."

"Don't know what to tell you."

Stalking off, thinking it's weird, her not knowing Luka. Hookers I used to share the Baron Square with knew every-thing about everyone. Chat your ear off dishing. Can't imagine times have changed. It's with this thought that I cruise over a couple blocks to where Bill's houses are located and start knock-ing on doors. Someone around here's gotta have a story worth listening to.

Most knocks go unanswered, disproving my half-assed notion that the folks around here are largely unemployed. First two that answer don't habla Ingles. Few more no-gos. Then comes 2877 Pacific. Black woman wearing a powder blue warm-up suit, ash hanging off her cigarette at least an inch long.

"What?" she says.

Show her my yellow, crooked teeth. "With the *News-Telegraph*. Have a sec?"

"Maybe."

"You know the guy owns that house?" Point across the street. Small white house. Dirty as fuck. On my list as a WJC property.

"Nope." Doesn't even look.

"How about that one?" Next one over. Yellow. Also sinfully soiled and also on the list.

"Nope."

"Ever see anyone go in either one? Contractors, maybe?"

"Nuh-uh."

"You here all day?"

"Uh-huh."

"Every day?"

"What you want already?" Big puff, then she ashes across the threshold. "Got food on the stove."

"I just wanna know if you've noticed anything out of the ordinary about either of those houses."

"Them's bad mojo, all I know. You can feel it."

"You can feel what?"

"Ain't never seen nobody come in or out, but there's people in there at night."

"You've seen people in there?"

"I know people's in there."

Point to a house that isn't on my list. "That one, too?"

This gets a long, slow nod, like I'm finally getting her. "*Big voodoo on that one.*"

"Thanks for your time."

Door slams and I hit the bricks again, blowing into my gloved hands. Try a few more houses in vain before giving it up. Kick a dented Coors tallboy up the street toward my car. Punt it into a storm drain across from Maggie's and decide to swing in for a quick bite instead of going somewhere that probably won't give me *E. coli* poisoning, because it's close and I'm famished. Arch, the bartender, is dropping quarters into the juke while his Doberman, Sammy, mans the bar. The place darkens dramatically when the door closes behind me. Group of teenagers clustered in a booth in the back corner, pile of Falstaffs on the table.

Maggie's, it's a speakeasy of sorts. Arch's family—brothers, dad, grandfather—they've always been cops. His dad was president of the police union till last year. Problem is Arch is a little slow. Slow enough, anyway, that he wouldn't pass muster at the academy. Family didn't want to see him pushing a mop or pumping gas, so they set him up with this place. Building was delinquent for years on property tax, so his dad got it for a cool seven hundred bucks at auction. One-bedroom apartment upstairs is where Arch lives. Self-contained and out of the way. Arch serves anyone who walks in and can speak English. Never had any problems and never will because cops drink free.

Arch, his Led Zeppelin tunes picked, walks over to the bar (door on sawhorses, technically), lights a swisher and says, "Yeah?"

"Falstaff," I say. "You cooking today?"

"If I gotta."

"Burger," I say. "Well done."

He grabs a can from the oversized Igloo cooler at his feet. "Burger's gonna take a few minutes."

Pop the top. "Not a problem, amigo."

After Arch walks into the back, I try to get his dog's attention, but Sammy's less than impressed with my finger snapping, so I drink the beer sans company.

Kids over in the corner, who've been whispering since I walked in, must be feeling the "Kashmir." One of 'em's singing. Poorly. Swallow some beer, and Sammy hasn't moved. Stuffed and mounted, maybe.

Hear someone walking this way from the corner booth. Keep my back to whoever and put on a bored face.

"Ain't you afraid your boss is going to smell the beer on your breath?"

Keep on ignoring her, thinking she'll move along. Chatty Mc-Shitface can't handle her beer and I don't have the patience.

Poke at my shoulder. "Talking to you, Cockburn."

Now I'm puzzled. Not enough to play along. "Co-burn, and fuck off."

"Jeez, I'm just kidding. Got a smoke?"

Okay, familiar. Turn my head but not my torso because that'll show her. Yeah, mister not-impressed here can't be bothered. Head slung low and I peer over the top of my glasses. Luka. Ponytail today. Black shirt. Violently faded blue jeans.

"You're hanging out with those kids?" I ask.

"Thing I do. Outreach, sorta. Don't wanna see 'em end up where I am."

"Bull-fucking-shit."

"Seriously. And the competition would hurt. Fresh, young faces, guys go for that. So what are you doing here, anyway? Doesn't seem like your kinda place."

"Hard at work." I tip back my can to illustrate. "Just met some colleagues of yours said they never heard of you."

"Don't normally do street trade. Sorta fallen on hard times."

"You normally, what, then?"

"Whatever pays."

"I.e.?"

"Stuff. Doesn't matter to you. Ask me about something else."

Peculiar. "Sit."

She does. Grabs my cigarette pack from my breast pocket, fishes out a couple and lights us. "You wanna be friends with Sammy, give me a dollar."

"You his pimp?"

"Give."

So I do. The bill's dirty and crumpled all to hell. She folds it lengthwise and holds it out. "You gotta tip him." She calls his name and over he trots. Up on his hind legs, he snags the dollar with his mankiller teeth, drops the bill on the floor and returns to his spot. "See?"

"You teach him that?"

She winks.

"Comfortable?" I ask.

"Getting there."

"How's Bill?"

"How's who?"

"Dunkel. Your regular from the neighborhood watch. Guy you're fucking. Dishes you the dirt."

"That's some crazy bullshit you're talking."

"Cut the shit. He pays you well, I hope. You seen his wife? His kid? Feel bad for the guy. Him in his pink house."

"You went there?"

"Course. And I've talked to his dingbat friends. Have a date with them."

Empty the beer. No ashtrays, so I ash in it. She does the same.

"He told me you and he had talked," she says. "He said you're a dick."

"That's one possible interpretation."

Arch walks over, places the burger in front of me. Dripping with grease and served on a napkin.

"Don't have any ketchup," he says.

"Don't need any. Thanks."

He looks at Luka. "No trouble today, okay?"

She winks. "Course not, Archibald."

Arch walks over to the pool table and racks up a game of nine-ball. Sammy follows.

"Trouble?"

"Kids are stupid. Drink too much, think they're invincible."

Is she eyeing me, waiting for a response to that little barb? "Last time we talked, I thought you were borderline retarded. That an act?"

"What do you think?"

"I think you're fucking with me."

"Maybe I am."

Bite into the burger. Cooked all the way through and not entirely terrible. "Start talking," I say.

"About?"

"Don't play Pollyanna here. Posse of seemingly well-intentioned freaks who're starting to find themselves dead or nearly dead. Ones that are still kicking, they're pulling some petty garbage on the local riffraff, but one guy in particular, he's up past his nuts in some serious shit he's losing control of. How's it gonna end? Badly, most likely. So, what I want you to do is tell me what he's told you about him and them."

"Why would I tell you anything?"

"Because you want to and you know your boy's a fucking douche. So start with the money."

"They don't have any money. You've seen them."

"You're correct; I have seen them. I've also seen documents that show the city gave your man near eight grand. Small potatoes, I know, but it's felony money. And he's not spending it at home. Doesn't sound like he's showering you with gifts, so where's it go?"

"He could get in trouble."

"He's in trouble anyway. What's a little more?"

She looks, unnecessarily, over her shoulder at the booth full of kids.

"Lemme take a guess," I say. "Guns."

Her head snaps back.

"Him and his watch buddies, they're feeling powerful now, shaking down the little fish. Am I wrong?"

"Nope."

"Where's he get 'em?"

"Where's anyone get guns they don't want traced? Whoever's selling. His hookup is some white-trash skinhead lives in a trailer somewhere in the county."

Okay, so he takes city money and buys stolen guns with it. That, I can work with. Thinking now: if he stocked up, passed them out to his friends—which I assume he did—that's a criminal enterprise. Criminal enterprise involving firearms might pique the interest of the U.S. attorney. Guy's got a hard-on for gun cases, and, bonus, his office is on our complimentary subscription list. "He ever mention what he's doing with the guns?"

"Nope," she says. Do I believe her? Maybe.

"They just for show? Or is he planning some OK Corral action?"

"I said I don't know."

"You ever ask him?"

"Couple times, yeah. But he always says don't worry because I won't get it."

"Get it." I make a gun with my thumb and index finger and shoot her. "Get it?"

"You're retarded, you know that?"

"Just asking, is all. What else's he say?"

"He's a nice guy."

"He's a fucking creep-weirdo and he'll be in prison soon enough."

"You gonna put him there?"

"He's putting himself there. Course, that's okay by you, I'm sure. Someone'll have to look after all those houses he's buying."

I've seen some things, but I've never seen a hooker do a double take. Till now.

"What houses?"

"Picked up a few of 'em around here on Pacific. Told you about it, I'm sure. Him and a couple friends of his went in together. Course, his buddies, they're not doing so hot. One's dead. Other nearly ate it in a car wreck."

"Don't know nothing about it."

"Why don't I believe you?"

"Not my problem."

"Sure it is. I'll just keep on badgering you. Follow you around. Make it difficult to work."

"Why you gotta be such a dick?"

"Just doing my job. So?"

"I mean it. I don't know anything about any houses."

"Why would he tell you about the illegal shit he does, but not the aboveboard stuff?"

"Trying to impress me, I guess."

"Did he?"

"You know what he said once? He said he'd take me any-where. And I believe him."

"And he probably said that right after he rolled off of you, no?"

"Fuck off."

"Look, you really think you and he'd get together, run away?"

"I didn't say that."

"But you'd like that."

"What do you know?"

"Much too much."

"You don't know shit."

"I know I get a bigger charge out of letting you dick me around than I do when I'm at home with my girlfriend." Atta Burn, turn on the charm.

"Maybe you should dump her, then."

"Can't. She's *avec enfant*."

At this, Ms. Luka barks out a jagged bolt of laughter. "That kid is going to be *messed*."

"What? Grow up to be like you?"

"If you're lucky."

And we find ourselves in one of those awkward silences. It's cut mercifully short by what sounds like a beeper.

"That's me," Luka says. She pulls a pager from her tiny hand-bag.

"You carry a *beeper*?"

She checks the number and puts it away. "Don't want to be that in touch. Borrow your phone?"

"For?"

"Guy wants to score some coke, so I'm calling him back."

"You deal, too?"

"Why not?"

"Use the bar phone."

She does, and the call's brief. A few *uh-huh*'s and she tells the guy half an hour.

"Gotta run," she says.

Dare I? "What's it go for these days, anyway? Blow?"

"How much you looking for?"

"I'm not."

"Fine, how much is *your friend* looking for?" All snotty.

"Maybe a gram or two."

"For you, one-fifty."

"One-fifty? I get a blowjob with that?"

She leans in so my coat's touching her shirt and I can smell my cigarette on her breath. "Cut you a deal on E if you don't touch that, either. Special K. Roofies."

"That your niche? Party stuff?"

"You could call it that. You in or out?"

I'm thinking out, but feeling in. Still have plenty of time to fuck up and make Allison hate me. So consider this my first shot at torpedoing my dipshit verbal (read: nonbinding) agreement to move into that god-awful apartment. And I feel a crash bubbling in the wings. Bump or three never hurt anyone. "Not really a party guy, so let's stay with the coke."

"Gimme an hour."

"Better idea—you're working tonight?"

"Haven't decided."

"Date with your sweetie?"

"Not that it's any of your business, but, yeah, maybe. So what?"

"Hope you charge him full price, is all, because he's not doing you any favors."

"You want that blow?"

"Gotta be this evening."

She grabs the pen from my breast pocket and jots down what I assume is her beeper number on the flap of her matchbook. "Just make sure you have enough dough." Her hand lingers a little too long on my chest when she returns the pen, so I take a half step back and extend my filthy paw for a shake. She leaves me hanging and heads out.

Few kids still over in the booth. Two sitting with their backs to the wall got distrustful eyes watching me walk over. Two guys, one girl. None of 'em older than seventeen. Smarmy-looking, the trio. Poor and desperate.

"You know her?" I ask.

"Maybe," says the girl. Ghastly bangs sprayed up big like she doesn't know better.

"What's she working you for?"

Dude No. 1, with his bleached hair and three-inch gold hoop earrings, says, "Fuck off."

"She got you selling? E? Special K?"

"How we know you're not a cop."

"I probably am. Most guys come in here are. You fucking stupid or something?"

"Just stupid-looking," says the girl.

"Not that I give a shit, because I don't. But whatever you're doing, it's gonna end badly. Guess I'll hear all about it in court."

One dude hits the other's arm. "Told you he was a cop."

Anyone over eighteen who wears anything other than ratty jeans is a cop to these dolts. Oughta correct them, but it's sorta pleasing in a very shallow, impotent way, to make them uncomfortable.

"Just trying to do you a solid, is all." I'll spare them the *I've seen what can happen* discussion. Nobody wants to hear some jerkoff reminisce about some stupid shit he did for a couple bucks when he was in a bad way. And how lucky he was to weasel (blackmail, anyone?) his way out of it. Otherwise, well, he'd be force-drinking out of a prison toilet right now. Truth be told, he oughta be. Chickenshit, amoral, recklessly endangering heathen like him sure as fuck has no business procreating.

fourteen

Stop at the convenience store next to the office and pick up a packet of those obnoxiously marketed and minimally potent low-grade uppers. Dick shrinkers, the kids call 'em. Dry-swallow the bastards and head down, knocking into Manny, looking uncommonly dapper (read: gay) in a navy suit and pink button-down.

"What's the news, chief?"

"Goddamn, boy," he says, "you smell like a distillery."

"Point of order—brewery."

He retrieves a stick of gum from his pocket and thrusts it into my face. "Here."

"Mmm, Juicy Fruit," I say.

"A lot of people wish they could have jobs like yours, you know."

I'd like not to interpret his flippant bullshit as a thinly veiled threat, but. "Speaking of, where's Nemo?"

"Who?"

"The inturd. Nemo. He in?"

"Oddly enough, boy, he's out chasing down a story."

"He's devouring the scraps I so generously tossed him."

Manny bounds awkwardly up the steps. I worry for a second that he might slip and hurt himself something awful. Broken neck, maybe?

"Oh," he says from the landing, "pencil me in sometime tomorrow."

"Only if you tell me what you're up to there with the suit."

"Not a chance." And off he goes.

Smack the back of Donna's head with the NüCorp envelope. "What's cooking, sugar pea?"

"I'm smoking again. Give me one."

I light us both. She's got photos spread on her desk. Looks like ten pictures of the same chair. Different paint jobs on each. So I ask.

"Décor spread for next issue. Crackle painting. Make new stuff look old. Genius, huh?"

"Fairly."

"You look like shit."

"Didn't go home last night."

"You're a dick."

"Not like that. Thing Manny's got me doing."

"Doesn't sound like Manny."

"Started out sounding like Manny. Looks bigger now. Better. You might even like it."

"Lemme guess—has something to do with someone getting murdered and you're going to make it sound really droll."

I ash on one of her photos. She blows off the debris.

She says, "How's Allison?"

"No comment."

She gives me a look dripping with motherly disappointment.

Something she must've had a lot of practice at, because it works.

"She wants to move." I hold up a slick Baron Square one-sheeter. "Here."

"Gross."

"Pretty much."

"She won't go for the abortion, huh?"

"Nope."

"That sucks."

"It does."

After a while, she says, "Well."

I dig around in my pockets for something. An answer. But what I find is this: "Yep."

"I've got a bunch of baby stuff still. In the basement."

Look at us, having a moment. "I gotta work."

Mosey the few steps to my desk and dump the NüCorp crap Charlene gave me. Two-page release goes right into the garbage, leaving me with four sheets that are full of tables and pie charts and numbers. Possibly some data in here worth culling. Finance breakdown, tax-increment-financing junk, debt paydown forecast, and, hello, a list of local contractors NüCorp is proud to do business with. Among them? Curtis Fixtures—bang: Bill's day job. WJC Investments—bang: Bill's mysterious landowning partnership. The dots, they're connecting.

Fetch a clean sheet of paper and map it out. NüCorp's at the top, next to Weed/Seed. Dunkel's below and has lines connecting him to *WJC*, to *stolen guns*, to *Wozniak* to *Korbes* to *Luka* to *local whacko patrol*. WJC's hooked up with *Korbes, Wozniak, NüCorp* and a dotted line to *stolen guns* because maybe the one he used to waste his daughter was hot. Korbes is hooked to his buddies. Gotta get to him. Other question is can I connect the city pigs with NüCorp? Or is Dunkel feeding from a couple of independent troughs?

What bugs me, suddenly, is Manny's apparently tight with NüCorp, as well. Hence the assignment. Hence my assumed complicity. Hence what the fuck is wrong with him? And, if he's roped in with these clowns, then I probably oughta not leave my notes lying around. Not that he won't have to read the story at some point, but I'll figure that out later.

Dial up Curtis and ask the receptionist in which sort of fixtures, exactly, does Curtis deal?

"Lighting," she says.

I say, "How illuminating," like a jackass and hang up.

Next call is Charlene. Get her number after digging in the garbage for the press releases I tossed. Office line goes to voice mail. Cell gets to her.

"It's Cockburn. From the *News-Telegraph* and earlier."

"How's the mayor?"

The fuck? "Drunk as usual." Oh, right. Had to ditch on her. "But, have a question for you about WJC Investments. Listed on the handout you gave me as a local contractor, right? What do they do?"

"I'll have to call you back."

"Please do. Real quick, though, what's the deal with the Loomis Building downtown?"

"The what?"

"Your company's buying another property, right? Across from the library downtown."

"Oh, South Fifteenth. We're looking into it."

"Break my heart if you run out the shine guy on street level."

"I'll pass that along."

Ring up my guy over at the morgue and tell him I'd appreciate a copy of the Wozniak autopsy report. Guy's a half-dead booze and cooze hound, so I'm thinking I'll hear back by the twelfth of never. Fire a burner and stare at the phone like I can make it ring. And, hey, I can.

It's Charlene.

"Consulting," she says.

"Consulting what?"

"Political consulting."

"What's the contract valued at?"

I hear some paper shuffling. "That's not a matter of public record."

"Actually, it is. Get it from you or I'll get it from HUD, so do me a favor, okay?"

"You'll have to get it from HUD."

"If you make me run through the FOIA drill, it's going to look very bad in the article how secretive NüCorp is about how it uses public dollars. I can see that getting some very prominent placement."

After a brief moment of dead air, she says, "Can you tell me what your article's about?"

"Not sure yet. Just going wherever the trail leads me."

She clears her throat. "Hundred-twenty thousand."

"And the Curtis contract? How much?"

"Seventy-three."

"Who's your contract compliance person?"

"I guess that'd be me."

"Okay, so I'm going to need copies of all the invoices and whatever else you have that deals with payments and charges."

Is that a pen click-click-clicking in frustration I hear?

"Look," I say, "I'm not trying to be a dick, okay? Just doing my job. My editor's a hard-ass." Using the *we're both victims here* tack, it does wonders. Sometimes.

"Manny's concerned about this?"

Et tu, Man-nay? "Why wouldn't he be?"

"You are aware of how much money we're spending on advertising."

"Not my concern."

"I see."

"Do you?"

"I really don't have time, Mr. Cockburn, to do this right now."

"You going to help me out or not?"

"Not."

"You got a boss?"

"If you're thinking you're going to get me in trouble, you're mistaken."

"All I want, Charlene, is information." Synonymous with power, that which I lack. "And unless the name of your boss is confidential, I don't see why you can't divulge that. So?"

"Perhaps if you read the materials I provided you, you wouldn't have to ask."

"Last question," I say. "What's the deal with the umlauts?" One final, percussive pen click before she kills the connection we never quite made.

Shuffle through the releases. Scan through three grafs of fluff till the first canned quotes from the NüCorp brass: stilted horseshit about saving a historic treasure from the wrecking ball, and it's attributed to one Mather Grimes.

Mother. Fucker.

Greaseball son of a bitch, this guy. Starters, he was one of the several dozen gajillionaires, politicians, untouchables and kingmakers implicated in the Douglas Credit Union meltdown twenty-whatever years ago. Before my time, obviously. Deal was Grimes, the credit union manager, was under investigation for accounting irregularities. Investigation went wide. Way wide.

Turned out he was allegedly running kiddie-fuck parties for politicians, real ones—including one who would later be a one-term
president, not to name names—and billionaires. Ended up the
special prosecutor died in a car wreck. His brakes, see, they went
out. Grimes did a few years for cooking the books. Only other
person saw the wrong side of the bars was a 21-year-old kid. Said
during grand jury testimony he was forced at gunpoint, and at
the tender young age of 13, to suck off a U.S. senator. Also said
there was a video of it, and the then-Omaha cop chief was the
cameraman. Kid got nine years. For? Perjury. Three weeks in, he
got shivved and bled out in his cell. Meanwhile, Grimes's released
and no one hears a peep from him. Till now. Maybe thinking his
celebrity status is long dead. And he'd be right. Nexis says the
only thing the daily's run on NüCorp has been a bullet-point graf
tacked on to the end of a city council roundup story the week
the tax package was rammed through.

Course, all that is circumspect. Anymore, it's just local folk-
lore and fodder for conspiracy theorists. Or, if you believe the
stories, it's a reminder that you can do whatever the fuck you want
if you're rich. So, what's a guy do? He calls the mayor's office.

"Seth Thomas," Seth Thomas says. Hate this prick. If for no
other reason than I know how little he does to make the fatty
checks he cashes. Swinedick here got a $25K raise six months
into the job. His raise, I pointed out, was more than my, and the
majority of Omahans', salary. This elicited a stifled chortle and a
no-comment.

"Seth, Cockburn from the *News-Tel*. What do you know about
this Baron Square redevelopment deal?"

"The mayor's, uhh," shuffle that paper, "going to be at the
ribbon cutting. Next week, I think."

"You know anything about NüCorp?"

"They're doing a great service for Omaha, and the mayor hopes other developers follow NüCorp's lead and—"

"Can the bullshit. Why's the city doing business with a child molester?"

Pause.

"You know what I'm talking about, Seth. I know you do. Now, come on."

"He wasn't convicted. Wasn't even charged."

"Who wasn't?"

"Grimes."

"With what?"

"The crimes you're alleging he committed."

"Guilty or not, he's tainted. What were you guys thinking when you were working this deal?"

"Think about this, Bernard. Do you want to come off like a paranoid conspiracy kook? That's how it'll play."

"You have this talk with the daily hacks?"

"They don't need to hear it from me."

"What do you know about the Loomis Building sale?"

"We're in the first phases of negotiations." What pisses me off is the stuffy tone he employs, like the shitbird's permitting me to use this bit in a news story. "The mayor hopes the city and NüCorp can continue our vital work of improving areas that have become blighted over time."

Cockspeak, all of it. "You do know the deal with Grimes, right? Kiddie-fuck parties?"

Seth clears his throat.

"Mayor's office invite get lost in the mail?"

"Bernard, seriously, you'd be wise to—"

"I bet if I checked the mayor's campaign filings, I'd see some contributions from Grimes or NüCorp or both, wouldn't I?"

"Very possibly, along with donations from hundreds of other individuals and employers. Anything else?"

"You maybe might wanna have your finance guys take a look at how the police department is handling its weed-and-seed dough." Click. Prick.

This story, it could work out. Unless Manny's crossed over. Have a hard time imagining he'd wanna join that club, but do you ever really know anyone? He does, after all, have some nast-o-riffic porn on his work computer. Who the fuck knows what he's got at home.

One of the many bitches of this is today's payday. Buried in my inbox is my check. Handwritten in Manny's sloppy, childish block letters is my semimonthly disappointment. Perhaps larger now than ever before. In terms of disgrace, not dollars. Fucker even wrote it out in red ink when he shoulda used yellow. So, tomorrow, when we have our talk, he's probably going to yank me from the story. And give it to whom? Donna? He's gotta know that well's poisoned. So he'll farm it out at ten cents a word to someone in our freelance hack stable. Surefire way to get a lame-shit story, assign it to a lame-shit writer. Or the intern. Cocksucker. Could try to dupe him. Fuck it. Play those angles tomorrow. Now I gotta find my shoe guy.

Stall's closed for the day. Hit a couple bars. Nothing doing. Local yokels been sitting on these stools for years. "Looking for Leroy," I bark in a few faces. "Leroy the Shine?" Fat white lady in bar No. 2 says try the library. Obviously. Main branch is around the corner and across the street from his shop. Prowling the stacks, I find him in a reading room. Pile of today's papers in front of him.

"What's doing, Leroy?"

Doesn't look up. Got a toothpick in his mouth he's loudly chewing and sucking. "Some news today, boy. I tell you."

"You tell me what?"

"See this?" He jams his middle finger down on a *Miami Herald* article on a judge accused of taking bribes. Or at least that's what the headline suggests.

"Don't know anything about it."

"You wouldn't."

"Friend of yours?"

"Like I got friends in elevated locales, motherfucker."

Pull up a seat. "You and me both, my man."

He turns the page, scanning away. Black smears on the table-top. Shoe polish or newsprint or both.

"You hear anything new from the Krauts?"

"Told 'em I ain't moving."

"And?"

"And that's it. I ain't."

"Got a question for you."

"You owe me two-fifty."

I fish out three singles and hand them over. They go in his pocket. "What you wanna ask Leroy?"

"Remember that credit union deal way back? One had all the—"

"Perverts in power got away free like damned birds?" His attention returns to the paper.

"That'd be it."

"Yeah, so?"

"You catch any buzz back when about same thing happening other places?"

Leroy rubs his bald head and puts down the paper. "Why you asking me about that now?"

"Curious, is all."

"I ain't got time for your games, suckahead."

"Help a guy out. One working stiff to another."

"You work?"

"Not really."

"Appreciate your honesty. Didn't hear nothing like that. But a betting man might think if that business was going down *here*, it'd be going down other places, too. Cleveland. Chicago. Minneapolis. Kansas City. Denver." Punctuating each city with a bang on the table. "So what you got for Leroy the Shine?"

"Stay offa Saint Mary's. Getting ugly there."

"Why the fuck I'm gonna go to Saint Mary's, anyway?"

"Good, so don't."

"Buncha hookers and winos is all. Think they want their shoes fixed? They can drag their black asses downtown like everyone else does. Telling me shit I already know. You got something real to share or you just wasting my valuable free time? Library closes at eight, you know."

"Not even six yet."

He pats the stack of papers. "Got all these to get through yet."

"I'll leave you be, then."

"Come see me soon." He eyes my shoes. "Looks like you need a new brush."

<u>fifteen</u>

After depositing my $479 check, my balance is $396. Running names and possible conspiracies in my head, waiting for the Eureka moment that doesn't hit. Plan is to stop at the apartment for a change of clothes before Allison gets there. Disappear before she arrives, because that'll show her. Got the blinker on to turn into the lot, but I kick it off and hit the gas. Parked next to Allison's car: a fucking Volvo with UNO parking stickers plastered on the rear windshield. Hang out with her folks? I think fucking not.

Quick stop at the Warwick. Room's in tatters. Paper scraps tacked to the wall. Scribbled notes on the floor, on the mattress, on the rickety little desk. Can't read a fucking word I've written. Sanskrit-looking. Dig around for the bottle, shake out a couple screamers and chew 'em. Taste like dirty quarters. Stop at the community pisser in the hall to take a whore's bath. Feeling just as filthy, I fall into the car and cruise over to the freeway. Billboard that musta just gone up by the on-ramp. *Smile*, is all it says. I power off my cell. Don't wanna be disturbed.

Heading north. If I remember correctly, Wozniak was on Redick between 35th and 36th. Turns out I'm wrong. Thirty-sixth

and 37th. Three streetlights on the block, two of which aren't
working. No biggie, because there's a couple houses that are to
the nines with Christmas lights. Didn't notice that the other day.
Course, from where I was, I couldn't see them. Grab the four-
C-cell Maglite from the trunk and head out. Cold as fuck, so I
flip up my collar and throw on a wool watchcap. Navy issue, a
prowler staple. Cut around to the backyard and try the basement
door. Locked, but, glass being glass, the windowed top half shat-
ters when I smack it with the Maglite. Knock out the remaining
shards and undo the dead bolt.

Basement's done up like a rec room. Pool table, beer signs,
bikini girl posters, dartboard. Steel tip, so it's good he keeps
(kept) it real. Find the stairs and head up. Keeping the beam
away from the windows, I see the ground floor is filled with
thrift store furniture. Nothing matches. Smells like body odor
and a house that's seen its inhabitants murdered. Which is to say:
grim and musty. Bowling trophy on top of the console TV. Not
going to find any good loot down here, so it's upstairs. Kid's
room is plastered with shit boy pop star posters, and it skeeves
me out to be in here, so I close that and hit the room down the
hall. Door's thin—hollow and made of pressboard. Big Papa's
room is bare save a twin bed jammed in the corner. No dresser,
no nightstands, nothing on the walls. Check for scrape marks or
dust outlines or something that might hint the cops felt it necessary to requisition the furnishings, but come up empty. Master
bath has a medicine cabinet stocked with all sorts of goodies.
Pocket the Ambien and OxyContin, but leave the remainder.
Check the closet. Nothing but clothes. Fuck me. No other rooms
up here.

Starting to think that maybe my first B&E is a total waste of
time. Not that I came here with any specific goal in mind other

than maybe finding something that'd be, oh, I don't know, helpful? Germane?

Back downstairs, I go through the kitchen and come up empty. Coat closet, surprisingly, is filled with coats. If I recall correctly, the roof here is steepled, so guy's gotta have an attic. No trap door in the hallway. Nothing in his room, nor in his closet. Don't wanna do it, but I hit the kid's room, and, sure enough, the ceiling of her closet, it's a door. And it's hanging open. Not only that, but there's an upside-down bucket on the floor. Motherfuck. Someone's been here. Only been a couple days, and the cops were here in force all day Monday and most of Tuesday, I'd assume. So, recently. Today, maybe. Tonight. Fuck. Spooking myself out. Whatever. Normal thing, right now, to be freaked. Dead guy's house. Saw him get wasted. His associates are armed and nuts. The fuck am I doing here?

"Asshole," I shout up into the dark maw. "It's the cops." Count out a four-Mississippi. Nada. "We're pissed and have bigger guns than you." Oh, what the fuck am I doing, stepping onto this bucket and trying rather ungracefully to pull up my unfit body? This can only end badly. I'm panting and my forearms are sore and scraped when I heave myself onto the subfloor. Frantically shine the Maglite around the room. Plumes of dust I've kicked up dance in the beam. Yes, I'm certainly alone up here. Just me and the seamless, fucked-up montages of Jesus paintings and unicorns pictures and photos of gross trauma victims and, of all things, cutouts from cereal boxes. Giant mural covering the walls and ceiling. So yeah, okay, full-blown four-F, this guy. Desk over in the corner. Monitor, keyboard and mouse on it, but no beige box. So no jackpot. Aerial map on the desktop with seven properties highlighted in pink. Jot down the addresses and cross-reference those later. More than likely WJC holdings.

Single drawer holds a slew of paper clips and pens and the like, all coated with a patina of dust stuck to something yellowish and sticky. Way in the back is an unlabeled floppy. This, I take. Poke around looking for something other than, say, the Count Chocula with two mangled snatches for eyes. Small wire mesh wastebasket wedged beneath the desk. Kick it loose and out flutter two sheets of yellow legal. One is top-to-bottom scrawled in Sharpie, over and over:

you did this. My civil rights have been violated.

Other is tri-folded and dated last week.

James David Wozniak—
This letter is to inform you that you're status as a share-holder of WJC Investments has been liquidated and you're no longer a party to the partnership. Please don't be upset. Business is business but I'll take care to make sure you get your part of what's coming.
                                        Sincerely,

Guess who.

Bill's shoving out of the Woz put him over the edge. Why didn't the cops take this? Open-and-shut case of a nutjob going nuts, so why bother? Or perhaps it's simply irrelevant.

Fuck notes. I pocket all this shit and triple-time it down the hatch. Once I hit the cold air outside, I feel like I'm on fucking fire, man. Race downtown and run down the office stairs, loot hot in my pocket. Got the shakes either because it's cold as fuck or I'm juiced or because I just B&E'd a dead guy's house.

Fire up Donna's computer and I'm drumming my fingers

on the floppy's edge waiting on this fucking junkpile to get its shit together. On the verge of clobbering the box by the time the thing's finally ready. Jam in the disk. What I got? First up: spreadsheets. Bank account numbers, transactions, balance info. Most recent entry is five days ago. Two accounts. One for the watch group—broker than me, which is saying something. One for WJC. Far from broke. Sitting on just over $105K. All seven outlays are eight- to ten-grand chunks. Down payments. Three deposits. One mirrors the consulting contract value Charlene quoted me earlier; second is 28 grand, even; third's (the first, sequentially) in the neighborhood of eight grand—there's the weed-and-seed money. Cross-reference the date with the watch group's books. Bang, same amount debited a day prior. Lamest shot at laundering I've ever seen, this playground shell game.

Payment to a bogus consultant. Misappropriation of city grant money. Vanilla graft and corruption, but it can work. Get it solid and I've made some prosecutor's case. But what are these clowns doing with the houses they're buying? Slumlord come lately? Thinking long-term and banking the real estate value'll jump? Fuckpads? Meth labs? Bill's not going to talk. Wozniak's dead. Korbes goddamn near got himself killed. Why? Drew too much attention. Guy in the driver's seat wanted to keep shit quiet, as they often and understandably do. Grimes had to have a reason to want them involved in the first place. Doubt he'll grant me an audience. So who's gonna tell me? That's right: Korbes.

sixteen

Nothing doing on Korbes's street. Few TVs on in living rooms here and there, but Korbes's place, it's dark. Hope this guy's just the quiet, creepy, sit-in-the-dark-and-stew type, because I don't wanna break any more windows tonight. Bang on the front door and I'd be lying if I said I'm surprised there's no answer. Round two nets the same bit of nothing. Let myself into the privacy-fenced backyard. Guy's got a serious barbecue pit. Thing's big enough to cook up a whole pig. Wind sock hanging limp off a pole in the middle of the yard and a couple-few cement lawn ornaments. Donkey pulling a cart. Gnome sniffing a flower. Takes me a second to remember Korbes is in a wheelchair. Has been for a while. And there's two sets of tracks in the snow back here, neither of which were made by a wheelchair. Both lead from the back door to the gate I just walked through. Wish I had been a Boy Scout. Probably a merit badge or some shit in track reading. Could be nothing, but my dander's way the fuck up.

Like a dipshit, I finish the walk to the door by putting my feet in the tracks that are already here. Go straight for the knob, and it's locked. There is, however, a doggy door. It looks like it might be big enough—body can fit through any hole long as the shoulders go through, right?—which could be a bad thing, because if his dog needs a door that big, it could certainly, say, tear off my face. Give the door-within-a-door a kick to hear if anything this way thunders, but nothing does.

It's a tight fit. Off with my coat, and as I'm squirming and writhing, I'm wondering, again, what it is I hope to find. Really gotta work on the planning end of these things. Or not. Didn't matter last time.

Crawl through and end up in what appears to be a laundry room of sorts. Genius didn't think to bring the Maglite this time. Smells like fabric softener, which ain't an aroma I'd've expected. I stay prone for a little bit, listening for anything that'd hint someone's around. Give up after a twenty-Mississippi and start slowly moving my way to the front of the house. Small place he's got. Looks like just a main room at the end of the hall. Kitchen's to the side and pitch-black, being windowless and all. Weird butcher-shop type scent coming out of there. Hold my breath and keep moving. Damn near piss myself when my head brushes something hard and bristly. Doing my best Helen Keller, I deduce it's the taxidermied head of some beast or another. Sharp teeth. Noggin about as big as a volleyball, but lumpier.

Sickly yellow streetlight leaking in through the miniblind slats up front. From what I can see, there's a couch, a chair. Something like a bureau. TV and stereo on a stand to my right. What the fuck *am* I doing? You hate cops, dickfuck, so why are you playing one? Nosing around some cripple's house. Even if you find anything, how the fuck are you going to attribute it? *According to documents obtained by the* News-Telegraph . . . *said a source who did not want to be identified for fear of retribution* . . . Hokey smoke-and-mirrors shit that might fool the readers, but what about

Manny? Feel like I'm sinking right here in this freakshow's living room. Guy's gotta have at least some beer in his fridge, because that's what this rarefied situation calls for: a depressant. Parched, anyway. Fucking hate uppers.

On the way back, I dodge the mounted beast and duck into the kitchen. Reeks in here. Must be something rotten somewhere. Feel around the walls till I find the fridge, pop her open and pull out a tallboy of Bud. Six-pack of 'em are nestled between the fridge's only other contents: loaf of Wonder Bread, package of generic bologna.

I'm trying to remember what my rationale was way back when. Why'd I go to j-school? Pop wanted me to. Whatever you wanna do, he said, do it while you can. Got plenty of fires to start before you settle down. Translation: don't end up like me. Now I'm—what? Thirty. Ish. Pulling Mickey Mouse cloak-and-dagger shit because I have a hard-on to break someone. When did I become so vindictive?

Let's just say I chase this fucker all the way down. Grimes gets his, right? For whatever symphony of felonies he's pulling. Maybe another fish or two. Bill and his guppy buddies. Then what? City's full of bullshit stories waiting to get their ink treatment. Write some profiles. Couple hundred humdrum homicides. Planning board meetings. Go home at the end of the day to what? Idle banter and a fistful of downers. Oh, fuck. Home. There's a pretty picture. Oughta just hang it up now. The prospects, they're bleak. Burn Cockburn, PR guy, adman, corporate communications flack, doomed coulda-been-a-cocksucker walking stooped like his old man. Get a place with a lead-filled yard and ride the mower out into the sunset.

Crack the tallboy and leave the door open. Using my head, see. Light and all. Turn to see if there's a stool or a chair or—

dear me. There is a chair. It has wheels. And it's occupied by what I assume is Korbes's corpse. Two neat holes up front. Wicked, chunky spatter congealed on the wall and ceiling behind and above him. Explains the smell.

Been a while since I've been within touching distance of someone who'd met a violent end. Without a viewfinder to hide behind, it's unsettling. Got the juice pumping now. Okay. Okay. Fuck. Okay. My prints are all over the house. The back door. The doggy door. The kitchen. Einstein here demolishing the tracks out back with the tread from his worn-down Dexters. Fuckers gonna try to hang this on me. This time around, they'd make it stick.

Options: Wipe down the place and get the fuck out. Wipe down and call it in anonymously. The right thing to do is the latter. Get the pigs in here, let 'em root around and see what they can see. Already contaminated the hell outta the scene. Erasing evidence of my presence would really butcher it. Cops coming means the daily and the TV guys come. TV jocks are a joke. But the daily, they start looking into this guy's background—which they will—it's not impossible that they'd stumble across my— repeat: *my*—story. Put a couple reporters on it and drop it before I can. Them and their fucking resources.

Yeah, it's a shitty thing to do, leaving Korbes here to rot, but.

Do as thorough a cleanup as I can. Dump the beer down the sink, pocket the can. Use my coat to smear around any prints I might've left (the bitch about my prints, see, is they're on file) and I'm back out the doggy door. Kick my way through the snow, obliterating any forensically usable trace of my tracks. Car turns over on the second try. Kick on the headlights when I round the corner, and I'm thinking I could either go home or hit Bill real quick like. Shit, not even a choice.

Smoke a cigarette on the way over to the little pink house. Guy's such a weasel, I have a hard time believing he did it himself. Have an equally hard time thinking he would have someone else do it. Which leaves my main man Grimes, who's proved he's not above such things. Dying to know why he's gotten himself tangled up with the local lowbrow crew. Getting the rubes to do the shitwork, maybe. He was an organizer in the kiddie-fuck business before, so why bother getting dirt under his nails on the new venture? Cook up a scheme, piss a few dollars down on some schmucks who've never seen what real money can do and watch the little pissants bust their humps trying to make you happy. They're thinking if they do a good job, there's plenty more to be made. What they don't realize, obviously, is it cuts both ways. That money can make you. Push the digits over a column and you've got nothing. A check gets cut and someone uses the contents of your cranium to paint the walls. And who's left to give a fuck? Not your buddies; they're busy sucking the tit.

Drop the butt in the snowbank piled up around his mailbox. Lights burning inside. Breathe in a few deep ones to compose myself, roll my shoulders and march up to the door. Knock thrice and put on a happy face. Lips, they're twitching. Hope it doesn't show in my pupils.

Door opens as wide as the safety chain will allow, which is to say: not very.

"Yes?" asks a woman.

"Sheila, right? I'm looking for Bill."

"He's not home."

"You always tell strange men who show up at your door at night that you're home alone?"

"I'm not alone and I'm not worried. Is there a message you want me to give him?"

"Actually, if I could, I'd like to ask you a question or two." I pull out a card and thrust it through the slim opening. "Bernard Cockburn. I'm a reporter."

She snatches away my card. "And?"

"Know where he is?" I do. As I stand on this porch, he's getting his prick sucked. And he'll come back here later and nuzzle up next to her, probably tell her he loves her, and he might mean it, too. And what bugs is I can see this little routine of his turning into one of mine a little further down the line. "Or when he'll be back?"

"He'll be out late. He's on patrol."

Can't help but picture him wearing a little plastic badge. "I'm writing a story, see, about the neighborhood. How it's coming up and how the neighborhood organization's making things happen. Good things."

"I suppose we are, yes, but Bill's a better person to talk to. He's more involved."

"He and I, we've chatted a time or two already. Here's my dilemma—all my sources so far, they're men. I'd like to hear your take."

She shifts her considerable heft and blocks out more light. "Now isn't a good time, I'm afraid. It's late and I'm about to put my daughter to bed."

"Okay, sure. Tomorrow, maybe. Tell you what, you call me whenever you want. And let Bill know I stopped by tonight. I just talked to his friend Creighton and—"

"Creighton? What'd he have to say?"

"A lot. Between you and me, he's pretty bitter about how things went down, what with getting forced out of the business and all."

"What business?"

"That consulting thing he and your husband have going. What's it called? PRQ or something."

"You must be mistaken. Bill's a salesman. And I don't want to talk out of turn, but I wouldn't put much stock in whatever Creighton told you. He's not all there."

I clear my throat. "Which is precisely why I want to talk to you and Bill. But, really, call me. And tell Bill I dropped by."

"What did you say your name was?"

"It's on the card."

seventeen

The assault begins before the door closes.

"Why is your phone off?" Allison demands. Her car isn't out front, so why is she here?

"It is?" Heh.

"It's been off for hours. We had plans, remember? Dinner?"

"It's only"—check the watch—"ten. Plenty of time to eat."

"You're not drunk."

"What the fuck sorta backward nonaccusation is that?"

"Thought you were out drinking."

"That would be incorrect."

"So? What were you doing?"

"Working."

"You look like shit, you smell awful, you're stoned on something. What is going on with you?"

"I was working." This time, I say it with a tone of finality. Case motherfucking closed.

"Tell me the truth."

Like all good relationships, ours is based on a deep, biding, unfounded and sincere mistrust. The truth here is, basically, I'm more enamored of this story than I've ever been of her. But tell her that? Set her off? I think fucking not.

"I went by the office," she says. "It was closed up and the lights were off."

I don't know if I'm offended or flattered. "The thing about journalism, honeysnake, is it's often done in the field." *In the field.* Wanker. "And, might I add, sorta weird for you to be checking up on me."

"I was worried. You could have called, at least."

"Tied up. You know, interviewing, shooting photos, blah blah blah. Lost track of time. And I've got this deadline and a monster story, and, you know, gotta keep Manny happy."

"What about me?"

"You know this is what I do. Always have. Always will."

"Never say never."

"I said always." Walk past her with the intention of scaring up a bottle and pouring a stiff one. Got some goosebumps going, either because the last kitchen I've been in was an egregiously fucked-up scene or because I can feel Allison shooting hatchets at my back.

"Not that you care, but the reason I'm mad is because we had plans. If you knew you weren't going to make it, all you had to do was call."

I grab the bottle and poke my head around the corner. "You sure it's not because you had your folks over here and you wanted us to share the good news?"

That she says nothing says everything.

Dangle the bottle where she can see it. "Want one?"

"A drink? No."

"You gone straight since the other night, wild child?" Pour a stiffy in an ice-packed tall juice glass. Probably not any more than

I'd normally pour, but it looks bigger. Image, as we know, is everything. "So what'd you tell 'em?"

"I didn't."

Dishes piled up in the sink. Unwashed. "They just came for dinner?"

"Right."

"You know I woulda been very pissed if things went as you planned."

"Swear to God, you are such a fucking baby."

Drain the drink. "Needs his ba-ba." Pour number two. Enough of these and I can forget for the rest of the night what I've been up to. Or, at least, the specifics. If I can do that, then maybe I can convince myself that Korbes's number had been plucked before I started nosing around. Because now, with a little distance, I'm thinking maybe I might've had something to do with it. The hastened capping of loose cannons. Shut 'em up before the paperboy gets to them. Unpleasant, to think, suddenly, that I might have been one of many causes. It's one thing, you know, to report. Quite another when you're part of the story. Makes me wonder how the old man did it all those years with his formulas and sending a preapproved number of flyboys out to get shot down. *Acceptable loss.* That's what it was called. Or so he said.

Allison flips on the TV and leaves it on the news. An entice-ment, perhaps. So I join her. There's a cushion's distance between us. Car commercial on TV set to the Buzzcocks. Ad guys, if they were smart, woulda bought the rights to "Everybody's Happy Nowadays," but they didn't. Life's an illusion, love is a dream, indeed.

"Hey, look," I say, "about that apartment. I'm out."

"Too late. I signed the lease, remember?"

"I didn't."

"I told my parents we're getting a new place."

"Sounds to me like you unintentionally misled them."

"I borrowed the money to pay for everything."

"You took out a loan?"

"From my parents."

Figures. "Forget it. Dickface here pays his own way." Pride, they call it. Bugs me, the idea of her folks—or anyone, really— trying to help. Because to accept help is to be in the hole to someone. And I resent her for having the cushioned support that I lack.

"What is it that's got you so worked up? Afraid you can't handle what you've done?"

"What I can't hack, dearest, is someone fucking with me. And that's what you're doing. That kid of yours, child protective services is going to take it away because you are ultimately flighty and irresponsible. And, besides, it'll probably be a waterhead."

"You're trying to pick a fight, and it's not going to work."

"Weren't you going to be a stripper once?"

She changes the channel. Lands on a cop show rerun.

"Come on, babe," I say, "gimme a show." Pluck a dollar from my wallet and wave it in front of her. "See if you can't grab it with your cooze."

Her jaw clenches. Good. Good. "How was your day, Burn?"

"You can't really believe you'll be happy with me and the kid. Not if you think about it."

"I'm not happy now, so what's the difference?"

"You never answered my question. About this not being an accident."

"Jesus. Again?"

"Till I get an answer I believe."

"You mean, until you hear what you want to hear?"

"Same thing."

"Fine, then. Yes, I got knocked up on purpose. I want a baby so bad, I stopped taking my birth control pills a few months ago. You're smart enough, so why not pick you? And you might think you're a cold prick, but you're really just a pussy and I know you'll cave in and do the right thing." Pause. "Happy?"

"Ecstatic," I say.

"If you think I did it to trap you, you need to get your head examined." She turns off the TV and drops the remote on the coffee table. "Look at me."

I do. Suspiciously and from the corner of my eye. Which ain't good enough for her, apparently, because she grabs my jaw and cranks my head over. This irritates me. Tremendously.

"I do not need you, okay? And I don't want you around if you're going to be a fucking asshole. I'm moving out. I want you to come. If you don't want to, that's fine. I'll do it on my own. If that's how it happens, then I never, ever want to see you or hear from you again. Are we clear on this?"

"What is today?"

"Thursday."

"You move when?"

"Sunday."

I draw an ice cube into my mouth and crush it. She hates it when I do this. "So now what? What's the score here?"

She looks the other way. Out of principle, I guess. Get up and hit the head. Deposit the Ambien I acquired in the black bottle, put the Oxy in the orange. The red is conspicuously gone. Go into the bedroom and stuff a couple changes of clothes into a garbage bag. Walk out and see Allison putting on her shoes.

"Leaving?" I ask.

"Why not?"

"No arguments here." I drop the bag as she reaches for the doorknob.

"When you die, who do you think's going to give a shit?"

Let her have the last word so she can leave with a sense of accomplishment. Thinking she'll slam shut the door. But she doesn't, and I feel cheated.

Anyway, get situated on the couch. It's quiet now. Wind's barreling down Harney and Farnam streets so hard you can hear the tree branches whipping over the howl.

Got my ankles hanging off the edge and my head propped up on the armrest, so I examine the brown amoebic stains on the ceiling. There's a few hairline cracks connecting them. Only a matter of time before the whole thing comes crashing down. Hopefully, I won't be sitting here when it happens.

Trying to piece together what I've got. Not exactly piece together, I suppose, but trying to figure it out. The *why*. Which normally isn't a question I ask. Woman drowns her baby, government schmuck takes a bribe, whatever, "why" concerns me not. Why? Because people, being people, do fucked-up things to themselves and to one another. Everyone that's ever been shot dead was turning their life around, or so their relatives will tell you. Anyone who ever did some underhanded shit with public dollars was trying to pocket a little sum-sum on the side. And then there's these jokers, who, for all their funding, don't have their shit together. Hillbilly fucksacks given carte blanche to terrorize the undesirables, the operation bankrolled inadvertently by the cops and advertently by the moneyed motherfuckers they oughta hate.

Which makes me think: all these neighborhood improvement jackasses, they can't be in on the take. That Denny guy with the oxygen cart, no way that guy knows the extent of the shenanigans going on around him. So who of them does know? And if Bill's really stocking up on hot heat, who gets it? And to what end? Could be the guy's some fucked-up crusader, bent on biblical shit and has given himself the task of cleansing, if not the world, then at least his neighborhood of the degenerate heathens. Would explain why these clowns are tear-assing around and bullying the sex and drugs peddlers. Could be something as tame as Bill gets an order from Grimes to clean out the scum and he's doing his part to earn that consulting fee.

But: why (again, there's that word) him? Whatever. Maybe I can schmooze him. Get him to turn on Grimes. He's the trophy here. Nail that freak for the assbag he is and watch him get his. For real this time.

Shit. I'm sick of thinking. Gotta have my head on straight for my powwow with Manny tomorrow. Shut him down before he does it to me.

<u>eighteen</u>

Second time this week I wake up on the couch. Morbidly hungover. Neck hurts. Throat hurts. New cigarette burn on the upholstery where I nearly killed myself last night, I guess.

Allison's gone. Make a couple cups of lukewarm instant, quick shower and throw on the duds. Tie today. Green one with narrow blue stripes. Knot's crooked, and I'm fucking with it when I hear some serious banging at the front door like you might expect from, say, the Grim Reaper. Times like this I wish I had a peephole. Or a pistol. Creep over and put my ear against the door. Don't hear anything. Instead, whoever-the-fuck beats on the door again. Like getting my ears boxed. So I swing open the door. Two guys, big like mules, in shitty suits and mirror shades. Mustache on the charcoal suit, graying buzz cut on the brown with cream pinstripes. My bowels run cold. Done this once before. Bad news.

Guy in the charcoal suit holds out one of my cards. "This yours?"

"You're holding it. My guess is it belongs to you."

"You want to tell us," Brown follows, "why we found it in Creighton Korbes's pocket?"

Well, fuck. "Wanna tell me who you are?"

"Chumley," says charcoal. Thumbs over to his partner. "This is McKinley. Savage sends his regards."

"Tin me, please. Gets me hard." Stalling, seeing if I can't place these names. Chumley's ringing a loud bell. McKinley, not so much. Savage—fuck him in his ear.

They treat me to a cursory badge flash. Deeply blasé, the presentation.

"Dig the leatherette," I say. "Very public servant."

"Cut the shit," McKinley says.

"Maybe. You boys are here because a what?"

McKinley: "He's dead."

Chumley: "And he had your card in his pocket."

McKinley: "We want to know why he had it."

"Gave it to him few days ago."

"Why?"

"Story."

Chumley says, "On what?"

"I know you from somewhere?"

"Answer the question."

"Neighborhood makeover."

A dim, strange look crosses his face. Gone just as quick, and he's wearing the stone mask again. "What's that got to do with Mister Korbes?"

"Guess I'll never know. Wouldn't talk, so I slipped it in his mail slot."

"Not the doggy door?" McKinley's turn. Nicked himself shaving this morning.

"We done here?"

Chumley, he turns to McKinley. "I think he's not being honest with us."

"That bullshit ever work on anyone?"

"Do you own a pistol, Mister Cockburn?"

"Co-burn. Nope."

"Nothing unregistered?"

"Kids, I know you're just doing your job, but, really, I'm a busy man. So, look, I'm going to tell you everything I know about this dude, and then we can go our merry ways. Ready?" Pause for effect, and they just stand there in their overcoats and suits and I'm freezing my nuts off trying to shake as little as possible. Don't wanna give 'em the pleasure. "Working this story on the renovation going on over at Baron Square, got a possible lead on some lightweight embezzling bullshit. Didn't pan out. Source of mine, turns out he was very wrong, pointed his crooked little finger at someone who works with Korbes. Which is how I ended up at the Korbes residence. Satisfied?"

"You never spoke to him?"

"Told you I put my card in the mail slot."

"Answer the question."

"Never have I ever spoken to Creighton Korbes."

"You shoot him?" McKinley asks, staring hard through those glasses thinking he'd catch me slipping.

"Yeah, three in his fucking belly, bang-bang-bang, just like that because the cocksucker wouldn't open his door. The fuck you think?"

McKinley reaches into his coat, for his cuffs, I imagine.

Okay, I fucked up this time. Stick out my hands and shut my trap thinking they'll beat me less if I'm suddenly docile.

He withdraws his hand, and in it is his card. He wedges it between my fingers. "I trust," he says, "you'll be available if we need to speak to you again."

"You've got my card." The three of us stare at one another for an uncomfortable moment. Easier for them, as they've each got only one guy to ocularly scold. I've gotta switch back and forth between the two and try not to look skittishlike. Truth be told: I'm a little rattled. McKinley coughs and spits a ball of phlegm at my feet, then the two of them walk down the steps and around the corner. Odd they didn't park out front.

Throw on my coat, lock both locks and head downtown. Yank off the tie en route because it's choking the life out of me.

Nemo's sitting at my desk, rifling through a pile of press releases.

"Anything titillating?" I ask.

"These three." He hands me the sheets he's set aside. Homicide last night—some guy shot to death in his driveway way up north. The name sounds familiar, though I can't place it. Second one is a missing kid. Sixteen, been gone a week. Rich family. Reward. Photo of him on the fax, but, then again, it's a fax, so. Last one's from the county assessor outlining new valuation protest procedures for next year.

"One and a half out of three ain't bad. This dead guy, I don't know how I know him, but I do. See if you can't figure it out. Then get a decent pic of this missing kid. We run short this issue, it'll eat some space. And do me a favor. Call the cop PIO and find out who was the lead on James Wozniak from the other day. Guy that killed his kid—"

"And shot himself."

"Very good. And, since you're digging, want you to talk to the fine folks in Chicago, Kansas City and Minneapolis, see if whoever's in charge of recording deeds has any transfers in the last six months that involve—"

"Wozniak?"

"Or Bill Dunkel or Creighton Korbes-with-a-K or NüCorp or Mather Grimes."

I wait for him to act suddenly interested at my mention of that last name. But he doesn't. Too young. He dutifully writes down his assignment and scurries off to the courthouse, leaving me alone in an office that's empty if you don't count the sales-douches, which I don't. Feet on my desk, I try to place this morning's homicide victim. Terrell Henderson. A black guy, so he couldn't be an acquaintance. I'm clicking my tongue and squinting at the wall when I hear Donna and Manny walk in. They're almost on top of me before they see me.

"Holy crap, boy, what are you doing here?"

"I work here."

"Not before noon," Donna says.

"Too bad he wasn't here a little earlier," Manny says to Donna. "Coulda had a free breakfast."

"Breakfast is for the weak and fat."

"If you're going to get all sore about it, how about a coffee? Come on, boy." He pats his leg.

On our way to the coffee shop, I ask Manny if Terrell Henderson rings any bells.

"Yeah, we did a story with him, oh, years ago. He works with Mad Dads, remember?"

Probably second or third profile-slash-feature I did. Guy'd spent a few years locked up on weapons and drug charges. Got out, went legit and ran this ex-con outreach thing to scare the wayward ones straight.

"He got shot last night," I say.

"Tragedy. Get it written up."

"Nemo's on it," I say, leading us to the counter. I order a

coffee with a couple shots of espresso dumped in. Manny gets a green tea.

I wait at a smoking table while Manny chats up the counter staff. When he arrives, double-fisting Styrofoam cups, I pull out my pack o' smokes. "So we need to talk, huh?" I toss Manny a smoke, stick one in the corner of my mouth and light us both.

"Here's the deal," he says. "I signed a contract with a new printer yesterday. Cheaper, and come first of the year, I'm going to renew the lease on the office. I've been haggling with them, and it looks like I'll be able to talk them down from what we're paying now. So you're wondering what this means to you, right?"

This is not what I expected to hear, so consider my silence a sign of surprise.

"Word around the campfire is you're going to be seeing some new expenses in the not too distant future." He pauses and gives me time to either confirm or deny what Donna probably told him this morning over eggs and bacon. He continues: "I know that what you're making now means you'd have to either work two jobs or quit and find some job somewhere you'd hate. I don't want to see either of those things happen, so, being the nice guy I am, I thought maybe I can help you out. What would you say to a raise—nothing big, maybe a couple hundred a month—and an insurance package—no dental?"

So he's coming at it sideways with the payola. "I'd ask what you expect in return."

"I'd expect you to work regular nine-hour days."

"And?"

"Nothing. That's it."

"You'd pardon me if I said 'bullshit,' wouldn't you?"

"Nine hours a day, that's it. You've got to work for at least six of those."

"This would start when? Now?"

"First of the year."

"So, what, do we spit shake?"

"Whatever you want."

He takes my bony appendage in his, and we shake. Dry, because we're civilized. "Now," he says, before letting go, "talk to me about Park-Leavenworth."

Down falls the hammer. "You know. It goes."

"They called me yesterday."

"They, who, they?"

"NüCorp. Said you were asking a lot of weird questions about subcontractors."

"The questions were few and straightforward. Woman I talked to asked me a weird question. Would you like to hear it?"

He sharply exhales; Mannyese for *stop fucking around.*

"Two questions, actually. One—was I aware of how much they were spending on ad space. Two—does Manny know what I'm doing."

"What do you make of that, boy?"

"One take is they think they bought more than advertising."

"Keep going."

"Another possibility is they did buy more than advertising."

"Have I ever butted in on something you're writing?"

"Nope."

"Have I asked you what you're up to with this one?"

"You gave me a softball story to write."

"Did I make you agree to stick with it?"

"Nope."

"Do you think I'm going to kill this story?"

"Depends."

"On?"

"What the story is. And, let me tell you, it's looking huge."

"Care to elaborate, boy?"

"Mather Grimes."

"Credit union guy. Long gone. So?"

"You know he's chief over at NüCorp?"

"Not until this moment."

"You know he awarded a bogus consulting contract to some bullshit LLC? Two of the three shareholders have met very violent ends recently. Third's still alive and he's bilked the city out of at least eight grand. Little, I know, but felony, nevertheless. This guy, he's taking the dough and buying up shit properties with it. Picked up seven already, and they're all within a block of one another. Plus, the guy's apparently building a small arsenal."

"You can prove all this?"

"Monster paper trail. Working on the human side."

"What's the deal with the lots he's buying up?"

"Don't know."

"The guns?"

"Don't know."

"Get it."

Here's a dumb question, but it's gotta be asked. "So, you're not on board with them?"

"No."

"Not at all?"

"Sold them some ads. That's it."

"Swear?"

"What's wrong with you, boy?"

"Got a visit this morning from a couple cops. They found my card on one of the dead guys."

"You have a lawyer?"

Bluff. "Don't see why I'd need one."

"Never hurts. I know a guy owes me one if you want."

"Names ring any bells? McKinley? Chumley?"

"Chumley. You haven't talked to him?"

"Just this morning."

"He's the guy runs the community programs out of southeast. Weed and seed. Organizes night outs. Take-back-the-neighborhood initiatives. He was at your house about a homicide?"

"Trying to rattle me."

"Looks like they did."

"Mildly."

"If you'd done your job correctly, boy, you would have interviewed him a few days ago."

"Had Donna do it."

"Doesn't answer why he's knocking on your door playing murder cop."

"Other guy sound familiar? McKinley?"

"Nope. Maybe you can have Donna figure that one out, too."

Cock. "Anything else you need to drop on me before I get moving?"

"Just watch yourself." He knocks on the tabletop twice as he stands, and I follow him out the door. On the corner, I pat him on the shoulder.

"Manny, this is where our paths diverge. Peace be with you."

Whatever he says to me is drowned out by a passing bus. I shoot him a thumbs-up and begin the short walk to the garage. Dial 411 on my way and get the address for Curtis Fixtures. Jot it down in my notebook. Too early to ambush him on his lunch break, so I drive over to 28th & Pacific, where all of Bill's real estate ventures are located.

Didn't notice this morning how wretched cold it is, but stepping out of the slightly heated car with the Canon slung round my neck, it's like getting kicked in the snout. Do a cursory walk around the block. Circuit takes twelve minutes, and in that time you can walk past all of his houses. Nothing stands out on any of them. Just like the rest around here, they look like the construction equivalent of spousal abuse. Shoot a roll's worth for GPs.

Back by my car. House across the street is faded yellow on the front, blue on the flanks. Dirty siding. Missing some tiles off the roof. Snow's pretty thin on the yard. Entirely melted in spots, and what shows through is frozen mud. Check the mailbox. One letter, and it's from the EPA. Pretty much anyone who has a yard and who lives east of 45th's gotten plenty of these. Though this particular piece of correspondence isn't a form letter. The print's different—all caps. So I open it up. Inside are two sheets. One is a plotter drawing of the yard that shows the parts-per-million density of lead found in the soil. According to this, a guy could break his jaw chewing a mouthful of dirt. Other sheet's a notice, says a lead abatement crew will be here Monday to scoop off the top eight inches of dirt and replace it. Weird that these guys work during the winter, the ground being frozen and all. Then again, with thousands of yards to replace, a backhoe's gotta do what a backhoe's gotta do. Postmark on the envelope is ten days ago. Nobody's going to miss this, so in my pocket it goes.

Door's locked, but there aren't any curtains or blinds. Gotta press my face up to the grimy windows to see in, and this place is entirely bare. Looks like the carpet's been ripped up. Floor's plywood and dotted with industrial staples. Fuck, man. Was hoping to find—I don't know—something. Stepping back, I notice an alarm company sticker in the corner of the window. Put on recently, because the gunk's been scraped from the window where it's stuck. Cop response time to home alarms is notoriously horrid, but, what the fuck, anyway. See if it's at least hooked up. I bang on the window enough that it oughta trip the thing, then mosey back to my car. Back it up so I'm not sitting right out front and mark the time. Figure I'll give it a half hour, so I throw in a dubbed tape of *Double Nickels on the Dime* and wait. Tape starts in the middle of "Shit from an Old Notebook," and just as the second verse of "Political Song for Michael Jackson to Sing" kicks in, a car pulls up. White Ford sedan. The kind that you get from any car rental agency. Jot down the plate. Car sits idling for a bit, then a tall, suit-wearing motherfucker steps outta the passenger side. Bad-looking dude. Sunglasses. Short cropped hair. Walks with purpose. Thinking for a second I'm looking at one of this morning's murder dicks, but this fella, he's too young. He walks around the place, checking points of entry. That done, he unlocks the front door and goes inside, closing the door behind him. Peculiar. Certainly not guys from the alarm company. If they even bother sending people out to check, guys'd definitely have some cheesy fucking wannabe cop car and polyester uniforms. Maybe even hats. Badass mofo guy's in there a while. Driver hasn't stepped out of the car and "Corona" is starting up. Suddenly have a flash of inspiration.

Kill the car, cross the street and walk up on the Ford, looking as innocent as a guy can. Hands in my pockets, I whistle a tuneless tune. Just a fella enjoying a brutally cold late morning stroll. Driver's got his window down and I'll be damned if he's not listening to Blondie.

"Morning," I say, tipping my imaginary hat.

He smiles, slightly. Looks like it hurts him to do so. Jowly motherfucker, this guy. Shaved head, no neck and wearing a cheap suit with the seams frayed all over.

"Gonna catch pneumonia sitting there with your window open, day like today."

"Thanks for the advice."

More a benevolent advisory, but. "Pneumonia, it's some nasty stuff. Had a bout with it two years ago, I guess it was. Put me in the hospital. Hell, I'm still paying that off. But I guess you probably got insurance, huh? Most do, I think. I was outta work see. Ain't that always how it happens? Murray's law, right?"

"Murphy's law," he says, looking straight ahead. "Enjoy your walk."

"Pretty rare I see someone I don't know around here. I was born a few blocks over. You wanna split hairs, I was born at Saint Joe's, but, you know. I grew up here. Still live here. My mom's here. Dad passed. Roots, you know. Got 'em planted deep. You looking at buying? Might not look like much, but this neighborhood, it used to be pretty. Great place to raise a family."

Nothing.

"Pete Lipschitz." I thrust my hand toward him and he makes to block it and maybe break my wrist, but stops short. "Woah there, fella. Just saying hi."

"You've said it. Have a nice day." He rolls up the window.

I shuffle up the sidewalk, looking back plaintively a couple times like my feelings have been hurt. As I'm rounding the corner, the badass motherfucker walks out of the house. Shoulda waited another minute; coulda had 'em both. When the Ford drives past, the fat guy honks twice. I look over, and he waves. I respond in kind like the neighborly neighbor I'm not. To think: some people live like this.

I dial up the office. Nemo answers.

"Kid, jot this down, okay?" I give him the plate. "Call my guy at the DMV and find out who the car's registered to. He's in my Rolodex." Yeah, I have one. Fuck off.

"Some guy called here earlier. Denny something."

"Amsterdam. What's he say?"

"Wants to know if you're, quote, meeting up tonight."

"Gimme his number."

I scribble it down. "Call me after you run the tag."

"On it."

Call Denny. He picks up on ring four. "Yes," he says, not asks.

"It's Cockburn."

Denny clears his throat. "I am organizing tonight's patrol and am wondering if you will be in attendance."

"Don't worry about cleaning up for me, Denny. I'll be a fly on the wall."

"I will see you tonight?"

"Be there. Eleven?"

"Eleven is fine."

"Probably bring a shooter, too."

Pause. "A shooter?"

"Photographer. Gonna have room for two?"

"It can be arranged. Good-bye."

Weird fucking bird, Denny. Love him. Hop in the car and call up Curtis Fixtures. Feeling like a smooth operator now. Couple rings, couple transfers and Bill answers his line like a good sales rep. All pep.

"Bill, I'm looking to renovate an old warehouse and turn it into yuppie pads and I need like a million bucks in light fixture things."

"First things first. Your credit card number?" He chortles. Really. "Just joking. Can I get your name, please?"

"It's Cockburn. From the paper. We had coffee the other day, remember?"

"Oh, yes." Extended exhale. "You had me going there."

"Yeah, well, it was a cheap shot. Listen, though, we gotta talk. Soon."

Sounds like he's shuffling through a stack of papers. "Um, Mister Cockburn—"

"Call me Burn."

"Mr. Cockburn," he continues, his voice increasingly shakier, "I don't think I have anything to say to you."

"What makes you say that?"

"You frightened my wife."

"Last night?"

"She said you were trying to intimidate her."

"Bill, my man, you know that's not like me. I was looking for you, you know. But you were, ah, occupied."

"And, I don't like drug addicts."

So many ways to respond to that. So many. Softball it. "Which is why you're involved in the community, no?" Turn onto the interstate and head west. His office is, what, ten minutes?

"I'm talking about you."

"Must have me confused with someone else unlucky enough to have been given such an extraordinarily cumbersome name. Though I find that hard to believe."

"State of Nebraska versus Bernard Alvin Cockburn. Docket number—"

"C-R nine eight dash two four three nine? That's all you got?"

"You pled guilty."

"Pleaded. Nolo contendere. Thirty days and probation. Not my proudest moment, but we've all done dumb shit."

"Narcotics, Mister Cockburn. That's not child's play. And giving alcohol to—"

"While it may give you a little jolt of superiority to possess that tiny nugget of incomplete information, it sure as shit ain't scaring me, so, let's cut to it, okay? I'm going to pull up in front of your office in a few minutes, and I'd be pleased as a waterhead at the petting zoo if you were waiting outside."

"I certainly won't be."

"Okay, so all of what Creighton told me last night, I'll just assume it's all on the level."

"Creighton can't talk. His jaw is wired shut."

Awful quick on that ignorant rebuttal. Didn't even flinch. Makes me wonder. "Maybe you oughta give him a call."

Needle's hovering at 75, which is as hard as I dare push this nag. Exit at 60th Street is less than a minute away.

"I will."

"Do that. And I'll see you tonight."

"I sincerely doubt it."

"You didn't hear? I'm going out with your boys. Gonna check out all the nice toys you picked up with the weed-and-seed dough."

"You'll find everything's accounted for."

Call waiting beeps. Number's blocked, so it's the office. "Bill, you wanna wait one?" Click over.

"Babylon Security," Nemo says.

"You get an address or anything?"

"Yeah, it's—"

"Check the reverse directory and find the phone—"

Kid blurts out the number. "One step ahead," he said.

"Good boy. Go work."

Click over as I'm hitting the off-ramp. Line's dead. And I was having such a good time needling the chickenshit cocksucker. His extracurricular shenanigans aside, I dislike the guy. Not because of anything allegedly immoral he's done, per se, but because I don't want to be him. Wife. Kid. House. Job. All of which he hates, whether he knows it or not, bless his entrenched little heart. And now he thinks he can fuck with *me*. I find this to be somewhat infuriating.

Cell rings again.

"Oh, and Wozniak?" Nemo says, "Detective Franklin Mc-Kinley."

"Thanks, kid. Go buy some cigarettes or something." Pulling the phone away when I hear him shout *wait*.

"Hit me," I say.

"NüCorp bought a tract of lots in Minneapolis last month. Defunct factories."

"Minneapolis gave you that already?"

"Just called them up."

I hate him. "Have them fax over whatever they can and put it on my desk."

"Can I ask you what this story's about, exactly?"

"Tell you when you're older."

Brain's lining up the pieces, seeing what sticks or clicks. McKinley draws the Wozniak case. Closes it out quiet like. Hell, everyone saw what happened. Chumley, he's a desk jockey dealing softy, feel-good police programs. Signed off on Bill's weed-and-seed grant. Tenuous connection to two out of three.

Three: nobody coulda reported Korbes since I saw him last night. Okay, devil's advocate: *If* someone called it in—maybe saw me creeping around—okay, the cops show, there's no way I'd be the first stop. And *if*, for whatever strange confluence of reasons, I was the first person they talked to, they woulda dragged me in. However, Chumley wouldn't have been one of the dicks standing on my porch. Conclusion: Obviously, they're in on it. It, being whatever the fuck Grimes has going now. *It*, also being what I must find out if I'm going to nail this story. Right now, *it*'s all conjecture and coincidence. The connections are there if you look for them; they're not if you're not. Gotta cement these things.

It occurs to me, as I'm veering off the highway, that the addresses for Curtis and Babylon put them on the same block. Now, isn't that convenient? Dial the security place.

A nasal voice that was born for the phones says, "Dispatch."

Jokers. All of them. "Think my wife is fucking around on me, you guys do that?"

"Surveillance?"

"Whatever you call it. With the pictures and the like."

"You want a detective agency, sir."

"Ain't you?"

"Babylon is a security company."

"Six of one."

"I suggest you look up a detective agency in the yellow—"

"Kinda work you *do*, then?"

"Building security."

"Like if I wanted to put an alarm on my house like my neighbor's got?"

"We only do commercial work."

Interesting. "That's who she's fucking, is how I know."

"Okay, well you have a nice day, then."

"Hit a trip wire or something when I was crawling around in the bushes with a cleaver. Swear, if I'da caught them in—"

Guy hangs up, but, whatever. Cruise over to the Curtis address. Small, squatty, steel-sided warehouse. One of several on the block. Babylon's in a corner strip mall. Shares a back parking lot with Curtis. Handy. Pull in across the street in some electronics wholesaler's lot next to a Texaco and see what I can see. Maybe I shoulda been a cop. Not a cop-cop. A fed. U.S. marshal or some shit. DEA? Nah. ATF I could handle. Got its paws in all the fun stuff. Shit, if I'd have joined up straight outta college, be almost halfway to a pension right now. Assuming they work on the same system the navy does. Twenty years, bang, you're set. Worked out well for my old man. Sad as he was and nobody but myself to blame, but he did okay. Enough to buy that fucking big-ass lawn mower he didn't need. Full-on tractor, that thing. Think he used it twice. Went for twenty bucks at the estate sale. I'd cleaned it up. Which got me in some trouble. Evidence, then detective Dick Savage said. And I was destroying it. Evidence of fucking what? I asked, scrub brush in one hand, hose in the other, watching the EMTs wheel off the chewed-up, pulpy remainder. Fell off the fucking retaining wall. How am I supposed to know that? I just fucking told you. Maybe you can tell me again after you spend the night downtown.

And that's when I gave him a blast from the hose and had a giggle about it.

Anyway, downhill from there. Pepper spray. Bruised ribs. Filed a complaint. He got yanked down to patrol. Bumped up to public information—a shitty detail no one wants. His presence there, it's put a bit of a crimp in my workdays.

Reverie's broken by my ringing cell. Caller ID's some number I don't recognize. Almost don't answer it, but I got nothing better doing at the moment.

"Cockburn."

"You left me hanging last night." A raspy woman's voice.

"Left who hanging?"

"It's me. Luka."

"The fuck'd you get this number?"

"I want something, I get it."

Admirable. "You want it, because?"

"That ski trip you were thinking about taking?"

"Yeah, nevermind about that."

"Fine. One-twenty."

"Don't want it."

"Hundred. That's a friend price and I know you can use it. Come on."

"Eat shit."

"Got some dirt, too. Throw that in for free."

"I got more than I can shovel at the moment."

"Not like this. Better than dirt. Mud. It sticks."

"To whom?"

"Listen to you, mister grammar. Where are you?"

"Working."

"Didn't ask what you're doing. Where are you?"

Eye the nearest street sign. 58th & J. "Driving. One-twentieth and Center."

"Yeah, sure."

"You got me. One-eighteenth."

"Sure that ain't you sitting in the parking lot by the Texaco, slick?"

"The fuck?"

"Yeah, like I said. I got some mud. You want it?"

"If you wanna pull that same shit Bill tried earlier, you're S-O-L, because that's nothing."

"Yeah, I know. He got a hard-on over it, though. Sad to watch him get all worked up."

I don't say anything. Nothing really to say. Other than *who the fuck* are *you, anyway?*

"So?"

"Where and when?"

"Soon as you can get to my apartment."

"I gotta bring a hundred bucks?"

"You don't think it's free, do you?"

She gives me her address, and I'm there sooner than I oughta be, which is to say, I arrive. Broke.

nineteen

It's an unremarkable yellow two-story in the middle of a block filled with the same. Based on the degree of decay most show, I assume they're all rental properties. Two unmarked doors on the front and lights burning both upstairs and down. My first instinct is to try the door on the left. Presumably, it has a flight of stairs behind it, and for whatever reason (yeah, fine, because of that goddamned Suzanne Vega tune), I imagine she lives upstairs. Reaching for the buzzer when a white cat jumps onto the windowsill to my right. So I knock on the other door. Luka peeks between the curtains and unlocks what sounds like a dozen chains and dead bolts before the door swings open. She's wearing a pair of black-faded-to-gray Jordaches and a hot pink pocket T-shirt.

"Entrez."

She obviously tried to straighten up before I came over, but the cat hairs that cover her few pieces of assembly-required furniture give the place away. It's like a cat exploded in here . . . probably fur balls in the ice trays, even. The place itself is your standard low-end rental property. Got the twenty-year-old shag carpet that probably started out white, but is now yellow-brown, the fifty layers of white paint on every vertical surface, including the woodwork. Furniture's straight from Target. Wood-grain veneer and plastic done up like stainless steel. Kicker? A fucking macramé owl hung on the wall between the windows.

"Where'd you get that thing?" I point to the owl.

"Salvation Army. Have a seat."

I do. The couch, which isn't all that bad to look at, is all that bad to sit on. The plywood just eats into your spine.

"Got my cash?"

I note she's still standing. Which is an odd choice. Power emanates from he who sits. Suppose disgrace does, too, in certain instances. "You got my mud?"

"Money first."

"That'd make it look like I'm paying for what you're going to say. And I don't do that. So, spill."

"Nobody's watching you."

"I am. So?"

She tosses a little baggie of white powder on the coffee table and joins me on the couch. "You've got the boys all worked up."

"That's all you got, I'm not going to be mad, but I am going to be disappointed."

"Gram is what you wanted."

"Talking about your quote-unquote dirt."

"What boys you think it is I'm talking about?"

"Judging by your question, the wrong ones." Stealthily eyeball the blow. Probably a dude hiding in the closet with a camera waiting for me to pocket it. It sounds preposterous, but, I fear, isn't. I wonder if anything is, anymore.

"That's right, wrong ones. Last time they got upset about someone, that someone isn't around anymore to upset them. Get it?"

I do that dumbshit gun gesture again. "*Get it*. Get it?"

She shoots me the bird.

"Okay, well, riddle me this—who am I pissing off?"

"I can't tell you. But I can tell you to ease up if you wanna be around to see your kid born."

I wonder if she sees me wince. "These guys recently get pissed at a guy named Creighton Korbes?"

There's a nearly imperceptible twitch in her throat. Ding.

"Saw what they did to him. Blew his fucking brains right out. All over the wall, the ceiling. In his kitchen, for fuck's sake. And the guy's a cripple, so, heartless, these goons."

"Gonna be tough for you to talk that game with a gun in your mouth."

"You putting it there?"

"Asshole, I'm trying to save your ass. Now, look, just write your story, but stay away from those houses."

"Houses?"

"Don't get wise."

"Can't. They're part of the story. Hell, sounds like they *are* the story. So help me and tell me what I shouldn't know. Otherwise, just might have to get myself in a real bind. It's a sickness, this curiosity of mine."

She draws in a deep breath and scratches the part in her hair. "Okay, I'll tell you anything you want to know about Bill and that stupid club he's in. Give you enough to write whatever it is you gotta write. But I'm not talking about those houses, and, if you're smart, you'll forget about them."

"Why, Miss Robeson, are you helping me?"

"Doing a favor for a friend. Get out your notebook."

I do as I'm told. "Ain't your heart just golden?"

"It's not you I'm doing the favor for. Now shut up and listen."

What she tells me, distilled, goes like this:

Okay, so the degenerate detachment—the pushers and hookers and junkies and drunks—they'd more or less had the run of the neighborhood since the eighties, and nobody really gave a shit. The local squares were used to it and didn't cause a ruckus, and the degenerates, they didn't fuck with the squares. A happy little experiment in letting victimless crime just do its thing unchecked. The cops, every now and again, would run a sting and round up some low-level players, but, whatever, gotta pay to play.

Fast-forward to last summer. July, probably. The blistering days and nights always bring out the worst everyone has to offer. So Luka here, she's working one night, and she's just finished with a guy swinging the world's tiniest pecker. So she crawls out of the backseat of the guy's Pinto and she's barely got her skirt untwisted when this white Nissan pulls up. Couple guys up front. Doofy-looking dudes, all camo'd out, and not lightweight jungle fatigues, either, but those heavyweight woodland BDU jobs. So, the passenger, he rolls down his window.

Passenger, he's the bigger of the two. Not quite sunglasses, but definitely tinted specs. Yellow-brown, if she remembers right. Trimmed mustache that made the guy almost look gay and a sailor sorta tattoo on his forearm—anchor with a banner reading *Susie*. Anyway, this guy, he jerks his thumb over to the driver, who leans over so his face just catches the streetlight. Clean-shaven, small mouth, eyes set far apart and eyebrows that looked like a couple chinchillas were napping on his forehead. He cleared his throat, and his voice sounded like it had a patina of threat on it, but consisted mostly of fear and insecurity.

"We're here to tell you, ma'am, that things are going to change, and if you're smart, you and all your friends will pick up and leave."

So what's she do? She spits in the window, and the big guy, he gets an eyeful. The gunk runs down his cheek, slowly, and he doesn't do anything to clean it up. He sits there and looks at her with his one nongoobered eye.

"You've been warned," says the driver. Spit-eye rolls up the window and they putter off.

"So," I say, "Bill, he's the driver. Who's the passenger?"

"One of his buddies. Forget what he calls himself. They all have dumb names. Code names or whatever. Idiots."

She continues: A few other girls she talks to, they got similar visits, but that was it. Cops didn't swoop down, the concerned citizens didn't start trying to take back the streets, nothing. So business continues as usual. Couple weeks later, the next wave hits. Six, eight cars cruise around the high-traffic areas all night. Back and forth with their brights and hazards on, "all blasting that classical music song. Goes like *dah DUM da da dah dah, dah DUM da da dah dah.*"

"Wagner," I say. "It's from a movie."

The tapes weren't synced up, so the effect was "freaky as hell. It was like a nightmare that wasn't scary, just really uncomfortable." And then they start taking pictures. Flashbulbs going off every thirty, forty seconds. But the cool thing, she says, is after maybe an hour, the squares, they start coming out of their houses and yelling at the car guys because the noise and lights make it hard to watch TV and sleep. Little bit later, a cop cruiser trolls through and the music and lights die and off scurry the troublemakers. Cop finishes his circuit, the squares go back to their TVs and the street people continue conducting their street-people affairs.

"This get good anytime soon?" I ask.

"Got somewhere better to be?"

"Carry on."

So things, they're status quo again. Everyone's getting high and laid and making money. Everyone in the world should be so happy, really. One night, the white Nissan returns. Driver's by himself and he pulls up alongside Luka.

"Hey," he says.

She doesn't play along, just keeps on keeping on.

"How much?" he asks, his car crawling along, the wheel covers scraping against the curb.

She gives him the finger. He dangles two twenties out his window, so she snatches them.

"What'd I just buy?"

"You just made a donation to the Salvation fucking Army," she says. "Congratulations."

"I'm serious."

"Fuck off, Rambo."

"No, look. Here."

She does, and he's pointing at his crotch. Two things strike her. One, this guy's got a raging full-on thrusting up out of his undone zipper. Two, there's a pistol on the seat next to him. Looks like an antique or something.

"I prefer 'em small," she says. Trying to keep her cool, but the gun's got her spooked, so she nonchalantly reaches for the folding straight razor she keeps in her back pocket. Her walking around with it there, it's visible, so half deterrent, half protection, she claims.

"Hold it," he says. She stops, thinking, Well, this guy's fucking crazy enough, so. "This?" He grabs the gun by its barrel, Boy Scout he is, and holds it toward her. "Isn't what you think. Here, take it. Doesn't work, just so you know."

Its handle is covered with thick, tacky grease. Heavier than she thinks it should be.

"It's a Luger," he says. "Genuine relic. German officers used to carry those."

So she's standing there, pointing this relic Nazi sidearm at him, and the guy's still got a boner.

"I've got more money if you want it. I don't know how much it costs for, you know . . ." He looks for the right word, and, thinking he's found it, says sheepishly, "Action?"

This idiot innocence of his, it's what does it for her. "Hundred bucks and you take me somewhere with a bed and a locking door."

So, short story shorter, they went to that motel on like 68th & Q that looks like a spaceship, and he wasn't into creepo shit. Wanted a blowjob and a screw, which is what he got. And then he took her back. Few days later, happened again. Same motel, but on the way back, she asked about the gun. He hedged, said it was a hobby of his, relic firearms. Ran down a quick list of his collection, M1 this, Civil War Sharp's that, Mauser something else. "The M1," he said, "is pretty amazing, in terms of design. You can break it down using only a thirty-ought-six round." Said they're all in shooting condition, but he doesn't want to sully them. Likes to hold them, he said, because they feel powerful. Probably saw combat and they probably were used to kill people. Not people, he clarified, "Enemy soldiers."

I interrupt story time. "That's all well and good, but where are you going with this?"

"Remember how I told you he was buying guns?"

"*Jawol.*"

"Okay, so this club thing he's in, they're sitting on enough guns to start a war. Not relic guns, either."

"And they plan on actually using them?"

She nods. "See, he and a couple other guys were really hot

on the idea before. So they got that grant money and used it to buy up all sorts of stuff. Guns and ammo and probably some other stuff, too. Bigger things."

"So, what, they're going to start some righteous blitz?"

"I don't know. Look, he's getting all strange now, like he's cranked out or something. Paranoid, sweaty, nervous, the whole works."

"You gonna tell me why you're telling me this?"

"Because he's going to lose his head and do something stupid. Maybe hurt someone. Maybe hurt you."

"What's that matter to you?"

"It doesn't. Like I said, I'm doing a favor."

"You're not going to tell me for whom, are you?"

"Not a chance."

"This person have dealings with Bill?"

"Twenty-questions ain't gonna cut it."

"Lemme think out loud here for a sec." I deal us each a smoke. She's quicker on the draw with the fire than I, and she politely lights me first. "You've been playing coy with me since day one, trotting out little bits of info you think I'd want, right? Keep me intrigued. Which, to your credit, has worked. And now you unload this, but you're still holding back the good stuff. You want me to take your scraps, verify them somehow, and then write up a story that puts away your man, no?"

"Pretty much."

"So, you're either afraid he's going to turn on you or someone who's got more juice wants him shut down, and you, you're the intermediary."

She's examining her fingernails, cigarette dangling from the corner of her mouth.

"I saw what happened to the guy in the wheelchair. Whoever

it is did that, why not let him finish putting his house back in order? One last nail to drive in."

"Bill has a child."

"And?"

"When you have yours, you'll understand."

Will I? Either have or understand? "Understand this—when I leave and you call up Mather to give him the update, tell him I'm not his bitch, either." Smiling, I kill the burner.

"He does something to Bill, it's hanging around your neck." Licks her lips. "Like those kids down in Papillion."

Wonder if she can see it, this meat hook in my gut.

"Someone bought them some booze," she says. "What was it? Vodka and wine coolers, right?"

"That record—"

"Sealed. But not very tight."

"I'm clean on that. Walked."

"Wonder what would happen if Manny got a copy of it. Or Allison. Or the TV stations. Bet it'd be hard to do your job once you're branded with something like that."

"What you want is?"

"Told you. Write your story. Put away Bill. Just leave the real estate out of it. That can be our little secret, too."

twenty

Never felt dirtier in my life. Head's splitting. Feels like I ate glass
shards. Burns when I breathe. Dizzy walking up the steps to my
apartment. Swing open the door, place is empty. At least, no
Allison. Boxes in neat stacks. Marked up. *Kitchen. Winter clothes.
Summer clothes. Books (1 of 3).* Been busy, she.

Standing in the middle of the front room, hands on hips, just
sorta looking around. General surveying the corpse-strewn battle-
field. Yep. Gonna have to find a cheaper place. Somewhere small,
so the next girl (there's always a next victim) won't have room
to insinuate herself. I never shoulda left the Baron Square. Whatever. Plenty of efficiencies near downtown. Stay here or across
the street once she's gone till I get it figured out. Won't have a
lot of stuff to move, I don't think. Which is nice. Really. Starting
over with nothing. Again. Just me and my bed. Which isn't *mine*
mine. My folks gave it to me. Actually, they didn't give it to me.
I took it before the estate sale scavengers showed up. Not-funny
running joke of my own creation is I was conceived on it. Which
may or may not be true.

Wander into the kitchen. This room's been picked through,

too. Only glass left in the cabinet is my rocks glass. The one with the heavy bottom. Stole it from a hotel in Chicago when I was there for some geek-shit IRE convention. Anyway, top off the beast, fire a burner and sit on a box of Allison's shit. Knives, probably.

Wonder what it is, exactly, I have here that I'm so afraid of losing. Then again, what's more boring than fearful introspection? And if we're not entertaining, well. We're nothing then, are we? Or, rather, am I.

Time the cocktail so I gotta refill when I throw the butt in the sink. Fresh one in hand, I mosey on over to the closet. Tucked up on the top shelf behind some shoe boxes filled with old issues (of the paper, natch) is a Hello Kitty photo album. Cheap plastic thing. Shelf's high enough that I gotta stand on my toes to reach all the way back there, and after a couple seconds of patting around, I find it. Only thing really worth salvaging, even though it's less than half full. Of? Dirty pictures of Allison. She was hopped up on something one night. I was wasted. Told her later I trashed the negatives. Which wasn't a lie, because I did. After I had prints made. So I'm sipping the Crow and flipping through Hello Kitty, trying to needle myself into feeling something, but I got nothing. Beaver shots, couple harsh-light, bad-angle blowjob numbers, jizz splattered on her back. Finger-painted a C with it. Throw the bastard back where it came from and set up shop in the living room.

Pathetic, this. Welcome, Cockburn, to the rest of your life. Guy sitting alone getting shitty in his shitty apartment. Day after fucking day. Just keep going at it till my liver shuts down. Yeah, so I'm wondering how this is any better than what's behind door No. 2. Booze isn't doing the trick. Can't hack the hot stuff. Which leaves the orange bottle.

Bathroom hasn't been packed up yet. Still got all of Allison's facial astringents and exfoliates and organic shampoo and shit on the shelf. Means, thankfully, the medicine cabinet is loaded. Grab the orange bottle and shake out an OC. Scrape off the time-release shit with my apartment key since all the knives have been packed away. Dry-swallow the bastard and wait for it to hit. Wait. Shoulda crushed it and snorted it. Can you snort this stuff? Total amateur hour here.

Laid out on the couch and I should just fucking swallow my finger and puke up this garbage. Fucking hippie, getting wasted so he doesn't have to hack. Can't even fool myself into thinking it's an *experience*. Maybe fucking *learn* something. Whatever. The truth, if there exists such a thing, is I wanna feel the way I think I oughta be. Neutralized, in a word.

God, what the fuck was I thinking yesterday? Allison. That god-awful apartment and all the compromises wrapped up inside of it. Easy to fix. What bugs is the spike of jealousy that sent me dashing across the courtyard. Juvenile. Come on, kid, haven't you convinced yourself yet that you don't need her? Remember how she used to be fun? Now she wants to turn you into a *fa-ther*. Foulest word you've heard. Yeah, keep trying. You'll believe it. Degenerate inbred white trash fuckstick oughta be across the street at the rat nest slime flop. But, no, he's here. Worth thinking about, kid. That you keep coming back. Maybe you wanna give it a try. Maybe you wouldn't fuck it up. Maybe you oughta quit hiding behind your bullshit excuses. Scared? Is that how you feel, Bernard?

Fucked up. Hillbilly heroin gets on top of me in a hurry, and I'm glad I'm on the couch. No way I'm getting up. Nor could I. Nor do I want to. Fitting. This, certainly, is how I take it: lying down. I could happily close these little peepers and never see anything ugly again. I just could.

But, through the thick mud that is my cranial contents, I hear a key twist in the lock. The dead bolt's thump. And I know, see, it's only a matter of seconds till in walks Allison, accompanied by a gust of punishingly cold air. Hits you like a vendetta, the winter wind. Think you're a poet now, faggot?

She stamps her feet on the rug like she's fending off a swarm of scorpions.

"What are you on?"

Apparently, it's that obvious. "Oxy."

"Where'd you get it?"

"Matters?"

"When'd you take it?"

I wave at her four or five fingers.

"You took one? Or more?"

"Uno."

She throws her coat on the back of the couch. The cuff of a sleeve, frozen stiff, brushes against my arm. Somewhat enjoyable.

"Having a good time?"

"Spose."

"You won't be needing this, then?"

She brandishes what appears to be a bottle of booze.

"Basil Hayden's," she says by way of clarification.

"Not cheap." Ever the observant one.

"Maybe tomorrow." Her voice trails off as she heads to the other end of the apartment. A door closes. Somewhere.

Yeah, so here I am. All fucked up and got another five hours.

I walk unsteadily to the bathroom. Allison must be packing up more of her shit in the bedroom. Door's closed. Not a hard trick to master, door closing, and I demonstrate this point by closing the bathroom door behind me. Lift the toilet seat and cram a couple fingers down my throat. Few dry heaves later, and out shoots the shit. Brown and thin, mostly. Shaking when I'm done, and the last burst was so violent I think I annihilated some blood vessels in my eyes. Mirror check confirms my suspicion. Throw some water on my face to quell the flushing and rinse off whatever stuck. Down a couple Tylenols because I'll probably be hurting later.

Takes me a few moments to correctly operate the doorknob. So, how long till this junk wears off, one might wonder. Soon, one might hope. Thinking maybe a nap might be in order. Wake up feeling refreshed. Only—what? Little after six, maybe? Plenty of time to snooze. Up by ten, ten-thirty and off to Denny's place, right as rain.

Making my way back to the couch, and the room twists. Or, rather, my perception of the room alters sharply and quickly. Steady myself with a hand on the wall. Moron. Make it, barely, to the couch. Still feeling queasy and shaky from the vomit episode. Wondering how Allison didn't hear my violent expulsion. She probably did. Didn't want to bother being bothered. Can't blame her. Only reason I bother with myself is because I have to.

Oh, kid, think you deserve pity? *You?* Tiny bump in the road and you lose your shit. Let your guard down. Eternal vigilance, you prick. The price of. Something.

Trying to keep my head together, staring at the water stain above me. Eyes following the hairline cracks that spiderweb across the ceiling. This place is gonna cave.

Hearing this obnoxious shrill noise. Comes and goes. Need some water. Maybe a beer. Something familiar might help. Fingernails scratching the cushion. Oh, shit. It's my cell, the bleating. Don't know the number.

"Uh-huh," I say.

"This Mr. Cockburn?"

" 'Tis, it is."

"It's Bill. Bill Dunkel."

"Greetings," I say.

"I'm worried about Creighton."

"He's feeling no pain."

"What?"

Dipshit motherfucker. "Gotta run, Bill. Sorta caught me—"

"I'm scared," he says, but doesn't sound really so much. "You wanna bust me? Fine. But I'm not going down alone."

"You got nothing on anyone. Especially me, so go fuck yourself, already."

"I'm not talking about you. I'm talking about Mather Grimes."

Work it, stoney. "Who?"

He repeats himself. Slowly, as if to lend some importance to his words.

"Don't know the guy."

"How can you not?"

"Fuck, man. You tell me."

"Come on. Douglas Credit Union?"

"Before my time."

"But you know the stories, right? Child molesting ring? Politicians? Come on."

"I'll bite," I say. "What do you have on Mather Grimes?"

"Eleven at Denny Amsterdam's place, everything's on the record."

"Gimme a reason to stay up past my bedtime to indulge your bullshit fantasy."

"You want to know what's going on with those houses I bought, right?"

"Possibly."

"I'll give you a guided tour. Bring a camera, because nobody'll take your word for it when you tell them what you've seen."

"But I'm supposed to take yours?"

"What's it going to hurt?"

"If you even begin to think about fucking with me . . ." I leave that thought menacingly incomplete.

"Eleven o'clock."

Lying on the couch, paying an undue amount of attention to every heartbeat and groan emanating from my body. The theory being I'll be able to detect the shift when the chemical nastiness begins to ebb. What's distracting is Allison, who lumbers out of the bedroom.

"Who was that on the phone?"

"Work thing."

"Didn't sound like a work thing. And you never yell at anyone."

"Wasn't yelling."

"You don't have to raise your voice to yell."

"I was yelling"—I loosely make those ironic air quotes with my digits, but decide mid-gesture that it looks stupid, so that little endeavor gets shelved—"at a source who's dicking me around."

"That same story? The one about the neighborhood watch group?"

"Focus has shifted, but, yes."

"How's that going?"

Her interest, feigned or not, it concerns me. "I'm not sure. Well, I think."

"You're putting a lot of time into it. Work."

Stare. Blankly.

"It's just unusual, is all."

Stare. Suspiciously.

"It's just, it's not very like you."

Look at the boxes. Look at her belly. Head's feeling heavy. Unwieldy. "Uh-huh. Can I get some sleep, maybe?"

"You're going out tonight?"

"Nap time."

"Because I was sorta hoping we could talk."

"Again? Seriously? We have nothing fucking left to talk about, okay? Get the fuck out if you're going. If you're staying, shut the fuck up."

"What the hell is—"

"You know right before I met you I sold some kids a couple bottles of booze for fifty bucks? I was broke, right? So this little blond suburban thing, all of seventeen, she sorta flirts with me and slips me some cash for a bottle of Smirnoff and a six of kiwi wine coolers. Says can she and her friend borrow my car for the night, too? Top off the tank and that's a deal. Why the fuck not, right?"

"Stop it."

"Off they go. Gonna stay drunk all weekend before graduation. Party fucking time, right? Next morning, banging on my door. Answer it thinking she's got my keys. Nope. Cops. Do I know where my car is? Where was I last night? Did I know Tina whats-her-face and Jill whoever-the-fuck. Did I supply them with alcohol? Fucking cops, they took me out there. Saw them. One girl, decapitated. Other one, cut in half. Car rolled right across 'em. And there's that bottle of Smirnoff about twenty feet away, mouth down in the mud. Hauled me in right there. Had some junk on me, too. Genius, right? But I'm a slippery, slimy mother-fucker, see. Squirmed right out of it." Pause. "What sorta pigfuck does that?"

So there's that.

She's staring at me staring at her staring at me staring at her thinking this's gotta end sometime.

"That suburban blond thing? One got her head knocked off? Cliff's little sister."

I expect her to leave. She doesn't. She's standing there, blank faced and I'm waiting for a wave of relief to hit. Settle for a trickle, even.

twenty-one

I'm sure there are worse ways to spend a Friday night, but I can't think of any right now. Tweaked and hanging out in the catering-shop-slash-neighborhood-watch headquarters at a little before eleven doing my fly-on-the-wall trick and watching thirteen grown men wearing everything from full camouflage to jeans and flannel and trucker caps smoke, drink and compare firearms. Escaped the apartment over Allison's protests. Stopped at the Warwick and sucked down an upper. Nasty metal taste in my mouth again. Shifting my weight back and forth from one foot to the other, hand working overtime scribbling jibber jabber in my notebook. Quick, uneasy looks around the room. Must look suspicious. Feel suspicious. Fuck, man, these guys have guns. One of them spots me jotting down notes and takes long strides across the room, a nonfiltered cigarette dangling from his mouth and a can of Coors NA in his hand. Wearing a white cowboy hat (because he's a good guy), an airbrushed wolf howling at the moon black T-shirt, stone-washed jeans with elastic cuffs, a hunting jacket and gray New Balance running shoes. What's that on his arm? Sailor tat. Score one for Luka in the credibility department.

"You the newsman?" he asks. "Here to make us famous, huh?"

"Cockburn."

"Sitting Bull said that."

Somehow, I doubt it. "Yes he did. You are?"

"Call me Cable."

"Okay, Cable, what's your name?"

"Cable'll work just fine for us. You gonna ride tonight?" He takes a long pull on his near beer.

"That I am. You wanna tell me how it works?"

"Shoot." He pats his jeans pockets. "Forgot my wallet."

"You know a fella named Bill Dunkel?" Hear that? How I ignored his non sequitur and adopted his peculiar vernacular. Sneaky way of alliance building.

"Bill the Real Deal?" Except he pronounces *Real Deal* like *Rill Dill,* so it all fucking rhymes. "Yeah."

"He around?"

"Why you asking about him?" Cable leans in over me, engulfing me in his hulking shadow.

"Supposed to rendezvous with him about now."

"He's normally a Saturday night trooper. Maybe he'll make it out tonight. Maybe he won't. Beer?" He gestures behind him to where there's a gaggle of five guys admiring the sixth guy's revolver. Looks like a Python or something else Dirty Harry would carry around. Got that new and hardly used shine to it. One nut wearing a pancho spins the cylinder and holds the gleaming, nickel-plated behemoth up to the light. "Purty," I think he says.

"Working, so I'll pass. But thanks, though."

"Come on over, I'll introduce you to the men."

I follow his size-fifty sneakers the few paces across the room and stop a little off to the side and behind him. A bit nervous. Feel sweat popping on my temples.

"Troops," he says, and I hope they don't see me cringe, "This here is . . . what's your name again?" I tell him. "Cockburn. He's from the newspaper and gonna ride with us tonight. So whichever one of you gets stuck with him"—Cletus or Cable or whatever the fuck his name is turns and grins at me, showing me his twelve-car-pileup excuse for a set of teeth—"take care of him. We don't need no civilian casualties, hear?"

The nutjobs grunt in approval and eye me suspiciously. I wave, and then realize I must look like a total pinko fag to these guys in my jeans, black Chuck Taylors, argyle sweater and coat.

"Okay, okay." Cable loudly claps his hands and everyone in the room hushes and turns. "We all ready?"

The crowd lets out whoops and huzzahs and a *Let's git 'em* or two, and I consider feigning diarrhea, because this can't go anywhere but down. Wouldn't really be acting all that much, either. I'm cramping up.

"Let us pray," Cable says in a rather solemn voice. Everyone links hands, and I step back, but Cable looks at me and says, "You too," as he snatches up my left hand. A scrawny motherfucker on my right wearing a POW bracelet and a bush hat intertwines his fingers with mine.

"Dear Lord," Cable continues, "we ask you to watch over us on this night as we work in your name to rid our homes and streets of evil. We thank you for your protection and guidance. Lord, through us, your will be done. Amen."

"Jackal," Cable shouts, and a runty little weasel gimps over from the other side of the prayer circle. Think he's got one leg longer than the other, because even with his orthopedic shoes, he walks something goofy. "You're taking the paperboy. Rendezvous back here at ought-thirty."

"Can do," Jackal says and grabs a pink-and-blue walkie-talkie from the crate. He shakes my hand and says, "Follow me."

I hesitate. "I'm waiting on the Rill Dill. Hate for him to show up and me be gone."

Jackal holds up his walkie-talkie. "He shows up, I'll find out, get you back here on the double."

Outside, it's windy and insidiously cold. Jackal pulls on a hunting cap with earflaps and leads me to his car, a rust-bucket Jetta from back when Volkswagens weren't the cutest little things. It smells like cheese and sweat, and every surface is coated in a sticky film, because that's just my fucking luck. He doesn't look at me or say anything as he pulls out of the lot onto 30th Street. We get as far as 26th before I decide this is too weird.

"So, Jackal. What's that short for?"

"Jack."

Obviously. "Lived in the neighborhood a long time?"

"All my life."

"And you like it, I presume."

"Can't say I do."

"So why get so involved?"

"Something to do."

"You know Rill Dill?"

"Bill? Yeah."

"And?"

"He's smart about computers and the like."

"How about Creighton Korbes or James Wozniak."

"Knew Weasel. Haven't spoken to Crater in a piece."

"Nice guys?"

"Decent, I reckon."

The walkie-talkie crackles and Jack holds it up to his ear.

"Jackal six here, over," he says. The toy gurgles static in response, but I can't make out a syllable.

"What's the word?" I ask.

"Suspicious activity in our quadrant. We're going to recon it." He replaces the toy in the center console and pulls from his pocket what might be a cap gun, but is probably a .38 snubbie. He sets the thing in his lap like your average citizen might do with a cell phone or a map. Terror drips down from the back of my brain. Fewer things in this world more dangerous than a man with a gun who thinks God is on his side.

"That thing real?" I ask.

"Yep. Supposed to leave it back at base."

"But you didn't."

"Nope."

We take a few turns, drive down an alley, and I don't know where we are anymore. Residential area, so there aren't any landmarks, and the streetlights are shattered, so it's pretty dark. He kills the headlights. This is just too fucking stupid. He grunts, taps my shoulder and points across my body and out my window to a mass of silhouettes clustered around something like a giant spool in a vacant lot. Jackal rolls up slowly, then stops. The bitch of this is I'm between him and the target, so whatever's about to happen has to happen over me. Jackal leans over and rolls down my window, elbowing me in the leg a few times. He picks up the walkie-talkie and whispers, "Jackal six, at the lot, have the darkies in sight. Over."

"You wanna see something?" he whispers, then before I can answer, he shouts at the top of his lungs, "Hey! Get lost!"

A couple heads turn, some fingers are pointed and a crotch is dismissively grabbed before a chorus of *fuck you*'s and *shut the fuck up*'s float our way.

"You better scram before the police come!" Jackal retorts.

The alleged miscreants ignore Jackal this time, and I hope he's satisfied with the point he didn't make.

"I don't get it," I say. "They're not doing anything illegal."

Jackal squints at me. "They're dealing drugs. Don't you know anything?"

"Couldn't they just be hanging out?"

"They don't do that." He reaches into the backseat and retrieves a Day-Glo orange plastic case. He sets it on his lap and looks at me like I'm supposed to be impressed.

"What's in the case there, Jackal?"

"My little friend."

"Shouldn't you radio to headquarters or whatever and have them notify the police?"

"And let them get away? Be at least ten minutes before the cal-vary arrives." The Jackal disdainfully shakes his illiterate head at my city-boy ignorance as he pops the latches on his little friend's case. He's got the thing turned so I can't see what he's got in there. "You got a camera?" he asks.

"I wish I did." Dipshit I am, forgot it in the car.

"Too bad. This is gonna be great." He almost giggles as he lifts from the case a flare gun. He looks at it adoringly, and I think he might be nursing a hard-on. "Just got 'er."

"From?"

"Same place I got the Snapper." He points to the revolver. "But you ain't gonna find any paperwork on it." Freak winks.

I look out the window at the crowd. Maybe a half-dozen guys all told, and part of me wants to shout a warning, but, really, to get involved would pervert the situation something worse than it already is. "The Snapper not doing it for you?"

His mouth tightens and kinda pokes out on the right side like he's thinking about my question. The walkie-talkie squawks, and Jackal says "Roger" into it. He pockets the .38, turns to me and says, "Rill Dill's back at HQ waiting. Get you there in a jiff."

Which is great, because now he can put away that fire cannon and I can do my thing and get the poop on what exactly the Rill Dill has been up to, and why is spastic fucktard opening his door? After slithering out of the driver's seat, he crouches next to the front wheel well and takes aim while I wish I had something to pray to. Jackal lets out a loud whoop, then a burst of something like *git-on-outta-hyah* about a half second before I hear a hollow *thunk,* and the blinding white and yellow fire from the flare bleaches the dark block. It arcs over the lot and explodes way past the target. The sparks and embers extinguish as soon as they hit the snow-covered ground, and just as quickly as everything became light, it's darker than before, because the burning magnesium fucked up my night vision.

"Run, chuckers! Run!" Jackal shouts.

I hear the unmistakable pop of a handgun in the not-too-distant distance to my right at the same time the window behind me explodes, and I've got shards of safety glass in my hair and down my shirt. I duck down and yell at the jackass to fucking shoot back or something already. And he does.

Jackal pulls out his revolver and fires one shot into the air. As soon as the report dies, he levels the gun across the car's hood and fires twice. The fire briefly illuminates his mug as he shoots, and he's got this twisted look of maniacal satisfaction on his face. The car rocks when Jackal jumps inside. In one motion, he throws the evidence onto the backseat and shoves the gearshift into drive. The tires spin and spit out gravel before the car lurches into motion. He's cackling and pounding the steering wheel with his left hand while piloting the car with his right.

"Didja see that?" he squeals. "Didja see them monkeys run? Think I winged one of 'em."

I don't justify his exuberance with a response, because idiocy does not deserve a reward. We're speeding at probably fifty down a narrow residential street, and he loses control of the car on a patch of ice. The car fishtails, does a 720 and I'm thinking *fitting* as the car slams into a parked hatchback. Impact throws me against the passenger-side window and I hear something crack. Actually, I hear a lot of things crack, but one is louder than the others. Turns out it's the window. My shoulder shattered the thing. Takes a second to refocus and I see I'm covered in tiny bits of glass, like I've been sprinkled with diamonds. Jackal's not moving or making any noise, and there's blood all over his face from where it bashed into the windshield and left behind a bloodied tuft of hair, but I can see he's breathing. Good enough. My door won't open, so I crawl out the window and over the hood of the car we hit. My right side hurts like a bitch, but my arm can move fine, so nothing's broken. As I take my first few steps I hear shards of glass tinkling as they fall from my clothes and land on the ice. Always the lucky one, me.

Limping away from the scene, I look for a street sign, but I can't find one. I'm on the crest of a small hill, and I can see all the way over downtown's lights and the Missouri River and into Iowa. A few defunct factories on the riverfront mar the view with their wretched metal mantislike towers and buildings. Hard to see any detail with the shitty light situation and all, but at least I know which way is east now. I hoof it northward about five blocks till I hit Leavenworth at 26th Street. Alone, busted up and freezing my fucking nuts off, I stop at a pay phone and call 911 like any responsible citizen does after witnessing an accident. The operator's disinterested voice repeats the vague details and tells me to wait for the police to arrive. You betcha, I tell her. I'm almost to 30th Street when I see the first cruiser speeding down the street.

Denny's the only person hanging out at HQ. Wearing all black, he's got a clove burning between his knuckles. Try to hide my limp, but my right leg hurts like a mother when I put any weight on it.

"Jack is not with you."

"You listen to that thing?" I point to the scanner.

"Occasionally." Denny draws on a clove.

"This evening?"

Denny shakes his innocent head.

"Jack," I say, "is going to be in some trouble."

"Is this better not spoken of?"

"Smart man, Denny. Bill here?"

"He was. He met two men and left with them."

"Two large gentlemen?"

"Yes, they were big."

"Nicely dressed?"

"Dark suits."

"He say if he's coming back?"

Denny cranes his neck over to the left. "His car is here, so I think he will be back."

"These guys he met, you ever seen them?"

"No, I have not."

"They say anything about 'Babylon'?"

"Nobody said anything except Bill. He said he would be back later."

"He mention names? Chumley? McKinley?"

"He did not."

"This was when?"

Checks his watch. "Twenty-three minutes ago."

"Bill look concerned? Worried? Nervous?"

"He always looks nervous."

"More than usual, then?"

"No, not more than usual."

"You ever use contractions?"

"I do not."

"Particular reason?"

"Yes."

"Wanna elaborate for me?"

"Not at the moment."

"I ask you something, you think you can give me a straight answer?"

"Possibly."

"You know anything about Bill buying houses?"

"I do not."

"Ever hear him mention a guy named Mather Grimes?"

"I have not."

"What about the guns?"

"What about them?"

"Why'd he stock up?"

"Self-defense in case we get into trouble out there. The police are not very quick to respond to 911 calls."

"You know your friends have been doing some bad shit, no?"

"I stay here and update the registry."

"Denny, you might wanna consider discontinuing your neighborhood watch membership. These fellas, they're gonna get in trouble. Hate to see something ugly befall you."

"I will take it under advisement."

And here I thought Denny and I were getting to be buddies. Executive decision time: wait it out or bail. Doesn't take but a second to decide on the latter. Don't wanna be around here when the troops reconvene and find out about the Snapper incident.

I express to Denny my heartfelt thanks for his candor and limp out to the Chevy. Hurting like I got worked over by a lumberjack, but I'm worried (yes, worried) about Bill. He's either duct-taped to a chair in the basement over at Babylon or he's getting worked over in one of his Babylon-protected houses. Fitting, the tragic coincidence of him getting his at a place of his own, so that's where I go.

I spot a white Ford parked in front of one of the WJC houses. Don't have a plan other than not to get myself fucked. Park around the corner and take my time getting over to the house. Quiet. No wind, even. Just the sound of my gimp-limping shoes on the gravel and rock salt. Clouded over, so maybe it'll snow tonight. Nary a house light burning. Single streetlight dies when I walk under it. Kicks back on when I pass. My mom used to say that's because of my guardian angel, floating above me.

House in question is dark and silent. I stand in the shadows across the street, looking for a flicker of life inside. Do that trick that ain't a trick for a while, give it up when my teeth start to chatter. What the fuck to do? Grab a chunk of concrete that's broken away from the rest of the sidewalk and chuck it through one of the windows. Duck behind a tree and listen to the satisfying sound of shattering glass.

Fingering the Zippo in my pocket like it might bring me luck. Maybe *luck*'s the wrong word. Fingering the Zippo like it might bring me two big dudes in suits running out of a house three doors down. Suitcoats unbuttoned so their shoulder holsters are visible. Takes a second, but I recognize them. Chumley and McKinley. They run up to the house, unlock the door and head in. Light inside kicks on, so I bring up the Canon and snap a few.

Hope the film's 3200. Too far away to hear what they're saying. Chumley points at what must be the concrete chunk I chucked. McKinley eyes the floor, pulls his gun and walks out of view.

Okay, so I'm thinking I've seen enough for tonight and I don't wanna end up, you know, dead on the street. Just about to walk away when a door opens behind Chumley. Looks like it's stairs to the basement. And who walks up? Luka. She's wearing this sleek black dress. Chain of pearls. Hair done up like she's going somewhere to be seen. So, what the fuck? Shoot a few exposures while she's gesticulating and looking righteously pissed. Talking fast to Chumley, and whatever it is she's saying must sting, because the guy's checking out his feet. In walks McKinley. She looks at him a second and slaps him—hard—across his mug. He's saying something, but stops when she starts poking his chest. Makes a big show of shaking her head, then walks back downstairs. McKinley jerks off his air dick and Chumley flips off the door with both hands. The pair of 'em stand around a few seconds more, then walk out and back down the street.

Make sure I'm outta sight till they pass. So, here I stand, behind a tree, wondering what the fuck what I just saw means, exactly. Other than the obvious, that Luka, whoever the fuck she is, isn't remotely what she's pretended to be.

Plan is, I'm thinking I'll go get some coffee and come back in a little. Make it late and hope everyone's gone to bed. Figure they'll have the window fixed up tomorrow, so, if ever there was a time . . .

Walk way outta my way to get back to the car. Don't wanna risk getting spotted now. That'd be, oh, painful, I imagine. Coming up on the Chevy and something doesn't look right about it. Like it's off-kilter. Which it is. Because both driver's-side tires have been slashed. Note stuck beneath the wiper—photocopy of a page of notes. *My* notes. Not from my notebook, it's some connecting-the-dots thing I scrawled out a few days ago. Written along the top in shaky, old-man handwriting is *Good work, paperboy.* I swallow, dry and hard enough that I can hear it. Drop the note and reach for my keys. Something hard and cold comes crashing down on my head. On my knees wondering if a tooth maybe cut through my lip. Round two up top before the lights go out.

twenty-two

Sounding aqueous, this voice.

"Do it again."

Something warm brushes my mouth. Click and a buzz. Guys laughing. Cold and wet all over. Sour-smelling musk. Open one eye. Then the other. No glasses, so things aren't clear. This a bordello I'm in? Red-tinted lights. Mirrors. Red furniture.

"Morning, sunshine." Got it. Luka.

"Madame," I say. Shift my weight. Hurting all over. Where the fuck? Four people, looks like, standing across the room. Squinting like it's gonna help.

"Give him his glasses," Luka says. Hulking mass walks over and slides them on my face. Right lens is cracked. Luka sits next to me. She's still all done up. I look around, and two of the guys I recognize—Chumley and McKinley. Looking like they're trying not to giggle. Third guy, he's old, bald, wearing a three-piece navy number with a yellow kerchief in the breast pocket. My Canon slung around his neck. Got these tiny wire-rimmed glasses perched on his pug nose. Hands clasped in front of his crotch like he's protecting something, looking rather pleased.

"Mister Grimes, I presume," I say.

"The pleasure's mine," he says, all squawk.

"You can get up," Luka says. "Take a look around if you want."

Head's scrambled. Flashes of standing outside. Shooting pictures. Getting cracked over the head. "The fuck?" I mumble.

"Told you to back off, didn't I?"

I grunt.

"But you didn't, did you?"

Can't quite focus on her.

"Bring over that mirror." She's smiling big and mirthful while one of the big dudes—which one is he? Chumley? McKinley? —hauls over a full-length mirror. Fancy job with a carved wood frame. The scene within that frame, though, it's fucked. Picture this: lipstick, rouge and blue eye shadow. Teardrop drawn in next to my left eye. Purple gown. Lace collar. Gaudy gold brooch. Still wearing my black socks.

"Looking sharp," Luka says. "Ready for a night out, I'd say."

Gown's soaked in something pungent. Sticks to me when I sit up. Peel it away from my chest and it leaves a cold, thin film on my skin.

"Urine," says Mather in his grating squawk. "Mine."

"Normally at least get a handjob before I let someone piss on me."

"You got more than that." He winks and shakes the camera.

"Can I go now?" I ask.

"Afraid not."

Chumley and McKinley, they set up shop. One on either side of me. Luka moves to a new seat and lights a cigarette.

Thinking I should test the waters with these juveniles. "Back in the day, you fuck those boys or just play bottom for 'em?"

"Hit him," Mather says. "But not hard."

McKinley's meaty fist plows into my stomach. Black out for a second.

"Next time," I say between painful hacks, "get me in the nuts, wouldja?"

"Give him what he wants."

Two-man effort. McKinley picks me up like the nothing I am. Got my feet dangling a couple inches above the floor. Chumley struts over and delivers a jab to my nuts that sends spiny bolts of pain up through my chest. Holds me a second longer, throws me onto the couch. Breathing heavy and trying to sit up straight. Throbbing all over. Feels like my skull's contracting at the temples.

"You were babbling while you were out," Mather says, then he stands there, mute.

I let that stand a while. "This the part where you tell me what I was talking about, right?"

He rolls out his lower lip and strokes his chin. "I'm thinking that purple isn't really your color."

"Is it anyone's?"

"True," he says. "Very true."

"So, can I go *now?*"

Luka tosses me a cigarette and a book of matches. "Get comfy," she says.

"It'd help if someone could tinkle on me again." Light the cigarette and drop the burning match on my dress. Flame dies with a pungent whisper.

"That's an expensive item you're trying to ruin." Squawk squawk.

"Can we cut the shit, *bitte schön?*"

Mather lifts up the Canon and snaps another. Flashbulb goes off in the corner.

"Your studio?" I ask.

"One of them. Process the film right there." He thumbs over his shoulder at a metal door. "My clientele demand discretion."

"Junior, who you trying to kid with this garage sale degenerate shit? You think anyone's going to sign up for minor league malfeasance in some shit setup in a shit part of town?"

"They're lining up."

"And paying?"

He nods, captain satisfaction.

"Anyone I know?"

"You've probably voted for a couple of them."

"I try not to," I say. "Vote."

"You should. It's necessary for a healthy democracy."

I scope the scene. Bordello, true, but with a KKK newsletter fringe: badly Photoshopped eight-by-tens of J. Edgar in drag, a grainy late-seventies porno still with JFK's pixilated mug rubber stamped onto some tattooed junkie in a sailor hat, and I can't begin to do justice to the myriad depictions of Clinton/monkey congress. Jesse Jackson, too, features prominently on this wall of puerile satire. And then, by the door? *Lolita* movie poster and a glossy of someone probably famous, though fuck if I can place him. So I ask.

"Roman Polanski," Mather says.

"So you're back in business." I venture. "And Luka here, she's in on the ground floor."

Mather looks perplexed.

"Told him that's my name," she says.

Which wins an understanding nod from Mather.

"Girl I grew up with. She's dead," not-Luka says.

"So," I say, "you are?"

"I don't see how that matters," says Mather.

"You go to British villain school or some bullshit?"

"Close. Exeter."

I finger my gown. "This really your piss?"

"Undoubtedly."

"Think you can tell me where I am?"

"Babylon, of course."

"Looks like a third-rate hillbilly whorehouse."

"Trash. It's this room's theme. I thought you'd appreciate it."

"So, there are others?"

"Several."

"Thematically different?"

"Ancient Roman, Wild West, hospital examining room, locker room." Sounding bored, this old man.

"And we're where? Baron Square?"

"No. That's a legitimate project. Do you remember the houses you were so curious about that you were warned to stay away from?"

"Got it." Underground—literally—fuckpads. I can almost dig how cheesy that is.

"If I had it my way, things would be different," Mather says. "But you have to cater to your demographic, and my people like to feel like they're being very, very bad."

"Which they would be, right?"

"And, it's so farcical that nobody'd believe it if rumors were to spread." He snaps his fingers like he's remembering something splendid. "Franklin, fetch me the carton."

McKinley walks into the other room. Light inside is red, so maybe they do process film in there. Comes out a second later carrying a small file box. Sets it at Mather's feet.

"The contents," he says. "Care to guess?"

I'm thinking a cartoon cat or some bullshit might hop out

of the box and dance a jig. Why the fuck not? "Notes. Mine."

Guy looks pleased. "That's correct." Removes the lid and shows me inside. Photocopies I've made. Notebooks. Scraps of paper with my scrawl on them. Rolls of unprocessed negatives. "I must say, I'm rather impressed." He plucks a sheet from the box. "You've industriously and wisely predicted NüCorp's expansion into the Twin Cities."

"More fuckpads there, too?"

"If there were, you wouldn't be so lucky as to stumble across them like you did here."

"I'm rather adept at stumbling."

"As are most drunks."

"Dig your rejoinders. So can I take my notes and leave now?"

He drops the paper back into the box and replaces the lid. Puts his foot on it, looking like he might plant a fucking flag at his feet. "Afraid not."

"Suppose you're going to burn them, right? Big dramatic production?"

"Actually, no. The ventilation down here isn't quite what I would like it to be. I think I'll end up shredding it all. Perhaps even have it recycled."

"Very PC."

"You know how it is, being in politics." He theatrically sighs, then chuckles. Squawks, rather.

"I'm curious," I say. "You've got her pretending to be a hooker—"

"Not pretending, exactly," she says. "I used to be. Years ago. How we met."

"I like to slum it," Mather says. "But, this one"—he strokes her head—"she's something special."

"Heartwarming."

"I wanted to have you killed before you came to," Mather said. "But she wouldn't let me."

"Mighty white of you, ma'am."

My smoke's down to the butt, so I yank it from my lacerated lips and flick it at Mather. Arcs toward him, bounces off his lapel and falls into my notes. Mather brushes off the ash, saying, "Hit him again." I'm clobbered from behind. Teeth rattling and I bite off a chunk of tongue. Hurts like a motherfucker and my mouth's filling with blood. Spit out a tongue chunk. Bloody. Hurt in my mouth is the only thing I feel.

"My girlfriend hits me harder." Sounding like I've got a mouthful of cotton balls. Warm blood, thinned by my spit, leaks down my chin.

Luka says, "I'm bored. Hurry up and let's get dinner already."

Mather reaches into his pocket and pulls out this twin-barreled Derringer. Chromed. Little gun, but it's got a big bore I'm staring down. "On your knees, please."

"Oh, can you go fuck yourself already? Please?" Too tired to be scared. Maybe too scared to know what I'm doing. Maybe this is too comical to be taken seriously; here, now, at this late hour, a gun. Probably a flag's going to pop out. *Pow!* it'll say.

"Help him out, boys," Luka says.

Which they do. One stands me up, the other kicks out my legs from behind. Once they have me down, the old guy, he takes the three steps over and holds the gun to my forehead. It's warmer than I think it oughta be. Faint smell of cordite. So maybe no little flag.

"If you want to beg, blah blah blah," Luka deadpans.

Spit a spray of blood for giggles. I could almost think this is amusing if I weren't bleeding. Thinking perhaps my survival instinct is defective, along with my paternal. Lean forward and look up at him. See a distended reflection of myself in his glasses, bruised and dolled up, thinking, whoever woulda thought it'd come to this? Watching the tendons in his forearm rise as he slowly increases the pressure on the trigger. Wondering why my life isn't flashing before me. All I've got is nothing. A big fat fucking void. Fuck, I'd think at least I'd see Allison. Can't even picture her. Mom, Dad—ditto. Manny, even? Nope. Just me, on my knees, puckering up for the big kiss. Biggest story I'll ever have, and I'm gonna be, at best, some daily hack's blotter brief. *Omaha police are investigating the shooting death of an asshole found yesterday in a vacant lot near 30th & Pacific Streets. He is survived by no one and nobody gives a fuck, anyway.* Then: bang. Loud. Head feeling like I got clobbered with a clawhammer. Try to scream, but what comes out is this thin screech like when a rabbit dies. Dazed. Left ear feels like it's on fire. Reach for it, but an apeman muscles my hand down to the floor at the old guy's feet. Loafers. Nice shine. Seeing tracers, hearing echoes. Voice coming down on me as if through a fan. *Which one?* Another explosion. Hole in my hand. Blood spatter on my glasses and in my mouth. Need to puke, but I fall forward instead. Fetal, howling, spitting, bleeding, heaving. Laughter as I black out.

twenty-three

Must've moved me. Come to in a different room. Splayed out on a dirt floor, drowning in pain. Gauze, heavy with blood, taped tightly on my left hand. Ears aren't working like they oughta. Still wearing that fucking gown. Least it's dry now. Wishing, really, the fucker just woulda put one in my brain. Not like the plan is to fuck with me and then let me loose. Try to sit up, but anything beyond blinking, it ain't exactly gonna happen.

"You're up, then."

I'm thinking it's time for round two, so I extend the middle finger on the hand that works and wave it indiscriminately.

"You wanted the tour, you got it."

Jaw's locked up, so I can't say *the fuck*?

A couple feet appear in my narrow field of vision. Blurry, me sans glasses and them being farther away than six inches.

"Can you move?"

I grunt my "No."

"They did a number on you. Here."

I feel my head being lifted. Left ear burns like a mother-fucker. Something's very wrong with it. Guy slips on my glasses.

Recoil in pain and wretch when he touches my ear. Refocus, and I see it's Bill. He's been worked over. Black eyes, crusted blood over busted lips.

"Can you hear this?" He reaches over by my fucked-up ear. I see his forearm move and hear his finger snapping, but not like I oughta. I shake my head.

"Your ear's damn near gone."

Gunshot at point blank, it'll do that, plus shatter an eardrum. If I get outta here, maybe I'll qualify for some sort of disability.

"Your hand—that from an ice pick?"

I make a gun with my good hand, point it at my bad hand and my bad ear.

"And your mouth?"

Show him a fist.

He nods, looking like a jackass in his BDUs and jungle boots, nevermind both are Vietnam-era surplus and it's winter in Omaha. Course, I'm wearing a piss-soaked evening gown.

He rubs his hands together. "So, how are we getting out of here?"

Thinking I might give talking a shot. "Where are we?" Bad idea. Serious pain.

"Long story short? Somewhere beneath the 2700 block of Pacific. Those houses I bought? Mather's got 'em all hooked up underground. For his parties."

I must look incredulous, because Bill continues. "Really. Didn't want his name attached to it, legally. Made me a sweet offer to be the middleman for site acquisition. Then he got pretty sketched out when James and Creighton got arrested, said I had to cut them loose." Here, he starts digging his boot toe into the dirt. "And you saw what happened there. James lost it. Creighton, well."

Even if I could talk, I'd stay quiet here. He's got more to say. Give him all the dead air he wants. The silence'll get to him, and he'll start up again.

"Thought I'd make some money."

Am I the only one who doesn't see anything fucking wrong with being lower middle class? Gesture to him to shut the fuck up. Don't wanna be pissed at the guy who's going to share my shallow grave. Yeah: *my*.

Check my watch. Timex is covered in blood. Scrape it away and see it's Sunday night, little after nine. Allison's moved her shit out by now. Nobody's gonna wonder where I'm at till tomorrow afternoon, earliest. Can't help but wonder if I'm imagining this whole ridiculous, impossible, preposterous setup. Maybe I'm really in a drunken stupor somewhere. Shit like this doesn't *really* happen. And especially not in fucking Omaha to fucking me.

"My guys, if they knew where we were, they could rescue us." He walks toward the door, knocks on it. Steel. "No breaking through here. Plan was to smuggle in some Mexicans, get 'em fake papers and have 'em start day-care centers upstairs. Totally legit, and it'd be better than working in the plants. Fine, I said. Let's get it done. And then Creighton and James messed up." He gnaws on his pinky. Spits out a shred of nail.

"Why guns?" Something that'd clotted tears open. Blood oozing out of my tongue. Fuck it. Just leave my mouth hanging open and let it run. Bill cringes. He faces the wall and starts talking.

"That was before. Wanted to scare off the dealers and prostitutes. Figured the cops can't do it by the rules, so we'd do it our way. Then that whore got her hooks in me, introduced me to Mister Grimes. You know the rest."

Cute, that he still calls him Mister. Think I might even be grinning.

"Anyway, there's your story." Few seconds later, he starts laughing. Light at first, but it builds, as if there's something really fucking hilarious going on here. "Happy? You got what you want. I just wanted to make some money." Pauses to wipe away those tears of joy. "Get a bigger house, take the kid to Disneyland this summer. You? Just doing your job. Your friggin' job."

If I could, I'd tell him it's all I have. That, and an apartment empty save the sagging bed in it. But I can't. So I don't.

"Jerk." Not laughing anymore. "Asshole." Getting steamed. "I could just . . ."

I try to say *What?* and make this fucked-up gurgle noise instead that sounds like *cunt.*

He balls his fists and punches the door. Hard. Gotta hurt. He throws another punch and I look down. Drenched in filth. Wearing this fucking dress. Probably still slathered with lipstick and shit. Don't see it coming when he kicks me in the jaw. Knocks me over and my vision flashes, dims, flashes again. Pain off the fucking charts. A shrill scream fills my working ear. Watch the gore splash against the wall, its dripping descent to the ground, the floor grit eating into my cheek. Heave, and bile shoots out. Burns like a fucking crucible. Bill goes to work on my kidneys with those boots, grunting out: *Mother. Fucker.* Over and over, syncopated to fit with the abuse. Shoulda taken a bullet in the brain. Kicking ceases long enough for me to hear a familiar squawk.

"William, stop."

Starts up again, faster now and he's screaming nonsense. Loud bang and it stops. He falls over me. Limp, heavy and a smoking hole where his left eye used to be. One eye that's left, it's open, staring at me. Strange thing: it winks.

Sound of shuffling feet getting louder. I'm moaning, hoping

he does it quick. Cross-eyed staring at a set of loafered feet. "Shit," I hear him mutter.

"Can you hear me?"

I nod. I think.

"I didn't mean to do that." He sounds just short of sorry. Like he might even *mean* it. "I intended to miss."

Shrug and wait a long minute. Hearing heavy breathing. Eventually, he kneels, holding what looks like a sheaf of paper. "Do you know what this is?"

Don't answer. He continues. "It's an insurance policy. Not a traditional policy, more a gentlemen's agreement." He sets a sheet on the ground in front of me. Black and white of me, dolled up before I got shot up, with a dick in my mouth. Dick's attached to a kid can't be older than sixteen, putting on a show with my head in his hands. Big hoop earrings. Right: kid Luka was chatting up at Maggie's. My bloody drool dribbles onto the dirt. "As I'm sure you've guessed, I have the negatives. I'm willing to make you a deal—I'll arrange it so you're found in your totaled car. One-car accident. Maybe you went out for a drive and fell asleep. Car careens off the road into a ditch. Familiar scenario for you. Here's the difference—you live. Very convenient way to explain away the injuries you've sustained, I'd say. All I ask in return is you forget about this place."

Can he see me extend that faithful middle finger of mine?

"I applaud your spirit, Mister Cockburn."

Which he correctly pronounces.

"But I'd caution you against making rash decisions after the day you've had. I'll check in tomorrow." He drops the rest of the prints and leaves me. Kills the light after closing the door so I can't watch the pool of brains and blood ooze toward my face. Try to squirm away when I feel the warm slop against my cheek, but I'm weak, down here in the fetid dark. Can't muster the muscle to shove off the dead weight. Black as pitch in here. Hear the occasional drip and I might be starting to lose my shit, half hearing the scrabble of rat claws on the dirt floor as the vermin surround me. Haven't felt any nibbles, so it's gotta be in what's left of my head. Thinking even if I make it out of here, I'm fucked. As if Mather'd let us go our separate ways. As if I'd go, anyway. He knows it. This is sport to the fucker.

Jesus. Need to get my head together. Throat's dry. Feels like it's bleeding. A twisted, constricted ball of pain, me. Less so than my dead companion. Almost wanna switch spots. Fuck almost. I do. Close my eyes and there ain't a difference anyway. Focus and see if I can't just disconnect.

twenty-four

My version of a Hail Mary: count to five, bite my lip and give
it hell shoving off the body. First time, count to four and get
psyched out when I move my fucked-up hand. Howl through
the pain. Soon as it dies down a notch, I kick and shove, getting
ripped to shreds, seeing black and red and the screaming in my
ear and the hot blood gushing are mine but the cold, thick slop
dripping and sticking aren't. Wet *thump* and it's done—he's there
in a puddle of his own and I'm here on my side, hyperventilating
in a dark world all my own.

Dense smell of blood rot. Head's burning. Fever sweat
scorching my face. Hear it drip, the pitter patter I'll never hear.

Suck. Exhale. Crying or laughing or both. Blink. Blink. Keep
'em closed and make a wish: Get me out. Please.

Creaking hinges and a blade of light cuts across the floor. Bill,
his emptied head beaucoup spotlit. Footsteps, soft. Form blocks
out the light.

"Jesus fuck," she says. "He did *not*."

Silence.

"Well? Where's the other one?"

"In there."

"Where? I don't see him."

"Didn't come out this way."

"I'm not going in there. Bring him out here."

"The body?"

"No, retard, not the body."

"What if he's dead, too?"

Pause. "He's too stupid to go that easy."

I grunt.

"See?" she says. "Bring him out."

Meaty set of rough paws shove beneath my armpits and drag me into the hall. More dirt. Metal beams above. Luka, casual now. Chumley, in his permasuit, needing a dry cleaning.

"Get lost," she says, and he does. She kneels down over me, and I can almost make out her features. Pink blur in a blue top.

"I'm not here to help you," she says, "so don't get all hopeful. Can you talk?"

Shake.

"Looks like you're ten minutes away from that." She points into the room. "But in my dress."

Had forgotten about that.

"You're curious about me, aren't you? Why I'm here, what you're in the middle of. Probably think you've got it figured out, don't you? Be honest."

Nod.

"You're half right at best. This is going to be the one that got away."

Shake.

"Mather's going to come down here in another half hour or so, and when he does, you're going to take that deal he offered. He'll stick to it if you do. But, if you try to fuck with him, ever, you're dead. And, if you're as smart as you think, you'll get your girl out of his building. He can be"—she hesitates—"erratic. You get me?"

Nod.

"Good boy. He asks if you have a deal, you say yes. Then you're out. He's got your car all arranged, and I'll put in an anonymous 911 call, so in another couple hours, you should be in the ER. Fuck up, you'll be in the ground. And he'll probably have your girl put next to you for good measure."

Nod.

"I told you to stay away." She pulls from her pocket a tiny syringe and jams it into my neck. Burns for a second, but I'm numbed out by the time she stands. I hear her say something to Chumley, ends with *gently*.

He doesn't heed her. Drags me back into the room by my feet. Clawing at the dirt, futile as it is pathetic. Gives me a taste of his Rockports before he leaves. Lights on. Don't even hurt anymore. Goofy. Smiling.

Sweating it out in here. Shakes. Maybe I shoulda done it different. Allison the only one left to miss me, and maybe she won't. It's wrong of me to want to see her again. It is. Where to begin with that? Where to end? Don't care. Warm all over and I feel like I oughta atone or stocktake, but I got squat: another square with nothing to show.

Tracers and motion blur when my eyes move. Feeling heavy, sunken. Damaged hand is bright red. Poke the bandage, watch the pus leak. Reach my right hand behind my left ear and snap my fingers. Nothing doing. Funny, I guess. Crippled and I don't have the story. Worth every dollar Manny pays me.

"You've considered my offer and have come to a decision, I trust."

Mather. He'd've startled me if I was capable of being surprised right now. Shoot him a thumbs-up. Trying to focus on him. Changed clothes. Looks like he's about to hit the links.

"Am I correct to assume you've chosen to take me up on my generosity?"

Keep wagging that thumb. He's got something in his hand. Lead pipe, maybe. World's Best Dad trophy? Shiny, small, cylindrical. Not a gun. He waves it.

"This? I nearly forgot. Are you in pain?"

Lie. Nod an affirmative.

"She thought you might be, even after the morphine." He crouches down in front of me. Junior bottle of Smirnoff. Telling me he knows that I know that he knows. "Think this might help?"

Booze is going to kill when it hits the mangled gash that is my tongue, but I'm nodding.

"Open up. That's a good boy."

Quick spike of dry pain. Largely muted. Can't taste the juice, but I can smell it. Swallow and open up for more. He touches the bottle lightly to my shredded lips and pours in another jolt. The wall shakes, an ominous rumbling above. He must see me look up.

"Traffic," he says. "Most likely a bus." Gives me another mouthful. "You're going to have to get good and drunk. I think it'll make the accident look better. What do you think? More authentic? You should know."

Wish he'd stop asking me these asinine questions I can't answer.

"The blood work will show you were intoxicated and on opiates at the time of the crash. It's amazing to me, the coincidences here." He burps a truncated giggle. "You'll just have to say the last thing you remember is leaving the apartment in a huff after fighting with your girlfriend over her pregnancy. Allison, isn't it? Building 4, apartment 3B. A little heavy for my taste, but I can see what she'd do for someone like you." He looks over at Bill's body. Coughs. "Okay, in it goes."

Another shot. He takes a pull. Wall shakes. Hard. A clump of dirt falls from the ceiling. Mather doesn't seem to think this is alarming. Maybe nothing is, down here.

"You're a little rough around the edges, but nothing I couldn't sand down. If I had a use for you, I'd put you on the payroll. I think you'd find the accommodations a bit more comfortable than that hole you call an office. Great benefits, as well. Right now, for example, I'm on my way to Havana. And I do so like to travel with company. That time in prison, as you probably know, I was in minimum security, but my colleagues? Simpletons. There was a time when I ran with the big dogs. It's true. Senators. I procured for the most powerful man in the world a sixteen-year-old Negroid boy. An Afro, he wanted. Africa medallion around his neck. And I delivered." Deep, wistful breath. "Granted, he was only veep then. But, still. Even locally—the mayor, that drunken louse, all he wants is blond 'tang. Young, eager to please. Can do. Uncreative, but I do what I can to make my clients feel like they want." Here he pauses, as if to give me the chance to ask him to continue. "And how they want to feel is untouchable. They can have all the money in the world, but what good is it if they have to abide by the same rules you do? They're better than you. They know it. You know it. I certainly know it. I just happen to facilitate the manifestation of that notion in a physically gratifying manner."

Feeling booze-woozy. Close my eyes for a second. Herculean lid lifting. Ugly motherfucker holding this shit vodka to my maw. Take a swing at his wrinkled puss. Comically slow and off target.

He puts down the bottle. "What did she tell you her name was? Luka, right? Disgusting name she picked. She said you'd be trouble from that first time she spoke to you. She wanted to disappear, but I thought I could use her with you. Have you clear up a problem or two for me." He gestures back at the body. "Unfortunately, I was wrong." Sip. "But, I'm a very old man and these knees aren't what they used to be, so I'm going to stand up now and take my leave. Chumley and McKinley will be in momentarily. And then all of this"—he holds out his arms and does a 360—"it'll be demolished and filled in by the time you come to. These houses will be torn down or torched and then it'll be like nothing ever happened." He tosses the bottle to me. Hits the dirt near my feet and skids to my hand. "Remember, Mr. Cockburn, I'm doing you a large favor here." He winks as I grab the booze. Wait for him to turn and then chuck it. Hits him hard at the base of his skull, and I must be way more fucked up than I thought, because it sounds like an avalanche as he stumbles, then falls. Rumbling above, the walls and floor shaking, Mather mumbling, grabbing his head. Dirt falling in streams, then clumps. This wretched screaming, nightmare tearing noise and the roof caves in the hallway. Mather rolling over, pulling his Derringer. Unsteady, wavering. Hole opens up above and the light pours in. Industrial motor noise. Yelling. *What the fuck? Back it up!* Scrabble backward as another chunk of ceiling crashes down. Metal support skeleton still standing. *The fuck is that?* Hard hats looking down. My yell drowned. Claw at the wall, drooling waving grab me now fuckers. I-beam drops, nails Mather's shoulder. He crumbles. Drops. Two pops, loud. Knocked back, chest burning, feel the blood rush.

twenty-five

What they've told me is this:

I'm at St. Joe's.

I should rest.

They being nurses. Been here fuck knows how long. Day. Maybe two. Left hand's bandaged tight, but it's still attached. No dearth of gauze and plaster on my person. Wrapped around my head. Curtains separate me from the other unfortunates in this ward, the specialty of which I know not. General trauma. Nearly wasted waste-cases. One-off fucktools. Whatever it is, the nurses don't really give a fuck and only appear long enough to jam a thermometer in my not-fucked ear, give me my pills and scribble on my chart. Curt smile and a rote *I'm sorry* when I ask what the fuck. Been keeping tabs on them. Walk-throughs every fifteen minutes, but I only get visited every two hours. One due any minute, actually. Hope it's the mean old lady. Sorta dig her and her moles. She appears on cue.

"Myrtle," I say. Still hurts to talk, but I've felt worse. What bugs is my audible impediment. Lispy now. Rather embarrassing. Can't use *s*'s now. Or, should I say, *etheth*.

"Ethel."

"Think I can get a paper?"

"I'll bring one next time I stop by." Jams a thermometer in my ear.

"Told me that already."

"I'm busy."

"I'm pissed." *Pithed.* Blood fills my face. Hot.

She twists out the instrument. Looks at it disgustedly and drops the plastic cover into the biohazard garbage can. "I'll send over an orderly to change your sheets."

"Would it really fucking kill to bring me a paper?"

"Would it really kill you to tell me your name?"

"Memory might get jogged if I had a paper to read."

"Think you'll be in it?"

"Maybe."

She hands me my pills in their little plastic cup and writes on my chart. *Patient is, as usual, a speech impediment-suffering fuckhead,* or so I imagine. She pulls the sheet up to my chin and taps the end of my nose. "You're going to have a visitor, so behave."

"When?"

"Soon as I'm done with my rounds and give her the okay."

Her. "No way. I'm too fucked up."

"Take your pills."

"Am I under guard? Cops hanging around?"

"Planning your great escape?"

"Could be."

"Take your pills."

Dry-swallow 'em. Good stuff, these. Few minutes, I'll be feeling no pain.

"Be nice to her. She looks upset."

As I assume Allison would. Who the fuck knows what the

cops told her. Probably had her in the interrogation room, typewriter cover over her face, slapping her with a phone book, screaming about how she better tell them the fucking truth. Brutes.

Or not, actually. Ethel doesn't know who I am, so she wouldn't know who to call. Unless, of course, the cops divined the identity of Mr. Doe and tracked her down. Though the boys in blue (black, technically) haven't stopped by to wish me good tidings and a speedy recovery. A peculiar lack of activity on that front, which worries me. That hammer's gotta fall. Or they'd send out an investigator to pitch me closed-ended questions, the responses to which could only make the department look faultless—spin it so the dead cops were working undercover, is my guess. As the only swinging dick left to provide a story that corroborates their sievelike explanation, I'd have to also be clean and shiny as a freshly minted nickel.

Visitor, then, is probably Donna. Sent to pick me up and whisk me out of here. If this scenario doesn't have the jejune tenor of wishful thinking, I don't fucking know what.

So, then, it's either Allison or Luka. Luka, who is presumably either dead or jammed up in another bed somewhere in the hospital, hopefully comatose.

In any case, I jimmy up the covers with my right (read: good) hand. Cover as much of my banged-up exterior as possible. Don't want whoever to see me looking so weak and vulnerable. Can't hide the catheter.

Groans further down the ward. Ceiling tiles full of tiny perforations. Same pattern on each. Thinking I'd kneecap a nun for a cigarette because that's simpler than trying to anticipate what I'm going to do if Allison walks in (she won't) and sees this damaged version of me. It's possible I'll get, say, emotional. Might not, and then feel remorseful about not feeling the way I think a person should. Feeling guilty about not feeling bad (or being overwhelmed at the prospect of an imminent redemption, but, truly, fuck that; redemption's the province of believers and amateurs) is not the proper state for a person to be in. At least not a person pissing through a tube.

I fucking hate being here. Nothing to do but think, and then poke holes in my thinking. Granted, I'm not strapped down, so I could yank out the catheter and the sensors wired hither and yon, but I'm so fucking hobbled I doubt I'd make it to the door before the orderlies arrived. And then there's the issue of clothing, in that I have none other than this glorified Kleenex robe. At least it's not purple.

Feminine throat clearing at the foot of the bed. Let my eyes drift down, and there she stands: not Allison. Luka. Three-hundred-dollar jeans (not that I know what three-hundred-dollar jeans look like, but these sure as shit aren't Levi's) and a black cashmere sweater. Objectively, not looking half bad. Feel my mouth go slack. Appearing, I'm sure, like a kid on Christmas morning finding that not only is there nothing under the tree, but the tree's been torched.

"You can't be surprised."

I reach for the nurse call button, and she lightly bats my hand, because we're such good fucking pals and all. "Knock it off. I'm disappearing in a little bit."

"Where to? Havana? Minneapolis?"

"Maybe Havana. Somewhere warm, for sure. Hate this fucking place. That apartment Mather put me up in? That disgusting pit? He insisted, thought it'd be *authentic*. Even got me that goddamned cat."

"You're not putting a pillow over my face. I can only assume you're here to make nice."

"Why would I do that?" All coy.

"Why the fuck you here, then."

"Curious."

"About?"

"Nothing."

"We hafta play?"

"What else you gotta do in here? Other than rot?" She fingers my catheter tube.

"Cut the shit. Cops are gonna come knocking and I still have a story to write." *Thtory to write.* Asshole.

"You gonna sound like that forever?"

"Gimme my thtory." Exaggerate cause I can. Figure if I'm poking fun, it'll be less appealing for her to do so. Freakshow.

"Sorry to say, but it's not yours anymore."

"Daily got it?"

"TV, too. Sorta. Your paper even ran something on it. Nobody got it right, of course."

"Who wrote it? Pete? Manny?" I think, but don't say, Donna.

"I don't know. Someone."

Useless. "What's the official version?"

"EPA was out replacing a yard and the backhoe hit a massive sinkhole. Foundation cracked and the basement wall collapsed, killing four and one damn near."

"Two cops, plus Mather and Dunkel?"

Nods. Checks her watch.

"Cops keeping a lid on it?"

"Trying."

"How'd you get out?"

"I wasn't there. Whole thing caved in. Cops are all over the place. Cave-in was pretty impressive. They're still digging out and haven't found the tunnels and everything else yet. But they will pretty soon, I bet."

"How long till they get torched or whatever? The houses?"

"I would've thought by now, but it's more difficult than I guessed it would be."

Arson. 'Tis a bitch.

"You still gonna write the story?"

"Maybe. Doubt it." True and true. "You wanna tell me some stuff I don't know? Makes for good texture."

"Like?"

"Fuck, I don't care. Where you're from. How this whole idiot scheme got cooked up. Why I ended up with a pisstube rammed up my dog."

"Ran away when I was thirteen. Did the homeless kid circuit downtown—bus station, warehouse squats, worked the clubs. One night, I'm working this old guy at the Diamond and this kid comes up to me, asks if I wanna make some real money. Sure, I say. He's not even old enough to shave and he's driving this black Jag. Cool, I think."

"Cigarette?"

She hands me a Parliament from the pack in her purse. Odd little bastard. Recessed filter. Ferret it away beneath my mattress.

"Takes me to Mather. Says he runs parties for rich guys. Really rich guys. Powerful. Gives me this big speech about the business he runs, it's so far out there, nobody'd believe it if someone snitched, but these rich guys, they get off on it, you know, doing whatever just because they can. So I'm in, fucking senators and the like couple nights a week, boatloads of cash in my pocket at the end of the night. Some of 'em wanted to get abused. Kicked, burned with cigarettes, liquor enemas, told they were maggot shit-eaters. Those were my favorites. Anyway, everything's going along fine, then Mather gets audited."

"And everything goes to shit."

"Like roaches when the light comes on, everyone scatters and disappears. He's not the snitching type, right? So he does his white-collar time, gets out and lays low. Moves to Brazil and burns through most of what he had squirreled away. So, what's he do?"

"Only thing he knows."

"Right. Meantime, I'd split town, been living in Seattle doing a bunch of nothing. Reading. Learned the violin. Got a parakeet, but it died. Anyway, Mather finds me, says he's starting his parties again, do I want in halfsies? Sure, I say. This was a couple years ago. Right? So he's gotta raise some funds and he cooks up this real estate deal. Digs it because his seed money is from Uncle Sam. Said it was payback. Whatever. Stop me if you know all this."

"Keep going."

"Problem is this neighborhood watch is very active. They're around all the time, on foot, in their cars. He's getting invited to meetings, getting sent welcome to the neighborhood fruit baskets. Morons think he's the best thing ever 'cause he's helping revitalize the neighborhood."

"Which is where you come in."

"Get close to them, he says, so we can control them. So I start playing hooker. That part I told you about how I met Bill?"

"R-I-P, by the way." Rewind the tape to that dead eye winking. Depending on how you count it, he's somewhere between my third and eighth. The two girls—certainly. Korbes—maybe. Mather—shouldn't count because he's an asshole. Chumley and

McKinley—ditto. Mom—debatable. Dad—coulda been averted.

"Sad, but, yeah. That was true. So I'm operating him, he's operating his gang, and Mather's thinking, okay, it's time to start up again."

"Then you run into me."

"There you have it."

"Why here?"

"Why not? Nobody gives a fuck what goes on here. And who'd think Mather'd be dumb enough to do it again, and here, of all places? But he's got the town in his pocket. City Hall." Sticks out one finger. "So no trouble with building permits and one hell of a sweetheart deal on financing the land and construction costs." Sticks out another finger. "Cops. But it's the little things that always bite you in the ass."

"You gonna tell me your real name?"

"You really gonna write your story?"

"Give it a try, but everything I had got buried." I'm not sure if this is a lie or a sick sort of optimism.

"Guess that'd be a problem, huh?"

"Pretty much."

"Hope you don't get fired."

"Or arrested."

"Guy like you? You'd do well in prison. Work in the library or something." She straightens out my sheet. "Met your girl, by the way. In the hallway. She's cute."

"How's she know I'm here?"

Not-Luka laughs. Certainly not sincere, but not patronizing, either. Sheepish. "Guess she wouldn't know that, huh?"

"Not unless someone told her."

"Relax," she says, "don't want you to have a heart attack. She's not here. Just fucking with you."

That she feels she has the liberty to fuck with me bothers me.

"Oh, those photos? Ones with that kid's dick in your mouth?" Like an afterthought.

I start to burn.

"Shredded. Burned the negatives. You're golden."

"Have my wallet, by chance?"

"Here." She fishes another cigarette from her pack. "One for the road."

"I'm not going anywhere."

"You should." Linger, linger. Ever the dude, I expect her to lean down and kiss me. Instead, she twitches her mouth, lifts an eyebrow and says, "Well, bye." One pathetic pat on the forearm, and off she goes. Hear her heels clack their way down the hall. Elevator dings, and then all's quiet except the electronic beeps from the machines hooked up to me and my wardmates. Try to find a rhythm, but, of course, there isn't one.

Matters not, I suppose, because the drugs are taking hold. Feel it first in my eyes, that boozy, swimming looseness. The word *unmoored* comes to mind, right before I start thinking of all the pop songs about everything and everyone being all right.

Could be it's the drugs, but I think I've got on this dumbfuck grin. Manny doesn't need me. Allison doesn't want me. I have no friends. So, what, then, is keeping me here? Nothing. Absolutely fucking nothing.